G

# Green Silk

Cathryn Cooper

HEADLINE
Liaison

First published in 1996
by HEADLINE BOOK PUBLISHING

A HEADLINE LIAISON paperback

10 9 8 7 6 5 4 3 2 1

ISBN 0 7472 5289 0

Typeset by CBS, Felixstowe, Suffolk

Printed and bound in Great Britain by
Cox & Wyman Ltd, Reading, Berks

HEADLINE BOOK PUBLISHING
A division of Hodder Headline PLC
338 Euston Road
London NW1 3BH

# Green Silk

# Chapter 1

It could honestly be said that Samuel Levy died with a smile on his face. Apart from that, he died with a hard-on, a fact which his more broad-minded acquaintances viewed with envy, and the more narrow-minded with disgust.

He was an old man, and thus his death was not unexpected, so distress was muted by acceptance – with the exception of the undertaker, that is.

Joshua Blondblaum, who guaranteed a good burial for a good price – which he interpreted as supplying as little as possible for as much as possible – was distressed due to his problems with getting an extra-large shroud to respectably cover the size and stiffness of the old man's John Thomas.

Such a predicament was enviable in a man of over eighty years of age who had just married a nippy little blonde of twenty-four, and envy was certainly on the faces of those that attended the funeral.

Like every other male mourner, Simon Tye was green-eyed with jealousy of what stood out so proud and so rigid from the old man's coffin.

With nervous excitement, he wondered whether the women mourners had noticed the fever of admiration and resentment that ran through the black-suited men who – it

1

had to be said – had not so much come to mourn old Samuel's passing, as to pay their respects to his stamina and see with their own eyes this rod, this obelisk whose fame had flashed from one male to another.

Their admiration was almost tangible, the same question running like a racing locomotive from one awestruck soul to another: how, at his age, and even in death, had he managed to maintain such a magnificent stiffness? Were the rumours purely wishful and envious thinking on their part? Heads shook in disbelief as their eyes merely glanced at Samuel's cold face, but lingered, wide-eyed, on his upright member. Testimony to everything that was being said, Samuel's rod was still stiff long past the normal period of rigor mortis.

Amazement and outright jealousy erupted in Simon's brain. Envy of Samuel, and disappointment in his own sex life grew into a whirling maelstrom as he studied the faces of the other mourners who had already gone up to the coffin and paid their respects. He saw their glazed eyes, the limp, lethargic look around their mouths. Their comments only confirmed what he had already heard.

'I don't believe it . . .'

'I only wish mine was as admirable . . .'

'What was his secret . . . ?'

'A Goliath, a veritable Goliath . . .'

Simon swallowed hard. Soon, he too would have to go up to the coffin. Could he face it? Could he cope with feasting his eyes on the sight of a man whose member, even in death, would not lie down?

He could not stop thinking about it, indeed, he could have stood there for hours thinking about it. But his thoughts were rudely interrupted by his wife, Ruth.

'Have you seen it?' she asked him, but did not give him a chance to answer. 'It's disgusting, an insult to heaven. Not only was he obsessed with such things in life, he's also taken to his box the same way. And as for *her* . . .' His wife spat the last word. Simon did not need to know that she was referring to the fourth Mrs Levy.

He managed to maintain his suitably mournful look, but his eyes sparkled as much as any other man's in the place as he furtively eyed the voluptuous form of the widow Levy.

But the question – the most important of questions – remained in his mind. How had old Samuel managed it?

The thought of having such an erection as old Sam's fired his imagination. His heart raced in his chest. Tonight, he would mention it to Ruth. Perhaps just talking about another man's weapon in private might ignite her flagging passion. For his own part, just thinking about it sent blood to colour his cheeks and harden his penis which, until that moment, had lain content – no – dormant in his pants.

He glanced down at Ruth who was muttering something disparaging about the young widow Levy to Mrs Goldman. On looking at his dearly beloved, his hopes that had – like old Sam's weapon – been as upright as obelisks, crumbled to dust.

He sighed. Before marriage, Ruth had been a raver. Since marrying, she hadn't. Sad, for a man like him. After all, what was the point of having an enormous hard-on if it had nowhere to go?

And as for other women, somehow he had either never found the time, or if he had, the ones who were willing were not the ones he wanted to do things with.

Thinking of natural and comparatively unnatural things made his eyes travel to Kitty Levy. What a little stunner! No wonder old Samuel had snuffed it on the job. But how had he acquired the sexual allure to win her and the stamina to keep her? True, old Sam had been wealthy. But were money and home comforts enough for a girl like Kitty? Wasn't it true that girls like her were physically demanding?

Even dressed in widow's black, she tantalized. Her face might be veiled and hidden, but the slim sheath dress she wore accentuated the curve of her bosom, the neatness of her waist, and the glorious roundness of her firm, ripe bottom. Simon licked his lips as he studied her pouting buttocks. How he would love, he thought, to push his own keen erection in between those firm globes and feel her muscles clench around his sensitive crown.

He imagined her skin; like satin, he decided, slightly shiny and soft to the touch. Her flesh would be firm. Her nipples hard and pouting. The hair that covered her sex like the veil did her face would be as blonde as the hair on her head, or if it was not, it would be shaved off entirely.

He salivated, and mindful that he was bordering on dribbling, licked his lips again. Without attracting his wife's attention, he tried to catch the eye of the luscious Kitty. But it wasn't easy. Was she looking his way? If she was, he didn't have time to find out. A sharp elbow dug into his ribs.

'Time to be going. I have paid all respects that are due to such a man as Samuel. Now hurry up and pay yours – not that the man deserves any respect after the way he lived his life. But Rabbi Bachman is his brother-in-law, and isn't the good rabbi my cousin?'

Simon swallowed, then nodded and pushed his way to the coffin. A tall man with a long face and very green eyes smiled and let him into the space where he had been.

'Admirable,' sighed the man as he turned away.

As Simon glanced up at the gaunt face, the green eyes, the wide mouth, the man's breath touched his face. Simon winced. A vision came to his mind. In it, he saw a place where strips of steel ran in red, molten sheets, where the air was laden with the smell of boiling metal, and men dripped sweat from every pore of their flesh.

Judging the man to be thinking the same jealous thoughts as he was, Simon again eyed Sam's stiff rod, then smiled up at him. The man was gone.

Quick mover, thought Simon, and turned his eyes and his ponderings back to old Sam. Normally, he would have paid his respects, then scooted off, glad to have got death over with, and got back to living. But Kitty, the grieving widow, came and stood next to him. His pulse throbbed wildly. His penis became painful, his heart brave. If he were ever to have a chance at ending up like Samuel – stiff, even in his coffin – then now might be the right moment to make suitable enquiries.

Taking off his hat, Simon looked down at the dead man. Yes, old Samuel definitely had a smile. Simon concentrated on the old man's face. Out of politeness, he averted his gaze from the sharp-topped pyramid that stuck up from the funeral sheet.

Kitty was near. He could sense her, smell her, her perfume like a bright cloud around the blackness of her outfit. Speak to her now, he urged himself, speak to her now!

Heart pounding in his breast, he turned to the widow

who just might need physical sympathy as well as the more usual kind.

Unfortunately for Simon, whose bad luck in love had caused him to end up with Ruth, whose idea of foreplay had more to do with golf than sex, the young widow – who was in fact wife number four – had been replaced by wife number one, who was overweight, and jubilant that she was still alive, and her ex-husband was not.

'Vengeance is mine!' he heard her exclaim, and he shuddered before he spoke.

'Mrs, um, Levy . . .' He tried not to sound disappointed, but it wasn't easy.

The first Mrs Levy was a big woman. She frowned down on him as much as she was doing on her dead and long since divorced, husband.

Vengeance might have been the Lord's by right, but on this occasion it was apparent on the face of the first Mrs Levy.

'Sex mad, that was the trouble with him!' she exclaimed. 'And didn't I know it. Every hour on the hour when he was young: too much for one woman to stand.'

Simon's eyes lit up. 'Is that really true?'

'Obsessed. He was obsessed. He got worse as he got older and his pecker wasn't as upstanding as it had been. Sold his soul for it, he did. And now look where it's got him – laid out flat whilst his member points disrespectfully towards heaven. Any normal man would have wilted by now. Now didn't I always say he was a wicked man? Didn't I always say he was more likely to go to hell than to heaven?'

'How come it is so . . .' Simon's voice trailed off as he

pointed somewhat nervously at Samuel's rigid rod.

The first Mrs Levy humphed and grunted and sniffed a bit. Like a pig, he thought to himself, like a disgruntled pig who has long been denied a decent boar.

'I blame his habits – those habits he indulged in down in that crummy warehouse and gentile office and never cared to bring home. They were what caused this, God rest his wicked soul.'

Simon waited for her to explain further. But Mrs Levy looked with triumphant loathing at a husband who had indulged in every sexual pastime and position it was possible to practise. Simon's patience evaporated.

'Something? What exactly do you mean? Can you tell me that, Mrs Levy?'

As she nodded, her jowls trembled then settled like limp jelly on her collar. 'He kept his dirty habits down at that warehouse. I would not allow dirty habits at home, so when he inherited that warehouse from his uncle, he spent most of his time there. Said his uncle had worked the place into the ground and it needed building up. All lies, of course. Uncle Maurice spent most of his time down at that place chasing the girls who worked for him. Swore that as long as there was breath in his body, he would indulge his passions for all he was worth. His wife indulged him too. Turned a blind eye, she did, but Sarah was a fool. The woman had no pride. I had my pride, and I told Samuel either the warehouse went, or I did. He chose the warehouse. Became obsessed by it, he did. But I had my dues. He had his women – his other wives, and more besides. I took my share of Samuel's money. Not that it seemed to worry him. Even Alexa, wife number three, had to go, and she was only halfway through her thirties. He said he needed a younger woman, something that was still on the boil, so to speak – someone who could keep up with his demands.'

Inside, Simon lit up like a Christmas tree. Down in his trousers, his rod beat a steady tom-tom against the front of his trousers.

He wanted to groan with desire, but coughed instead. 'Are you . . . is everything being sold?'

'I expect so,' she said. 'Ask that little trollop he married. Maybe she knows more than I do; after all, at the end of the day, it was her who got the benefit of his stiff dick, not me!'

Simon didn't find out until a few days later exactly what the young widow Levy was doing with her inheritance which included the apartment in Manhattan, the cabin in Maine and the condo in Florida. But it wasn't those things Simon was interested in. He wanted the warehouse, and the business stock, the stuff crammed into the old shirt-waister building at the back of Thirty-sixth Street where the Levys had been in the garment trade since before the gay nineties. The business was being wound up. Kitty Levy was off to Florida to chase the sun and the sea, and no doubt to obliterate her sorrows with bodies that were perhaps firmer than old Samuel's, but possibly not as virile.

And that was how Simon Tye came to buy a building, and a business that he didn't really need. Simon had plenty of businesses to deal with already. But that something inside him, born that day at old Sam's funeral would not go away. He was convinced that hidden somewhere among Samuel's artifacts was some secret item that had enabled the old man not only to regain his youthful vigour, but to surpass it and take his erection to his grave. And that was something that Simon wanted too.

# Chapter 2

Josie Morrison was thirty years of age, with dark hair and matching eyes. She also had a figure which although not slim was well proportioned. Josie was of the considered opinion that she had been born too late. She was very aware that in the earlier part of the century she would have been termed a fine figure of a woman. Her grandmother had told her that, and in all honesty her grandmother would know, seeing as she'd been one of the famous Gibson girls.

In order to back up her statement, her grandmother had shown Josie the faded photographs of girls with coy expressions, but also possessing bosoms and buttocks that were more than a handful for any honest man.

Her grandmother was also honest about how her charms had enticed the most discerning of men, and how in the darkness of a horse-drawn cab she had been enraptured by the sweet words of admiration poured upon her (besides the kisses on her bare breasts, and the exploring hands that crept up over her garters and into the slit between her legs).

Perhaps it was the way her grandmother described her youth, or the sparkle that came into her eyes as she recalled the comments, the kisses and the youthful caresses; perhaps a combination of both. Whatever it was, hearing the torrid history of her grand matriarch made Josie feel somewhat less than satisfied with her own love life.

Josie had been dating Rod Blackbull for years – from time immemorial it seemed – and although she had succumbed early on to his suggestions to join him in his bed, she still could not get over the feeling that she was missing something.

Rod was very gentle for a man who walked the high girders of half-grown skyscrapers, had shoulders that could fill the Grand Canyon from side to side, and the sort of native American face that had put the wind up General Custer.

But it wasn't Rod that was the problem. It was her. She knew it was her, but hadn't a clue as to how to sort herself out.

The trouble was she had listened to her grandmother in awestruck silence for too long. She had then decided that she could never hope to match either her figure or her adventures. If she managed one of those aims, she would be lucky. In fact she had been. She had inherited her grandmother's figure, and she gave thanks for that. It was the other thing she was having trouble with.

Rod Blackbull treated her as though she were made of china and was far more innocent than she had ever claimed to be. Somehow, she did not want to shatter that illusion. So from the start of their relationship she had acted the part, letting him make the first move, then submitting to him once they were naked beneath the sheets.

After a while, she became reluctant to break her sexual habits and let him see just how wildly uninhibited she could be. The more time went on, the more disinclined she was to let him know that. After all, a man who has been used to a

12

seemingly virtuous woman might wonder what activities could have occurred to turn her into a red hot mamma!

Josie had worked in the Levy warehouse for around eight years. It was her job to collate deliveries with paperwork, then transfer invoice information direct onto the computerized accountancy system. Not the most interesting of work, but it paid well, and she liked the people she worked for.

Old man Levy had been kind, and although his fingers had had a habit of wandering to her bra strap and snapping it open as she worked, she had taken his eccentricities in good faith. After all, he'd always given her a good bonus, and had even invited her to his third and fourth weddings. Not many bosses would do that, she told herself.

But now everything had altered. The old man had died – probably killed by the demands of his pretty new wife who used to be his secretary and had taken down a lot more than shorthand.

But it was all over now, and the warehouse had been sold.

She sighed as she wondered what the new owner might be like. Not that it would make any difference what she thought about him. He'd bought the place, so that was that. Anyway, she had already decided that if he wasn't up to scratch and the atmosphere at the warehouse changed because of him, then she was off to pastures new.

It was Josie's habit to wait for Rod to collect her on a Tuesday night, because that was the night they went bowling. On this particular Tuesday, he rang to say he'd be late getting there because there had been an accident on site, and he was needed by the union to take statements from those concerned.

After that there would be a meeting, and such meetings being the way they were and such men being the sort that liked to chew matters further over a beer or two, he could be even later than assumed.

Josie resigned herself to waiting for him, and because she wanted to give the new owner a good impression of herself she decided to clear out the cupboards in the small room next to Samuel's old office.

The key to the small room had been kept by the old man on a secret hook behind a batch of old-style sales ledgers that had no use whatsoever except to hide the key from view.

It was on one particular day when his hand had fondled her knee as well as her bra that Samuel had told her about his little room and where he kept the key.

'That's where I keep my real special stuff,' he'd told her secretively, then grinned and tapped his nose.

At the old man's invitation, she'd followed him into the room not knowing what to expect, and not being overly impressed when she saw what was in there.

Besides some unprepossessing furniture, and a painting that she tried her best not to look at, there was little except for an ornate white marble fireplace, and three closets of a clumsy style associated with the forties and early fifties.

'This is it,' he'd said to her proudly. 'This is where I keep the very best material that this firm has ever had the good luck to own.'

He'd licked his lips then, and looked at her with more than fatherly consideration. Time, she'd decided, to make a sharp exit.

But this evening, she could go into the room without the

worry of being fondled by someone she did not want to fondle her. This evening, under the pretext of sorting out uneconomic lines, she could finally see the things the old man had seen fit to keep secret.

But first, she had to find the key.

Perhaps, she thought to herself, it might already have been moved, taken by some junior probate clerk at the law firm handling the inheritance issues of the Levy estate. As always in these things, vultures flew from every perch to strip what flesh was still hanging on the carcass.

Josie sighed triumphantly. She was in luck. No one had taken it. There it hung, still half hidden by the black plastic folders of old sales made before the days of interactive computer programmes.

The lock clunked, and the door was easily opened.

The room had an uncommonly fresh smell, which was surprising seeing as it had not been opened for weeks.

It was, she decided, exactly how she remembered it. One brown leather couch, one water dispenser, one painting of a naked young woman with big breasts, and a bigger bottom, who was accommodating penises in every available orifice. Ranged against the walls were the closets she remembered.

Surprisingly, two of them were unlocked.

'Not so precious, huh, Sam?'

For an instant, she wondered if old Sam could hear her in that place where he had gone.

'Hope you find plenty of action there, Sam,' she said quietly, and felt a sudden surge of guilt at being in the secret room without him.

Pull yourself together, girl, she thought.

She took a deep breath, and shrugged her shoulders, then aimed the key at the first lock.

An avalanche of books, magazines and paperbacks rained out as she swung the closet door open.

Despite the front she put on for Rod's benefit, Josie was not narrow minded, so she did not blush as she knelt down and picked up one book, then another. The cover of the first was lurid and plainly advertised what sort of literature it contained. The second was more discreet in cover design, but on opening it and reading the first paragraph, she judged it as explicitly sexual as the first.

Another seemed very old and was entitled *The Perfumed Garden*.

Thinking this might touch on horticulture, and she did have an interest in potted plants, she opened it, and saw that it had been translated from the original by a man called Richard Burton.

The one that married Liz Taylor?

'No, you fool. This book was printed before either he or she were born,' she said to herself. She laughed, then covered her mouth with her hand, and looked nervously over her shoulder.

Dusk was closing in quickly, so it was only to be expected that the gathering gloom would make her feel nervous. Not that she should be too worried about her safety, for even if the warehouse was dark beyond the circle of light thrown from the office doorway, there was a security guard patrolling out there, and a security system scanning whoever came to the main entrance.

Before opening the second closet, she briefly skimmed the first paragraph of another of the books, and once she'd read the first, she had by nature to read the second.

What she read brought a flush to her cheeks and a throbbing to that black-haired area between her legs that Rod liked to stroke as if it were a sleeping pussy cat. A pleasant tremor travelled up over her belly, and she couldn't help but lick her lips.

'Are you all right in there?'

The book cover closed with a bang, and startled by the sudden voice, she gasped and clutched her chest. 'You frightened me.'

'Sorry, Josie,' said the guard, who was big, black and beautiful. His teeth flashed as he smiled. 'Just checking you were all right. Rod picking you up?'

She nodded and read regret in his velvet brown eyes. I wonder, she thought, if you'd lay me out on this carpet and spread my thighs if you didn't know Rod, and didn't know he was coming to collect me.

The very thought took her by surprise. Where had it come from?

Her cheeks reddened as she looked from him to the book before pushing the offending literature back into the closet and slamming the door.

'I'm just sorting out these closets,' she said, and brushed her hair back from her forehead. 'There's an order in tomorrow, and we need more storage space.'

The guard took off his cap, and wiped the back of his hand over his eyebrows. He shook his head.

'Fancy that. Getting rid of all the old man's stuff to make way for new. Don't seem right somehow, not with the way he used to care about this room and the stuff in it.'

He winked at her, and she knew then that he was as aware

of what those books contained as she was. Now her blush would never go away.

Purposefully, she moved to the next closet.

'I suppose you know what's in this one too,' she said to him airily as she opened the door.

'Toys.'

He said it at the same time as a bundle of brightly-coloured plastic dildoes and other false bits and pieces fell out of the cupboard.

'Oh, my God!' Now she did blush.

'Shall I help you with them?'

Josie had the vague impression there was a double meaning in what he was offering to do. All the same, he was down beside her, helping her to shove the oversize phalli, stimulators, and goodness knows what else, back onto the shelves.

Eventually, it was all back in. Red-faced, she slammed that door shut too.

The guard grinned and leaned against the door, his cap still in his hand.

Is this guy ever going? she asked herself. There's no way I'm opening that other closet until he shoves off.

She crossed her arms just below her chest and cast a look at the guard that should have left him in no doubt that she wasn't doing anything until he'd got the hell out of there.

The key got warmer in her hand as she waited.

'Mind you,' said the guard, a wicked gleam in his eyes, 'I never did get to see what was in the third closet. He never used to keep it locked, not until about a year before he died. He sure kept it a close-guarded secret.'

Sick of his grinning, and still unnerved by his unexpected

appearance, she made an instant decision.

'You can go now,' she said as she looked up at him.

He seemed disinclined to move. His eyes were on the third closet, but his grin did disappear.

'You sure you'll be all right?'

'I'm sure. Anyway, Rod will be here soon. I've got nothing to worry about, unless you leave him hanging about outside, and then he's likely to get pretty mad.'

Resigned to his dismissal, and knowing that Rod was bigger than he was, the guard withdrew from the room, went through the office, and melted into the darkness of the warehouse.

Josie turned her attention to the third closet. As always, it was locked, and for a moment, she could not help but regard it with more than a hint of trepidation.

What could be in there? Something as sexually descriptive as the books, or so obviously vulgar as the plastic sex toys?

And should she open it anyway?

Tingles of fear and the residue of old loyalty mixed with everything else she was feeling.

Please God, she said to herself, don't let it be a body, or whips, or something as primitive as a blow-up rubber doll!

The door creaked until it was open as wide as it could be. There was nothing horrific, nothing vulgar in the closet. In fact, it was pretty near empty except for one particular item, and that could not possibly give offence.

Josie breathed a sigh of relief. Leaning diagonally from the floor of the closet to its ceiling, was a roll of what looked to be fabric.

Relieved, she smiled, then reached out her hand and touched it.

Something resembling electricity shot up her arm as she touched the softness of the material. It's silk, said a voice in her head, green silk.

The throbbing between her legs that had started when she had read the opening paragraph of the sexy book seemed to intensify. The strange sensation now raced around her body, and the urge to take the bolt of cloth from the closet was uncommonly strong. It became something she just had to do.

It was heavy. That was the first thing she noticed. Funny, she thought, that a material so delicately woven could be so heavy.

The second thing she noticed was that as she held it against her, sensations that could only be described as extremely erotic spread like a fibrous blanket over her body.

It made her shiver, it made her tingle and want to rub herself more fully against the bolt of cloth as though it were a lover.

Sweet sensations occurred in her nipples, sensations that normally only the touch of Rod Blackbull's strong fingers created. The faint ache in her groin that had been created by reading the literature in the first closet now became more intense, more demanding.

The bolt of cloth still hugged close to her body, she caught her breath, then moaned as her hips began to gyrate and her limbs slowly rubbed against the soft material.

It wasn't easy, but she did manage to get the cloth to the brown leather couch.

She let it fall, and found herself falling on top of it so that her legs were astride it, her crotch exposed. The heavy mass of fabric pressed against her sex and made her gasp. 'Ooh . . . !' she cried as delicious sensations came into being. Her mouth stayed fixed in an 'O' shape. Her eyes were glazed. She was lost to touch, lost to strange visions that erupted in her mind. It felt as though she were riding an electrical charge. In her mind, she was riding a man. Energized by the charge, her hips began to move in a slow, yet growing rhythm.

Take off your panties, said a voice in her head, and she did so, flinging them away so that they landed on top of the water cooler.

Now, as she eased herself again across the fabric, she moaned at the coolness of its silky touch, a touch that, because this was a bolt of cloth, was also hard.

As her pubic lips rode over it, and her bud of passion was deliciously tickled by the exquisite material, her breathing became quicker, and her breasts heaved as if trying to escape the confines of her brassière.

Take it off, a voice said in her head. So she did. First her dress, then her underwear.

The end of her hair tickled the small of her back as she threw back her head, and cupped her breasts with her own hands. Her own hands, yet not her hands. Through narrowed eyes, she glanced around the room as if expecting someone else to be there. Yet there was no one. She was alone and riding on a plane of her own desire – her own subdued passions which were now bursting free. But in her mind, she saw a man, a long, lean man with dark hair, dark skin and very green eyes.

Her eyes closed, and her fingers did tantalizing things with her breasts and her nipples. Because her eyes were closed, what she was feeling was intensified. It was as though she were pulling all her sensations into herself, sucking them in so that their size was contracted, but their mass expanded. It was like reaching out and grasping at all the sexual abandon she had ever denied herself because of the image she wished to portray to Rod Blackbull.

The virginal, the chaste, the inhibited, were now cloaks she no longer wore. She had cast them aside, cut them from her, and torn them into shreds.

She licked her lips, ran her hands down over her rib-cage; enjoyed the feel of her hands; enjoyed the feel of her flesh. Like petals of a rose that has left it till late summer to bloom, her centre of passion flowered against the bolt of green silk.

Even when she opened her eyes, the details of the room – the water cooler, the fireplace, the picture, and even the closets – seemed to muddle together in a tangled blur.

Those sweet sensations, those tingling wings of delight, were now flocking around that neat little bud that hid behind her black-haired lips. Like water rushing into a fountain, it gathered, soared, then crested and fell to earth.

Her climax was over, and yet, when she opened her eyes and her gaze met those of the open-mouthed Rod Blackbull, her body was already refreshed and demanding more.

'Rod!' His name was little more than a rush of breath.

He was staring at her, trying to say that the security guard had let him in, but his words seemed no more than a jumble of incoherent gasps, sighs, and half-formed questions.

'Rod.' As she said his name, she smiled. Her naked breasts rose towards him as she held out her arms. 'Take off your clothes, my darling,' she said softly. 'Take off your clothes and join me.'

When he had first seen her, his eyes had opened wide, and his mouth had hung open. Now his face showed new understanding.

Her dress, shoes and bra were piled like an offering before the white marble fireplace and the painting of the naked woman and the lustful men. Her panties were still on top of the water dispenser.

As Josie dismounted from her inanimate sexual partner, she hugged it to her, then let it go. It fell to the floor and the silk unravelled.

Once it covered the floor in a green sheet, she lay down on it.

'Come on Rod,' she said, and patted the place beside her. 'I'm hot for you, darling. I want you now. Now!' Her body, creamy white and voluptuous, writhed against the soft green silk.

Rod, his pulsating length visibly grown, stared at her goggle-eyed, and paused as he fumbled for the right words to say – whatever words are right at such a time.

'I can't believe it's you,' he said, and for one moment, it looked as though he intended to run.

Then, the silk took a hand. Rod took one step – one only. The toe cap of his boot touched the selvedge of the spread silk.

He gasped, and looked down. His length, which had already started to respond to this woman, this woman who he thought he knew so well but who was now presenting a different picture than she ever had before, now jerked into new vigour and larger proportion.

He clenched his fists as he felt the irresistible tingling that started at his boot and shot up through his calf, his thigh, then whirled around his pelvic girdle. His clothes were off in no time, and as his breath quickened, and words of love and lust combined on his tongue, he fell beside her, sought her lips, cupped her breasts, and moaned with unbridled enthusiasm as her hand encircled his stem.

Never had he known her like this, so uninhibited, so blatantly wanton. Never had he known himself to be pumped so full of blood and desire.

His rod prodded at her belly. Her hands cupped the softness of his scrotal sac which, hanging loose against his thigh, felt as though it were filled with nine-carat gold ingots, rather than round little nuts made of flesh and gristle.

The silk was beneath their bodies, yet both had the impression it was covering them as softly as a layer of freshly fallen snow might cover the earth.

They rolled together, belly clamped tightly against belly, his thighs between hers, the coarseness of his pubic hair pleasurably scratching her skin as his rod entered her.

'Give me more! Give me more!' she cried, then sucked his lips into her mouth, clasped his head, and, abandoned to her desires, brought her feet up so that her heels rested upon his shoulders.

Was that electricity that played over their limbs? Without it being obtrusive, the same question was in each of their minds. Both were aware of the same green light shimmering over their flesh as their bodies fused together.

There was heat between them. There was also a feeling of union as their bodies clashed, clasped, thudded and tangled, then, at last, spasmed in climax.

'Where did he go?' asked Josie during the lull.

'Where did who go?'

Rod was smiling. His fingers were caressing his penis to new dimensions.

'No matter.' Josie bent her head and took him in. The very thought that she had seen a man with dark hair and green eyes faded from her mind.

It didn't end there. In fact, it didn't end until the security guard came walking in and stared in disbelief at the two naked figures, glowing in a pale green light, and entwined together in a tangle of vibrating contortions.

As their last climax came, then left them, the glow that they had all been aware of disappeared.

Wide-eyed, the security guard tipped his cap to the back of his head before he spoke.

'Well, I'll be damned!' His surprise was real.

He'd always had a fancy for Josie, an in-built desire to exploit the naivety he thought he had seen there. His eyes swept her body, but his desire was somewhat blunted. Josie, it appeared, was not quite as she seemed.

Suddenly aware that she was naked and not alone, Josie sprang to her feet. Her breasts jiggled deliciously, and her bottom shone with an innocent pinkness as she retrieved her panties from the top of the water cooler.

Rod Blackbull stepped off the patch of green silk, and all the tingles that had invaded his body seemed to seep out of the ends of his toes.

He was himself again – to a point.

'Don't put them on, honey.'

Josie stopped trying to stand on one leg while she put her other leg into her panties. Her eyes met those of her darling Rod, and something completely new and entirely wonderful passed between them. In a fresh spirit of understanding, she smiled, and took her panties back off.

'Okay, honey. I'll put them in my handbag.'

Rod's arm was around her as they left, and his hand rolled with her rump which was now naked beneath her dress.

Once they were gone, the security guard, whose suit was made of thick wool that could withstand wetness as well as cold, rolled the silk back up.

'Ouch!' At the same time as he said it, he let the bolt of cloth fall back onto the couch. 'Damned electric shock.' He rubbed his thumb against his fingers, then picked up the key to the little room, and locked the door. Frowning and still rubbing his fingers and thumb together, he left the key on the desk that used to belong to Samuel Levy, a man who had loved sex more than money.

That night, his two-hundred-and-eighty-pound wife had the benefit of his sexual attention even before she had chance to eat supper. She had it again after supper, and even in the early hours of the morning.

By 10.30 a.m. she was telling her best friend all about her husband's renewed virility.

By 12.30 a.m. her friend had bought some sexy underwear and had had her hair done in the hope that her best friend's husband had some virility to spare.

# Chapter 3

Waking and rising early was not normally one of Simon's habits, but this particular morning was not just any old morning. The lawyers and accountants had finished drawing up documents and checking figures with regard to his purchase of the fabric warehouse that had been the foundation of the Levy family fortune. Today he would finally walk into it as its new owner.

Apart from that, of course, today was the beginning of his quest to find the secret of old Sam's undoubted virility. That Sam had had exceptional staying powers, he did not doubt. In fact, it had even been rumoured that his less than grieving widow was pregnant, and although Simon gave lip service to the notion that he was not a gossip, what he said and what he believed were two entirely different things.

Determined to step into the new day and his new venture with a keen brain and a bounce in his step, Simon reached for the windows, flung them open, and breathed in the dubious air of the equally dubious New York.

He took another breath, and another, and felt better for it, until his wife raised her head and her voice from the pillow.

'What are you doing at this Godforsaken hour?'

As if to confirm his newly found commitment to good health, Simon took another big breath.

'Starting the day with some exercise and some air, my darling. I've made a decision to take better care of my body. If I take care of my body, I will live a longer life, a better life, and have more energy for my work – and other things.'

'Should I live so long,' came the returned mutter as his wife's head fell back to the pillow.

'You have no faith in me, my dear woman. Don't you believe I can be a new man, reinvigorate my energies?'

'Is an egg yolk purple?' came the reply.

Simon had learned to rise above such comments. 'It's a new day, and I have bought a new business. Can you tell me your day will be as interesting as mine will be?'

Ruth raised her head again and eyed him with the same look he'd got from a fish in Lionel Schumacher's aquarium.

'I'm going out to spend some of your money. I'm going to the auction at old Sam's house. That flighty little broad of his has put the whole schabang on the market. Lock, stock, and down below the barrel. Anything you want me to get for you? Like her dirty underwear for you to sniff at and give yourself a hard-on?'

Simon chose to ignore her. The sarcasm which she had brought to their marriage had increased in intensity over the years. He could do without it, and besides, he didn't want anything or anyone ruining either his day or his quest to find old Sam's secret of sexual longevity.

Tossing his pyjamas to one side and taking an easy pride in his nakedness and his not inconsequential erection, he strode off to the bathroom, and turned on the faucet before watching his erection disappear as he used the lavatory.

No matter. It would return, he told himself; then he sang as he sorted out his shaving equipment and all the other little things he'd bought to make his body more pleasant for himself and for others.

Once he was dressed, he smoothed back his hair of which nowadays there were only two patches and these on opposite sides of his head.

'Go to it,' he told the mirror, and he did.

The warehouse was red brick, and fronted half that particular block, not far from Thirty-sixth, but cornering Bruton and Morrison.

Smiling, he nodded at the faces of his new employees, noted the wariness of the men, and the glances of the women which he preferred to think were assessing him as a man rather than as the guy who controlled the size of their pay-cheques.

He also noticed more about the women than he did the men. Some were middle-aged, well blossomed, and no doubt good workers, so therefore valuable assets. Others were younger, some slimmer, and some most definitely worth more than a second glance. One especially drew his attention. She was dark-haired and creamy-skinned, with a look on her face that made him think she had discovered something exceptionally thrilling of late.

Not that he wanted to know what made her eyes sparkle. He had other eggs to fry, and as yet, she was not one of them.

As expected of him, he gave his new workforce a little pep talk about how pleased he was to be here, and how he hoped to continue in the proud traditions founded and carried on by the Levy family.

He smiled all the way through his talk, as though he truly believed what he was saying, but all the time old Sam's erection was uppermost in his mind. Like a large finger, it beckoned him, lured him, and at the same time, made him incredibly jealous.

Once his talk was over, he was off up a set of steps that led to a corridor, that in turn led to the offices that housed the paper pushers, the computers, and the desk and filing cabinets of the deceased Samuel Levy.

'Not bad,' he said to himself as he entered what was now his domain.

The office had two windows, one overlooking the warehouse floor, and one looking out on a small square that separated his building from a row of tenements opposite that had been converted into trendy apartments.

The office was adequate – not opulent, but comfortable. He nodded as he looked around it. All was in order. Both the office and the small room adjoining it had been thoroughly cleaned prior to his occupation. There was nothing there that should not be there except for a bolt of green silk lying flat out on the brown leather couch. He frowned at it, then eyed it from a different angle, and thought what a beautiful luminescence it had about it. But the office he concluded – his office – was not the place for it. He picked up the telephone and barked his first command into the mouthpiece.

'Get this bolt of silk put down in the warehouse. Should a man have his wares sat on the furniture with him?'

His order was carried out, though green sparks of charged static shot out from the bolt of cloth each time someone touched it. The first man who tried to lift the silk and take it to the warehouse tried twice to pick it up, tried again, then as a streak of electricity shot from the bolt to his fingertips, dropped it.

'Get some gloves. Get some help.' Simon was getting impatient. Not only did he want the cloth out, he wanted the man out too. He had something to do, something to find.

The man went off somewhere, and eventually came back, bringing with him a sheath of thick plastic which he wrapped firmly around the silk.

Once he was gone, Simon, his heart thumping in anticipation, began to do some snooping. Of course, he didn't really look at it that way. After all, the warehouse, the offices, the fixtures and fittings, were now all his.

He tried the black leather executive chair out for size, then began to open and close the drawers of the desk. As only to be expected, Samuel's personal papers had been taken from his drawers and his filing cabinets, but Simon had made it a condition of his purchase that all other personal effects should remain *in situ*.

Accordingly, he found a variety of items still rolling around in the desk drawers, though nothing to set his pulse racing; no magic potion to swallow, no exotic cream to rub into the area below his belly. It was disappointing, but it was the first day, he told himself, and nothing of any value was ever executed with undue hurry.

When the telephone rang, he was going over the more mundane matter of business organization with his financial advisor. He excused himself, though Jim, his pale-faced, pale-haired and bespectacled accountant, stayed in the office, and continued to wrestle through the wad of computer printouts and lists.

Simon took his glasses from his nose before speaking. 'Hello.' He was half expecting it to be Ruth on the other end of the phone. If it was, he could say something suitably suggestive, and as usual get a suitably sarcastic reply. Anyway Jim still sat rustling paper, so he could not let the conversation drop to a personal level.

'Mister Tye. This is Mrs Levy, Kitty Levy.'

Simon sat bolt upright. So did his penis.

'Mrs Levy. How nice to hear from you. How are you? What can I do for you? Are you well?'

Simon was aware of the accountant's eyes leaving the printouts. He frowned, and nervously fondled the receiver. The last thing he wanted was an audience when he was talking to the delectable Mrs Levy.

He cleared his throat and put his hand over the receiver. 'Do you mind?'

Recognizing that he wasn't wanted, Jim had already half risen from his chair. He tucked the printouts under his arm and left the room.

As the door closed behind the lean frame of the accountant, Simon was aware of Kitty Levy telling him she was fine, and that if ever he needed her help with anything regarding the old warehouse, anything at all, he had only to call.

A lump came to his throat, but it was nothing compared to the one in his trousers.

'That's real kind of you. I can't tell you how nice it is to hear from you, and as for your generous offer, what can I do but take you up on it?'

'Well, we could meet if you like, and you could ask me anything you want to know then.'

The bulge in Simon's trousers rose beneath the touch of

his fingers. It was so hot and hard that he had to reach for his zipper, pull it down, and let his rod break free. It leapt out of his trousers as though it were attached to his body on a tightly-wound spring.

Simon sighed heavily. 'I'd love to meet you. When can you fit me in?'

Just asking such a question made his member swell that much more. It waved like a magic wand about to cast a spell.

As Kitty told him when she was free, where they could meet, and at what time, he encircled his swollen flesh with his hand, then began to move it up and down.

The sensations developing in his groin were too good to let fade too early. The sound of Kitty Levy's voice, and the vision she presented, had started this exercise, but he had to finish it. He had to keep her talking.

'Tell me. What are you doing with yourself? Are you off to Florida?'

Her laugh was light and pretty and made him pull more vigorously than ever on his hot and throbbing male part.

'I should be in Miami before the end of the month, but I have a little unfinished business here in New York before I go. There's a couple of things I'm looking for, and Sammy doll might just have left them hanging around there in that warehouse, though I was pretty sure he only kept them at home. But he was getting a little old, a little forgetful.'

But still virile, thought Simon, but didn't say that. 'Well, if I can help at all, you just let me know.'

'That's good of you.'

For Simon, it was very good. Just the sound of her voice was enough to make his member leap even more in his hand. Wide eyed, he gazed at it, pulled it, and a dot of silvery fluid oozed out and sat like a crown on its head.

'Have you sold everything yet?'

As usual in a woman who knew her own worth and the effect she had on men, Kitty Levy started at the very beginning, until like the sensations in his penis, the telling rose higher and higher towards a final conclusion.

'There,' she said at last, as Simon's hot seed ran over his fingers and into his pants. 'Don't you think that little condo in Florida would be the best place for me?'

'Yes.' Simon gasped it rather than said it. 'Yes, yes. I think it would be a great idea. I holiday there, you know.'

'With your wife?'

Suddenly the shrinking of his erection seemed to accelerate.

'Sometimes,' he lied. 'But not all the time.'

He heard her sigh. 'I should have been in Miami by now, but as I told you, I've been looking for some particular items.'

'Something valuable?' He made a good job of sounding all attentive. The truth was that he was trying to concentrate on doing up his zipper without catching the delicate skin of his penis between the sharp metal teeth.

He sensed her hesitation before she spoke. 'Yes. They were valuable – to me anyway. Presents from Sammy doll. I might have left them back at our old apartment, but everything got a bit chaotic what with packing and sorting things for the auction.'

'And you didn't find these items when you were sorting things out?'

'I didn't sort things. My maid did.'

'Have you asked her about it?'

'No. I fired her.' Her voice suddenly lost its sexy undertone. 'She was Samuel's choice of employee, not mine. She and I never got on, so I got rid of her as quickly as I could. Besides, I had no intention of taking her with me to Florida.' She brightened. 'Never mind. No doubt it will turn up. We'll talk about it over lunch anyway.'

They said their goodbyes. The words ran out, but so had his semen. Eminently satisfied, but breathing a little hurriedly on account of surmizing where their meeting might take them, he put down the receiver.

'Yes!' he shouted as he clenched his fists and thrust them in the air. 'Yes!'

He was going to meet Kitty, and not only was she well worth meeting, she alone would know more about her late husband's virility than anyone else.

# *Chapter 4*

Carla Ferretti had worked for Samuel Levy and his first wife
long before Kitty had come along. Even though the young
bitch had treated her like dirt, she had kept her mouth
tightly shut, and thought of the dollars rather than Kitty's
disdain.

Before Kitty had arrived to warm Sam's chill bones and
his bed, Carla had enjoyed the odd fumble with the old man
even when the third Mrs Levy was still around.

But a few months after he'd met Kitty, and a few months
before marrying her, everything had changed, and only
Carla knew the reason why.

Samuel fell in love. He had the money to win any woman
he wanted, but the one he had been unlucky to fall for
wanted more than just his bank account. She was lusty, and
wanted his body to be as virile as his cheque book.

Beauty is as beauty does, was an old saying she knew, but
hadn't really understood until Kitty had come along.

Kitty had beauty, all right. Her hair bubbled around her
face in pale gold wisps. Her breasts were full, and her behind
fuller.

Any other blonde bimbo, thought Carla, would have
enjoyed the old man's money and left it at that. But not

Kitty. Kitty had a sexual appetite that would have been a good match for Sam's in his younger days. He did his best, of course, but the fact that his body was not as agile as his mind became more and more obvious.

At long last came the showdown, and Carla's ear happened to be pressed against the bedroom door when it came.

Kitty got fed up, and shouted at him to get it together, or she was off to pastures new.

'I'll do anything for you, Kitty darling,' he'd said to her. 'Anything. I'd sell my soul to be able to make love to you three times a night. Believe me, I really would.'

And that, in Carla's opinion, was exactly what he had done.

It was late at night. The third Mrs Levy had already filed for divorce, so old Sam was alone.

As usual, Carla took him his late night bourbon. Having been brought up to be wary of black candles and odd designs chalked on bare floors, she asked him if he hadn't better put out the candles and light the light.

'It's so dark in here, Mister Sam.' She crossed herself as she'd been taught to do. Her eyes flitted nervously between the flickering candles and the naked Sam. He told her not to worry.

'I've got a plan, Carla my love,' he said. 'A plan to give me the virility of a twenty-year-old, and the allure of Rudolf Valentino.'

She hadn't liked to say to him that old Rudolf was dead, and likely as not looking like a dried-up prune. Normally, she would have poked fun at his out-of-date idea of a star, but having judged the look on his face, and having felt a

38

certain pity for the state of his male part, she had held her tongue.

Not liking to leave him entirely alone, she had hung around outside the door, perhaps dozed, but perhaps not, and thought she'd heard voices – men's voices.

She knocked and went in only thirty minutes after that expecting to find someone else there with him. There was no one. He was in bed, sound asleep, and clutching a bolt of green cloth as if it were the woman of his dreams. Strange, she thought, that she hadn't seen it earlier.

She'd smiled at his childlike pose, clutching the cloth to himself as a small boy would a teddy.

Sweet, she'd thought, and left the room.

The very next night, Kitty Levy came to stay.

'You still here!' Kitty had scowled as she said it.

'Turned up again, have you? Like a bad penny,' Carla had retorted.

Most employees, having seen where things were going, would have left then. But Carla had confidence in her employer keeping her on out of habit.

Telling herself that she was purely concerned for her employer's security, Carla had long ago engineered a small hole in the wall through which she could not only see what the old man was doing, but hear it as well.

On that particular night, Carla eased her eye to the gap and saw that Samuel had on a pair of green silk pyjamas she had never seen before. Kitty wore a matching all-in-one body suit in the same silk, but with grey lace around the legs and across the bust.

What happened next was something she dreamed about in the days that followed.

They took off the green silk garments and lay on them. Then Samuel, a man in his eighties, made love to Kitty, a woman in her twenties.

Normally, this would have been exciting enough. As Carla watched, her breasts would have tingled, and her hidden lips would have pulsated with their own rising demand.

But there was something very different, and very intriguing about this particular lovemaking. Their movements were breathtakingly fast, frantic, yet incredibly sensuous. All the time Samuel's body slammed into Kitty's, and her back arched, and her hips thrust upwards to meet his, a strange, vibrant glow surrounded their every move.

What fascinated Carla even more was that he did not make love to her just once – adequate enough for a man of his age – but he took her again, and again, and the amazing thing was, neither of them seemed to tire.

Carla had made a point of watching them from then on. It would all, she told herself, end in tears. And it had: at least for those who had truly loved old Sam. One year exactly after that first frantic session, Samuel was dead. But in his coffin he was smiling, and his member was still stiff.

There was one thing above all others that she had noticed about these sessions. Samuel would always wear his green silk pyjamas, and Kitty would have on the same green body she had worn that first night. Once they were off, they always made a point of lying on them.

Carla was a woman who had experienced much sex and many men over the years. In the slums of Puerto Rico, two things were prevalent over all others: one was violence, a tendency her brother had inherited, the other was sex.

From an early age, Carla had been aware of the effect her fiery eyes and dark hair had on men. But as much as she loved having sex, Carla had become more mercenary with experience.

Good girls, she realized, get married, get pregnant and stay poor, or get pregnant, get married and stay poor. There was little difference. Bad girls got rich, but only if they chose lovers who had money rather than looks.

She had loved many young men, their bodies brown and firm against hers, but she had sought out the men of wealth, though not necessarily honour.

Marco was a man of power. She was not the first young woman he had invited into his car, then into his bed. On hot nights she lay in bed and remembered that first time he had slid his hand up her skirt and parted her ripe lips. As she pushed her own finger into her vagina, she pretended it was his, that she was sixteen again, and determined to be something better than she was.

Marco had lavished gifts upon her, gifts he could easily afford. Carla was shrewd. Looks, she concluded, as she surveyed her wrinkled mother and the other women of her age, are soon gone. Once they were gone, only money could give her the life she wanted.

Carla kept all the gifts he gave her. She never fenced the gold jewellery, the fine dresses, the dark green emeralds and the illegal substances that were as good as dollars. She kept it all safely hidden. One day, she told herself, she would need that.

The day came more quickly than she had expected. Marco was killed in a gun battle with government troops. Her brother came running to her and told her she too was in danger. Carla was ready, and although she would have liked more time in order to get a good price for her possessions, time was precious. She had to get out.

Clasping her dollars in her hand, she bought passage for herself and her brother. Soon they were in New York.

Carla had firmly expected to be Mrs Levy number four. Then Kitty had appeared. But she bided her time in the hope that Kitty would cut out once she realized the limitations of Sam's libido. It didn't happen. Sam suddenly became a super-stud.

Those clothes, Carla told herself, were the secret of sexual delight, and she had to have them.

When it came to sorting out the stuff to be sold at auction, Carla was there. Wearing pink rubber gloves, she sorted out what had to be sorted out, but made a point of finding the green silk nightwear which crackled with shots of electricity as she picked it up.

Without Kitty seeing her, she put the items in the bottom of a small wooden trunk that had brass hinges and clasps.

In order not to invite the attention of the newly widowed Kitty, Carla placed some old family portraits on top of them, portraits that someone like Kitty would never, ever contemplate having on her wall.

'I'd like to buy that little chest,' Carla had said to Kitty.

Kitty's scowl was something to behold. 'Over my dead body.'

'No. Over Mr Levy's. It's him that's dead.'

Kitty had a mouth that smiled like a hungry wolf – all width and teeth. 'That's right! He's dead, and this is all mine to do with as I want, and you are having nothing!'

Carla had seen red. 'Bitch!'

'Hag! Just you wait. No one will employ you when I've finished with you. This city will be too hot to handle!'

'So, no doubt will you – as hot as a bitch on heat looking for another dirty dog to plug her hole!'

A few things had got thrown, but Carla had left with a smile on her face. Not only had she seen red, she had also seen the details of the auction. The trunk and its secret would be hers.

So, on the same day that Ruth Tye and her friend went off to the auction at Samuel Levy's old apartment, Carla went too, her mind fixed on buying one item and one alone.

Someone had already bought the grand piano, and it was being lowered on ropes when Carla alighted from a taxi.

The best-laid plans can easily come adrift, especially when the guys shifting the furniture are young men whose minds are occupied with the events in the back seats of their cars the night before, rather than the sudden swinging of a suspended piano.

'Watch yourself, honey!'

'What!'

It was all Carla said.

The piano fell and pinned her legs to the floor.

'No,' she screamed. 'No. This can't be happening!' She fainted.

An ambulance was called, and a crowd gathered.

'Oh, God,' she kept saying to herself as she began to come round. 'Oh, God. This just isn't fair, this just isn't fair.'

A strong voice spoke near her ear. A strong arm was around her shoulders. 'Calm down, honey. We'll get you in the ambulance and at the hospital in no time.'

Carla sighed, then groaned and tried to look up at the face so near to hers. She smiled in far too alluring a way for someone whose legs felt as though they've been snapped in half.

Something flashed like silver. A shield, she decided, on a uniform, the uniform of the man holding her.

As the pain travelled up from her legs, she bit her bottom lip and reached for his hand. Perhaps he could go into the auction and bid for the wooden chest on her behalf.

'My chest,' she said weakly, and in too sexy a voice. With renewed interest in his chosen profession, the policeman rubbed her chest, and couldn't resist adding a slight squeeze to her right bosom.

'For luck,' he said with a smile, then winked. Carla fainted.

# Chapter 5

Ruth had arranged to go to the auction of Samuel Levy's furniture and effects with Hannah Goldman, whom she had known since they were girls. A taxi, Ruth decided, was the best way to get there and as usual Hannah did not argue.

'Will she be there?' Hannah emphasized the 'she' so that Ruth was in no doubt who it was she meant. It was like circling an item in a mail order catalogue. It couldn't help but stand out.

Ruth shook her small, dark head. 'No. Once the warehouse was sold, she bought herself a new apartment in some swanky block overlooking the river. That, so I understand, is to be her New York base, though when the snowbirds start flying down on United Air, she's more likely to be in Florida than here. Kitty Levy is not the sort of woman to let the grass grow under her feet. Besides, there's better pickings down there. She'll have a choice between beach boys with big muscles, and old men with big bank accounts!'

Hannah nodded her understanding. Ruth noticed her friend's lips were twitching. She instinctively knew what was coming next, but did not offer information unnecessarily.

'So your Simon bought the warehouse?'

Ruth was not exactly passionate about her husband, but she was loyal.

'Yes. My Simon is a shrewd man, a man who knows a good business investment when he sees it. He has plans, does my Simon, big plans.'

She kept to herself her suspicions that her husband had bought it in order to get nearer the not-so grieving widow Levy who had a very obvious bosom, and a big behind. Kitty was flying south – eventually. Everyone knew that, but until she was gone, Ruth would keep an eye on her husband. After all, he might not be the world's most exciting lover, but a bird in the hand . . .

Ruth Tye also kept to herself that in her youth she had been excited by sex, rather than a martyr to it. In her youth she had also been a keen movie-goer, though if anyone had asked her what films she'd especially liked, she would have been unable to answer.

Movie going had meant drive-ins, and drive-ins had meant her bare behind sticking to the leather of the back seat, her breasts exposed and groped by sweaty palms, nipples tweaked by inky fingers. As whatever boy she was with had slammed himself into her, murmuring to the point of tears against her ear, she had concentrated on achieving that scintillating moment when, if treated correctly, her sexual organs would release all her pent-up desire in one sensational explosion.

Concentrating on achieving an orgasm had been so all consuming, that at times the features of her lovers had seemed to dissolve one into the other. In her mind she assessed the pluses and minuses of each one in order to bring them together in one outstanding mixture. If this one's penis had been bigger, and that one's staying power had been that much greater, and another had done that, and another touched this. And if all the attributes of her lovers, whom she graded with utmost precision were added together, then her climax would be that much greater. Having been a maths major, she viewed it as a sort of $\pi R^2$ except that in the case of the bodies that had entered hers, it was more $P + T = C$: Penis plus technique equals climax.

Thinking about her youth and such things made her less grateful than she should be. Hadn't she got a good husband? Didn't he provide for her well?

Yes. He did. For everything, that is, except in the field of sex. When it came to those delightful moments when a man's heat enters the coolness that is woman, they should melt, mould themselves to each other.

She and Simon did not do that. She and Simon jarred, rather than melted.

Shame, she thought, it hadn't always been like that.

Kitty Levy came to her mind as they approached Samuel Levy's old apartment, and immediately she gritted her teeth.

'Come on, Hannah, or we shall miss all the bargains.'

The wool of Hannah's pale blue jacket was soft beneath Ruth's fingers as she gripped her friend's elbow and guided her past the paramedics who were on their knees beside some unfortunate woman who was groaning and moaning as some kind police officer rubbed her chest.

Other men were clearing up bits of wood, and chips of black and white oblongs that might once have made up a piano keyboard.

'I wonder what's been happening here,' said Hannah who couldn't help but be nosy, and even now was looking backwards over her shoulder as Ruth hurried her along.

'It's none of our business,' replied Ruth, sniffing as she pushed Hannah into the lobby of the big building where old Sam used to live. Samuel had lived in the penthouse at the top of the building. Today, his old apartment was heaving with people.

Samuel had been known as a hoarder and, as such, had attracted a lot of interest from people who dealt in old things that were still in mint condition.

Hannah intended to bid for some good quality linen, a selection of best Limoge china, and what looked to be a female figurine mass-produced in the twenties. The figurine was naked, and made of metal.

Ruth stayed cool, and was undecided about what might be the best bargain for her. She peered at this, poked a prying finger at that, and made a point of avoiding anything that Kitty might have come in contact with.

Not that assessing what Kitty had come into contact with was that easy. The bed for sure; bedding, chairs, sofas. Certainly not the saucepans. Kitty had made full use of Samuel's money to employ people to do the more mundane things in life.

As Ruth ran her hand over a mahogany chest with brass clasps and hinges, she felt a delightful tingle that not only coursed up through her arm, but travelled through her body and lay like the touch of silk upon her breasts. There was even a tingle in that more secret and little-used spot between her thighs.

She retrieved her hand, then deciding that she could

stand more of such sensations, she touched it again. At the same time as her hand landed on it, so did the hand of a man. Even without looking at him, she knew it was a man. His hand was broader, more coarse than her own, and yet it was finely made. She shivered. It was also very cold. He wore a gold ring on each finger. In the centre of one was a dark green emerald.

Strangely enough, he did not retrieve his hand as she did. Hadn't he felt the same shock she had?

She looked up at him, and trembled. The man's eyes were the same colour as his ring. Did he want the chest?

No matter. Here, she had decided, was a bargain. The residual sensations caused by her touching the brass-bound chest were still coursing through her body, teasing her nerve ends, and tingling those parts that had not been so tingled for a very long time.

'I'm buying that!' Her sudden proclamation seemed to take him aback, and for a moment she thought he was going to tell her that he would outbid her no matter what she offered, in which case she would have, of necessity, had to reconsider. After all, her husband might be a shrewd businessman, but his pocket was not bottomless, nor his bank credit limitless.

But to her relief, and surprise, the man smiled. 'At any price?'

She didn't like the tone of his voice. It had a hollow ring to it as though he were talking through the trunk of a dead tree. But she made up her mind. 'Any price!'

She didn't like his smile, which was wide, and lean as a sliding slug. But she did like the polite little bow he gave her.

'Then be my guest, madam.'

She beamed at the chest, then patted it. When she looked back up to thank the man for his consideration, he was gone. No matter. The bidding was about to start.

The chest was attractive, and Ruth had expected stiff competition from other bidders besides the man with the green eyes. To her surprise, she got it for twenty dollars when it must have been worth two hundred at least.

'I was going to bid against you for that chest,' Hannah said as they made their way home in the taxi. 'I thought it was real neat.'

'So why didn't you?' Ruth asked the question in a gloating way. After all, the question was purely academic now. The auction was over, and the chest was hers.

'I tried to,' Hannah replied. 'But I just couldn't seem to raise my hand. Something seemed to weigh it to my side.'

'Divine providence!' Ruth laughed after she'd said it.

'Or the devil's,' Hannah added, but Ruth ignored her.

Ruth thought about opening the chest when she got it home but there wasn't time.

Simon would be home shortly, and she didn't want any moans and groans about her spending money on useless rubbish, so she shoved it to the back of the closet where she put every 'bargain' she ever bought, until the time was right to bring it out.

Besides that, something about the guy with the green eyes who had left her to bid for the chest was still with her.

'I think he fancied me,' she said to her mirror as she rubbed her hands together. They were tingling like they did when she got ice from the freezer.

A dark-eyed, dark-haired woman in her thirties who was still attractive, looked back out at her from the mirror.

She pouted, and a wave of something warm and delicious seemed to flow through her body and make her hips sway.

'Ruth Lipman, you brazen broad, that guy stirred your hormones!'

She laughed at her thoughts, and her fingers traced down the coolness of her neck as she threw her head back. Her fingers and the hands they belonged to travelled onwards and took off her clothes.

Imagine, said that laughing voice in her mind, that there's a man with you, a man with green eyes.

'He was tall,' she said to the mirror. 'And he had big hands, but they were fine – like an artist, or a musician.'

Palms towards the mirror, she raised her hands, saw her life line, her heart line, and all the others she wasn't so sure of. Then slowly, those hands from the mirror cupped her breasts. In her mind, they were no longer her hands, but those of the man she was thinking about. Cool hands, warm breasts. Soft fingers, hard nipples.

The hands, the fingers, the touch of them, ceased to be hers. Only the sensations from her breasts registered in her mind.

Low mews of delight issued from her throat as the hands that were no longer hers ran down to span her waist, the fingers stretching to her belly.

Thigh caressed thigh as her hips swayed with a rhythm that was as old as time, and entirely irresistible.

How cool and firm her fingers were against her belly, how soft and smooth her palms.

Gently, one finger entered her cluster of pubic hair, then eased apart the lips beneath. That finger too did not feel as though it were hers. No touch registered from its tip. All she

51

felt was a presence entering the moistness of her secret garden and tapping gently at the flower within.

A mist clouded the mirror, or was it that her own eyes did not want to see what was there?

But it was her own reflection, surely? Only one part of her brain accepted that. Another, the part that was controlling this sexual scenario, saw another vision: a man in a black suit, gaunt frame, lean hands, green eyes.

It took over, this vision. Was it of its own accord, or was it because she wanted to believe he was there?

No matter.

The finger, whoever it belonged to, now explored the furled fringes of her inner lips. Moistness spread, and her legs spread too as waves of sensual delight coursed through her body.

Her mind was hazy, her sight was blurred.

More fingers pulled and squeezed her nipples.

Both nipples?

No, there's only one hand. It's not possible.

Were they also on her behind? Completely impossible.

Fingers invaded her vagina. Two? Three?

Or was it something larger, hotter, and harder?

None of it could be possible.

She closed her eyes so that the haziness was only in her mind. Her hips jerked against the intrusion, rode the thumb that so pleasurably tapped at her hidden bud.

Higher and higher she climbed the fateful path, the path that led to the peak, all white and gleaming against a sky of blue. A mountain, that was how she was seeing it. The path steepened, yet her progress quickened. At last the peak, crisp, invigorating, stupendous! Then, a sensation of falling like a feather, down, and down, to the valley below.

When she opened her eyes, it was her own hand that was between her legs, and her own that held her breast.

Before her was her reflection in the mirror.

Behind her was the room. A thin gleam of green light shone from beneath the closet door.

# Chapter 6

Celicia Corinne was as tall and thin as the fashion models she employed to show off her up-market creations. She also had an account with a Californian plastic surgeon to ensure her skin stayed tight across her classic cheekbones, her stomach remained flat, and her nipples pointed full ahead rather than at her toes.

Celicia was as shiny as the pages of *Vogue*, her hair as sleek, her make-up as perfectly painted as a work by Raphael or da Vinci. Celicia tried to look like the ideas she tried to sell.

Celicia was very successful in her field, and prided herself on making personal selections for the materials used in her fashion business, where creations were sold for a thousand dollars up, and were usually only worn once.

Josie had met Celicia before, and although it was not really her job, she had ended up with the task of taking her round the warehouse, and standing by for instructions as she made her selections.

'Tawdry!' It was a word Celicia was fond of using when she was not enamoured of the colour, pattern, or texture of a fabric.

Jose did her best to be helpful. 'What about this?'

She held up a bolt of rust-coloured silk, and let some of the cloth unravel and flutter onto the display table.

With fingernails red and flashing, Celicia felt, scrunched, then dug into the fabric.

'Nice texture. Wrong colour!'

Josie was beginning to tire of this. After all, Celicia had been here an hour or more now, and nothing had yet been selected.

Besides that, Josie's thoughts were on other things. Rod was coming over tonight, and after they had eaten and drunk wine, they would make love in many positions, and with more passion than either of them had ever thought possible. Then they would discuss their wedding plans.

Josie sighed. The rate Celicia was going on, she could be here all night. She made the decision to hurry her along, although Celicia did not normally like anyone infringing on her selection process. But Josie was desperate.

'What colour are you looking for?'

Celicia pursed her so perfect, so red lips. The nylon of her lashes swept her sculpted cheeks as she considered the question.

'Green,' she said at last. 'I want green, a special green, a vivacious green.'

Hopeful that she might get a decision out of her before five, Josie guided her to where the greens were stored.

Bolts of cloth, all of the same colour, but in varying shades and textures, were piled on shelves so that they resembled a prettily shaded grove of trees.

Celicia glided rather than walked along the rows of fabrics, her fingers lightly touching this and that. Her assistant scurried along behind her like some faithful terrier.

Celicia smiled secretively as she moved along between the shelves of fabric. It was nice to glide rather than walk, nicer than those watching could ever imagine.

Gliding was a result of not wearing underwear. Without the obstruction of silk, nylon, or cotton, it was possible to rub the satin smoothness of her inner thighs against her naked sex which was totally free of body hair. Therefore she glided, her narrow hips swaying alluringly on her long, lean legs.

Like a low current of electricity, she could feel her sexual awareness hanging like trembling leaves from her sex. It murmured through her body, hummed through her head; this sexuality, this constant companion.

But the current, the humming received a sudden jolt.

With a surprised look on her face, Celicia stopped in her tracks. What was it that had caused that?

She looked questioningly at the piled materials.

The humming in her head and through her body seemed stronger than it had been. She was aware of her nipples pressing against the lining of her jacket. There was no blouse beneath it, nothing to stop anyone from seeing the deep divide between her breasts if she chanced to lean forward, which was something she purposefully did as often as she could.

Bending over as far as possible was another thing she liked to do. If the onlooker was lucky, he – or even she – could glimpse the very tops of her legs, the very curve of her behind. If doubly lucky, the pale smoothness of her nether lips might also be smiling.

Sitting down was even better. When she sat down, she could cross her legs so that there was a momentary flash of something that might be termed her flesh, or something that might be thought to be underwear. The watcher would flush and wonder, and lick their lips, their eyes never leaving that region in case she carried out the same manoeuvre again; and of course, she always did.

But today something had affected that murmur, that constant hum of sexual readiness.

Her fingers traced back over the bolts of green cloth, then retreated quickly. Again, she felt that surge of desire, that irresistible need to throw off the last remnants of her business outfit, and leap on Serge, her assistant, or even Josie, and have them pleasure her. In return, she would pleasure them.

'I'll take this.'

She said it quickly, then stepped back, surprised to see Josie put on a pair of rubber gloves as she took the bolt of green silk from its shelf.

Josie saw the sudden caution in Celicia's features. 'I'll get it sent over,' she said, strangely worried that the fashion designer might change her mind.

Celicia only shook her head, and licked her lips. 'I'll take it with me. We can make room for something as special as this.' One hip dipped, and the other rose as she rubbed an inner thigh against the delicate flesh that peeped so shyly from between her hairless lips. A sound vibrated from her throat, then out of her mouth. It was a hybrid sound that lay somewhere between a groan of desire, and a purr of pleasure. The sudden surge she had felt earlier was still making her flesh sizzle as though she were being lightly suntanned.

Could it really have been the effect of a bolt of green silk cloth, she asked herself, then smiled. It sure would be fun finding out.

# Chapter 7

Serge wasn't the real name of the man who accompanied
Celicia Corinne, but in the world of high fashion, Clay
Lancaster Frazer didn't have quite the same mystique about
it that Serge Sevron had.

Serge Sevron was his choice. The name Clay had been
bestowed on him by his father who had been mighty fond of
boxing, and especially of Cassius Clay before he had become
Mohammed Ali and a Moslem. Lancaster had been his
mother's choice, because she was keen on movies, and an
avid admirer of all the big Hollywood stars.

On the whole, they were good choices as far as his looks
went. He was as brown and well muscled as one, and as
athletic as the other with a teeth-filled smile to match.

But in the world of high fashion, both sports and screen
personalities are people you try to impress, not ape. It was
the job of the couturier to persuade the rich and the famous
that their bodies would look especially good moulded into
the sheath-slim designs so beloved of the fashion designer,
and so sought after by everyone with a few score dollars to
spare.

Serge was grateful to have landed the job with Celicia
Corinne, that super-smooth harridan who was as sharp with

her tongue as she was in her looks.

Like a puppy, he followed her around, and just like a puppy, he lapped up her kind words, and was whipped by her sharper ones.

All the same, he dreamed of her. Dominant women had that effect on him. In his dreams, he imagined her narrow body, her nipples pointing through peepholes in clinging leather, her panties slashed high, almost to the waist. Her bottom would be exposed, a single strip of leather separating one lean orb from the other.

Although she would be wearing thigh-high leather boots and carrying a whip, it would not be her using it on him. Oh no. In real life, Celicia Corinne ruled him. In his dream, he overcame her dominance and ruled her. In his dream, he whipped that white bottom, those teasing pink teats that he saw every day as she leaned over her desk to snap out her orders.

Oh, yes. Corinne knew she tantalized him.

Perhaps one day, his dreams would come true. Serge didn't hold out much hope of that.

Everything changed the day he went to the warehouse with her and she came away with a bolt of green silk.

From the very first, she had seemed mesmerized by it. There was nothing wrong in that; it was a very fine bolt of cloth. It wasn't until he helped her get it into the back of the taxi that Serge realized it was something special.

Tingles of desire ran through his body as though someone was drawing hot, copper wires through his veins. His pelvis heaved off the back seat as the same sensation tangled in his testes, then slithered like quicksilver through his hardening penis.

'Do you feel it?' Corinne said, her eyes shining with excitement.

Serge, whose chest was heaving with the faster beating of his heart, swallowed and nodded. 'Yes. Yes, I do. What is it?'

Her eyes shining, Corinne ran her tongue over her bottom lip. Her fingers reached over the bolt of cloth that lay between them on the seat, and touched his arm.

'I don't know for sure, my darling boy, but I felt it from the very first. I think it has a power of its own. I think it has dark and sensual properties that can be cut to shape, sewn into garments, and sold for astronomical sums. Can you imagine the sensation such garments will cause?'

Serge eyed her fingers which were now edging across to his swollen member.

'Everyone will want it,' he managed to say before she undid his zip. 'It will be a sensation.'

'Of course, my darling boy. Of course they will. But first, we will try it out. Just you and I.'

Celicia's fingers probed for his member, pulled it from its lair, then wound around its stem. He gasped and glanced towards the driver. What would he think? Black plastic earphones protruded from the driver's ears and he was singing along with whatever he was listening to.

'We have time,' whispered Corinne before her head went down between his legs.

Groaning with pleasure, Serge heaved his hips towards her hungry mouth. As he did so, Corinne's legs came across so she was doing a cramped, but useful handstand. Her sex was close to his mouth, her legs on either side of his ears.

Was this real? Serge asked himself. He blinked and

61

blinked again. This was no dream. Not only could he see Corinne's sex right there before his eyes, he could smell her perfume.

Like a man wanting to swim the Olympic mile, he dived to his task, his fingers holding her naked lips apart as his tongue slid over her glistening flesh. Secure in his task, he placed one hand on her buttocks and pressed her against him. He did the same to her head with his other hand.

It wasn't the first time he had done such a thing, but never in this position, never in a taxi, and never with a woman completely shorn of pubic hair. But he liked what he was doing. The outer lips of her sex were white like satin, and soft against his mouth. Her inner flesh was pink and plush as velvet and smelt of musk, honey, and things too sweet to put into words.

Yes, he liked what he was doing. He also liked what she was doing to him.

He was aware of her hands encircling his engorged flesh, her mouth sliding up and down his stem, her tongue flicking and licking his stiff member.

Never had he experienced such an erection as he had now. Never had he come again and again into such a luscious, luxurious mouth, his semen enticed by such a strong, experienced tongue.

As his tongue probed her vagina and flicked at her clitoris, she jerked against his mouth, and her honey spread over his lips.

'I want you to come to dinner tonight,' she ordered, once they were back at the office. 'There will be three of us for dinner – you, me, and Angelo. Dress smartly.'

He hadn't answered. She knew he'd be there. He knew

he'd be there. And it wasn't because he was drained of energy by virtue of his experience in the cab with her. It was because he was still trying to take in that his dream was coming true. For the very first time, he had pleasured Celicia Corinne, and she had pleasured him. Tonight, she would pleasure him even more.

Upon arrival at the sheet glass and chrome doors of the apartment block where Celicia Corinne lived, Serge spotted Angelo Armarini coming in the opposite direction.

Both stopped before the doors and looked each other straight in the eyes.

Serge broke the silence first. 'You too?'

Angelo, whose father was Italian, and whose mother was Puerto Rican, nodded and looked the slightest bit frightened. He did, however, manage to speak.

'What do you think it's about?'

Serge pursed his lips and thought about the journey back from the warehouse when a bolt of green silk had travelled with them on the back seat of the car.

Serge grinned, partly at Angelo's discomfort, but also at his own. 'I think she's out to seduce us.'

'Shit!'

Angelo had received ballet training, so was lighter on his feet than most, and well able – so far – to keep out of the reach of his lady boss.

But there had been the odd moment when she had cornered him, and her lips had sucked at his whilst her hand had clutched his assets.

Striking as she was, Angelo could not bring himself to submit to her demands tonight. Not that she didn't arouse him. She did. It was just that he'd heard that she was one

63

hell of a performer, a story he believed to be true. After all, she was nearly twice his age and had no doubt experienced far more than he had. And hadn't he always been told that practice makes perfect?

On one of those occasions when she had cornered him, she had not stopped at just a grope of his rod and tackle, but had slid down his zip, her red-tipped fingernails burrowing in his pants to bring his member out from its hiding place.

Her mouth had dropped open once it was in full view, and her eyes had looked to be on stalks.

Not that she was the first to be impressed by the length and circumference of his measure, and neither was she the first to drop to her knees, crying, 'I don't believe it! What a beautiful cock.'

Like many before her, she had then delivered an adoring kiss on its glistening head. And like all the others, it had not stopped there. A kiss was followed by a suck, and in minutes, his member was halfway down her throat. And that was where all similarities ended.

Celicia Corinne had been the first to have the suck of a vacuum cleaner. It was like having your testicles drawn out through your penis. Only three sucks and he'd dispensed his load. Even then, she hadn't let him go. She had kept sucking him until he was hard again, until he'd come again, then she left him gasping and worn out so that he'd had to crawl into the fitment room and sleep for the rest of the afternoon.

He should have known it would not be the end of her pursuing him; after all, they'd barely touched on the more aesthetic aspects of sexual practice and deviation.

Sighing, he nodded at the doors. 'After you, Serge.'

'After you, Angelo.'

It worked out that they went through the doors together.

On the forty-fourth floor, Celicia, dressed only in a pair of high-heeled silver shoes, awaited them.

'Darlings, darlings!'

Her butler took their coats as she kissed each of them on both cheeks, and patted their groins.

As she turned her bare bottom towards them, Serge and Angelo exchanged looks.

The sight of the tight little cheeks of her bottom translated a sexual message to their sleeping members. Wake up, it said, wake up and follow me.

Their rods stiffened, and they did follow her, but each trembled. Serge trembled in anticipation of turning his dream into reality. Angelo trembled in fear that he might not be up to the job she had in mind.

The butler left the room which boasted a decor of burnt orange, warm creams, and subtle hints of beige.

She insisted on them having a drink, and offered each a green silk napkin to place in their lap.

'There now, my beautiful young men. See how I look after you?'

Hesitantly, Serge touched the napkin that lay so innocently on his lap. Immediately, it rose as his penis pushed against it.

He glanced at Angelo. The same thing was happening to him.

Celicia was smiling.

'My darling boys. Do not be alarmed. Feel free. Unzip your trousers and let your cocks break free.'

Her voice danced in their senses, but not nearly so much

as their male parts did behind the safe bastions of their trouser zips.

Serge slid his hand beneath the napkin and let his penis out from behind it.

He stared at it, sure it had grown since the last time he had examined his erection. For a moment, he had the impression it had changed colour and looked to be slightly green.

He blinked, sipped at his wine, then smiled as he saw everything was as it should be. Not knowing or caring whether Angelo had unzipped his trousers, he stared at Celicia.

Angelo did the same. Both were transfixed by the sight of her lovely naked body and hairless sex, opening like the soft petals of a rare orchid before their very eyes.

She lounged on the soft beige of her couch, and in a purposeful gesture, lightly dangled her own green silk napkin up and over her sexual mouth. Flashes of static dazzled and danced from the silk and around her groin.

Her white teeth flashed as she smiled, and although both young men were aware of the intense darkness of her eyes, the chiselled perfection of her cheek-bones, it was hard to tear their eyes away from her most treasured possession, so pink among its surrounding whiteness.

Wet tongues licked dry lips as each young man removed his clothes, and under Celicia's instructions, tied his napkin around his wrist.

Both were vaguely aware of an electric current travelling up their arms. Serge knew the nature of that current. Angelo did not, but took the view that certain materials can be like that. Some have more static than others.

Muscles taut, and honey-brown skin glistening with the sweat of expectation, each young man stood proud and beautiful before her, male parts gently swaying and pulsating as their erections swelled with desire.

Celicia smiled at them. Her eyes shone. 'On your knees, my darling boys. Worship me as you would wish to.'

Eyes staring, and pulses racing, the young men sank as one to their knees. Dipping their heads to the floor, and their naked and butter-brown rears into the air, they kissed her feet, their tongues dividing each toe from its neighbour as she mewed with delight above them.

Their mouths travelled up over the gleaming shins, the tight muscles of her calves. They licked her knees at the front. Obligingly, she lifted her legs from off the soft leather couch so they could lick them at the back too.

She kept her legs raised and spread them to the extent it seemed she might split in two – like a dancer might when doing the splits.

Their tongues licked the soft skin of her inner thighs, circling, kissing, sucking the sweet satin softness of her flesh.

As their searching mouths reached her sex, she raised one leg into a contortion she had learned from some oriental guru in her younger days. With the dexterity that only the very slim and the very experienced can achieve, she hooked her foot behind her neck. Without any prompting, her boys, the ones she had pursued for so long, now did her bidding.

Murmurs of pleasure escaped her rose-tinted mouth as one tongue flicked at her passion-filled bud so it rose from its sheath. The other tongue dived like an energetic penis into her moist and wide open portal.

Two heads, two tongues both sucking and licking the

same moist sex, arousing the same ecstatic sensations.

Rolling onto the floor, she got onto her hands and knees, and again, like two closely attached appendages, they followed. One young man paid attention to her clitoris and its surrounding flesh, whilst the other attended to her vagina.

As though orchestrated by the demands of thought alone, hands covered her breasts, and fingers manipulated her nipples in just the way she liked.

Now was the time she wanted them to enter her, yet she did not tell them that. She knew, just by thinking it, that they would give her what she wanted, and in return, they would be getting exactly what they wanted too.

One brown body slid under her, and as her lips met his, her sex enveloped his member, her muscles sucking him in just like her mouth was sucking his tongue.

She cried out, surprised by the size of his erection, and the feeling that she was so full, so firmly impaled on a rod as hard as iron, as hot as hell.

I'm full, she thought to herself as she groaned with the effort to contain him, but only half full.

Even as she thought it, she wondered whether she was being too greedy, too sure of her own sexual stamina.

But it was no good. The thought was already out, and the silken head of Angelo's glans was dividing the cheeks of her bottom.

Could she cope with this thing? Would it hurt? Would it split her in two, and sever one tight little buttock from its sister?

Fire burned in her belly, then in her behind. The heat and hardness of Angelo's penis was in her, and the crisp hairs of his pubic region rasped lightly against her buttocks.

Eyes staring, and groans falling from her mouth, orgasm overcame her; not just her own, but theirs as well. Semen poured into her like hot lava from very active volcanoes.

That fascinating electricity she had sensed in the warehouse, that curious static that had reached out for her and turbo-charged her sexuality, was now not just running through her body, but out of her. In turn, energy released in the form of their climax was charging between her, Angelo, and Serge, and along with it, something resembling lightning – green lightning.

It didn't stop there. Serge and Angelo were also tinged with that green light, and charged with that same energy by which she had been able to withstand the size of their weapons and the intensity of their onslaught.

Once her session was over, it was Angelo's turn. He had her kneel before him, and as she sucked and kissed at his new erection, Serge approached from behind.

Obligingly, Celicia tilted her bottom, and as Serge entered a willing anus for the first time, she took Angelo's penis into her mouth, which because of its length, meant her throat as well.

As Celicia could be such a contortionist, and indeed enjoyed being one, once that session was over, she hooked both feet up behind her neck so that the full extent of her sex was exposed.

It was as if she were all sex, her opening the only one she had, and the very centre of her body.

They lifted her, one on each side, each holding a foot as though it were a handle, and carried her to a closet which had two very convenient clothes rails.

They pushed back the rows of clothes, and hung her there, one foot either side, and as one stood behind her to hold her steady, his penis sliding enticingly between the cheeks of her behind, the other entered her.

Many more games, and many more positions seemed to erupt from their minds and take place before they finally succumbed to tiredness, and untied the green silk squares from their wrists.

In the early hours of the morning, once she had collected up the pieces of green silk and locked them away in the place where she kept all her most precious things, Celicia Corinne turned Serge and Angelo out into the darkness.

'Is that it?'

Angelo did not hide his disappointment.

Serge was non-committal.

'For now,' said Celicia. 'Tonight was play. Tomorrow is work.'

And anyway, she thought as she closed the door after them, I'm the gal who's made a real killing today. Think of how much money I can make with material such as that.

Then she went back to bed, and thought of how the green silk that she intended to make up into many different garments, would swiftly turn into green-backs once the erotic properties of the material were discovered.

# *Chapter 8*

Kitty Levy was talking to Simon over her green salad and mineral water. He did his best to look attentive, but was having trouble concentrating on what she was saying. The messages travelling from his eyes to his brain were overpowering the ones from his ears.

Outlined in pink, plump and curved, her lips moved enticingly as she talked. The sound of her voice ceased as she opened her mouth to receive a forkful of lettuce, tomato and cucumber.

Fascinated with the perfection of her mouth, and intrigued to think of all the other things those lips had done, Simon watched closely. He saw her mouth open, her lips part before the fork slid between them; almost, he thought, as though she were breathless, as though something more alive, much hotter, and much harder was entering her mouth.

His penis was hardening, and he felt hot. He pushed the thoughts away and took in the rest of her appearance. She was wearing a loose silk top with matching trousers. Her hair was brushed away from her face but fell to her shoulders. Looking at her hair made him think of burying his nose in it, smelling it, and even imagining the feel of it on his chest, on his belly, and falling in a ticklish cloud around his penis and between his thighs.

He imagined her shoulders bare, caught his breath as he imagined her nipples lightly kissing his chest.

Oh, how he would kiss those nipples, how he would reach out for them, finger them, twist them, rub them gently between his fingers and thumbs. And all the while, she would be riding him, her bare rump slapping in time with her rising and falling on the most enormous erection she had ever encountered.

His reverie was broken as he became vaguely aware that she was asking him a question.

'You are sure you haven't seen my things anywhere in the office?'

'What? Uh . . . no . . . I don't think so.'

'The pyjamas were green, and so was my body.'

'Your body?'

Simon had sudden visions of her firm white breasts, and imagined her nipples being as deep a pink as her lips. What did green have to do with it?

She giggled, as was only to be expected. After all, Kitty had no doubt known more than a few men in her time. It was no big deal to imagine what he was thinking. In her time, he thought to himself, she must have had to step over a fair few men, the way they threw themselves at her feet.

'Body. The sort of thing that covers from here, to here.'

One hand rested across her chest, the other just at the start of that scintillating valley that dived between her thighs.

'It was made of green silk and matched the pyjamas,' she told him, then reached across and touched his hand. Her face became suddenly sad, and her voice became girlish, almost silly.

'I would like to find those things. Sammy doll was fond of his jimjams, and he loved me in my little bit of silk. It really got him going, so for old times' sake, in memory of him . . .'

Her voice petered out, and she bowed her head towards her hand.

Simon patted the one nearest him.

'Don't worry,' he said to her soothingly, 'It's bound to turn up, and if it is in the office or the warehouse somewhere, then I'll get it back to you pronto.'

Her smile returned, and although her eyes didn't seem particularly moist, he could not harden towards her, except where it counted – in his trousers.

In his trousers, his one-eyed snake stirred like a king cobra waking up for a meal.

I wonder, he thought as he imagined his body in action, and hers lying underneath him. He made the effort to ask what she was doing that afternoon.

'Meeting an old school-friend,' she said, her smile and her eyes suddenly bright and breezy.

'Oh.'

Simon swallowed his disappointment, but the hardness in his pants swallowed nothing, and continued to jerk against his zipper.

She smiled, and her fingers moved over his. 'I'm sorry to disappoint you.'

There was a look in her eyes that he'd seen on a dozen girls in his time. All of them had given him the brush-off.

'I'll manage,' he said, and managed to smile. 'Perhaps another time.'

The look in her eyes intensified, and her tongue licked languidly over her lips.

'Perhaps I can help you manage.' Her voice was hushed, as sexy a tone as he'd ever heard. Her smile was as promising as her words.

What happened next made Simon's eyes become as glazed as glacé cherries. He gasped, but aware that other people dining at other tables might hear and therefore look, he choked on it before it could get too loud.

Beneath the cover of the table and the crisp linen cloth that covered it, Kitty had slipped off her shoe, and was pressing her foot against his groin.

As her toes teased his stem, and her heel pressed on his sac, she spoke in a sugar-sweet fashion about Sammy doll, about her life, about the weather, in fact, about anything.

Under the circumstances, it was just as well.

Simon could not speak at all. His penis was hard as granite, or perhaps like Lot's wife, it had turned to something like salt.

Everything about him was still except for the fluid travelling up his member. He heard Kitty, he saw her, but couldn't quite work out what she was saying. Despite that, her voice tantalized him, but not as much as the motion of her foot against his appendage, the toes that curved over its tip.

Stiff and lively, his rod pounded against his zipper. He swallowed, swallowed, and swallowed again as though he were trying to dislodge a plum stone from his throat. In fact all he was trying to do was hide the sounds that revealed he had come in his trousers.

Life had taught Kitty Levy many things, and one thing she did know about was men and the signs of ejaculation.

She removed her foot, and smiling sweetly, picked up her purse.

'I do have to go now,' she said in her prettiest voice. 'My old friend from my high-school days will be waiting for me. Pleasant days, pleasant times. I'm sure looking forward to rekindling old memories, so you'll have to excuse me.'

She leaned across and kissed him, then, suddenly wide-eyed and appealing, she reminded him of why she had asked him to meet her for lunch. 'Now don't forget if you find my night things. Sammy doll and I did have some cute sessions down there at the office, you know.'

Simon nodded. He didn't know, but he could guess. His mouth went dry at the thought of how sexual, how stupendous, how rod-jerking such sessions would have been.

Because he was thinking about that, and because the warmth in his trousers was now cooling and becoming too sticky to be comfortable, he almost forgot what he had meant to ask her.

'Kitty, I wonder, could you answer one question for me?'

She had already stood up, and now looked down at him before glancing at her watch, then smiling – a little impatiently, he thought.

'Sure, what is it?'

'Please don't think me personal.'

'I won't.' Her voice was sharper.

She looked at her watch again.

'How did old Sam . . .' he hesitated. This wasn't easy. 'How come your husband had a reputation for being something of a stud and still had an erection in his coffin? Did he have some secret formula?'

She pursed her pretty lips, raised her eyebrows and looked away from him. For a moment, he thought she might have something to hide.

But no, he told himself. Kitty was a pretty woman. Kitty wasn't like that. Kitty gave one hell of a jerk-off just with her toes and her foot.

'Tea!' she exclaimed suddenly, as she took the first step towards the door.

'Tea?'

'Yes. Tea. He drank gallons of the stuff.'

She hurried her goodbye after that, and didn't offer to pay her half of the cheque.

'Tea?' Simon was still saying the word even after he had counted out the twenty dollars or so.

There was indeed quite a selection of tea in his desk drawer back at the office. He had intended throwing them out, had even mentioned the fact to Josie, and Josie was incredibly helpful. Even now, she could be bundling up the bags and boxes. They might already . . . !

Oh no! No, Josie, no!

Rapidly and continuously the same words ran through his head. Visions of Josie throwing the packets of tea into the rubbish flashed before his eyes as he rushed back to the warehouse and his office.

Nothing could slow his progress. He slammed the gas pedal to the floor and ignored the sounding of taxi horns and the scattering of pedestrians.

'Jaywalkers,' he shouted at the ones who gave him rude signals, but were unable to throw him a punch.

Sweat broke out on his face. If only he'd thought to bring the mobile. He could have phoned and told Josie not to throw the tea away. But then, if he had brought it, he wouldn't have taken the route he had, and he wouldn't have found out that Kitty's old school-friend was not quite what he had visualized. The only reason that he saw Kitty with her old friend from high school, was because a red light was against him. The old friend looked as though he might have played full back, judging by the size of his shoulders. Like most of that ilk, he also had bulging thighs and a square chin. Blond, of course. That to Simon's mind was always the way they seemed to come, apart from those who were black skinned.

Being a relatively average man himself, he also believed they all had one other thing in common, besides playing football. A small pecker, he thought to himself, I'll bet he's only got a small pecker. Sporting types with large pectorals always have small peckers. It's because all their strength goes into building the other muscles of their body.

Whether they did, or whether they didn't, he put the matter from his mind. Kitty had given him a lunch-time treat that he could feed on for days, and he was grateful.

But he had a mission, a very important mission. With steadfast determination, he slammed open the door that led up to his office, took two steps at a time, and bounded towards his desk.

Just as he had remembered, there were the packets of tea. Earl Grey, Darjeeling, plain Liptons, China, and Ceylon. He was a coffee man himself, but this fixation of his was too big to allow for fads and fancies. What was a cup of strong, black coffee in comparison to a hard, thick erection?

He called Josie to his office.

'I want you to show me how to make this.'

'I thought you wanted me to throw it away.'

'I've changed my mind.'

That afternoon, once Josie had shown him how to brew the dark brown leaves to full strength as Mr Levy used to like it, he drank gallons of tea. He did the same that night, the next day, the next night, and the day after that.

On Friday, in the closeted secrecy of the men's washroom, he examined the contents of his trousers. His penis was as it ever was, not too big, not too small, and at this moment in time, more intent on letting out the gallons of tea he had poured into his system than on becoming stiff and ejaculating semen into some woman's body, no matter how voluptuous it might be.

But he persisted in drinking tea, and finally deciding that he must have consumed enough of the stuff for it to have fortified his stamina, he decided to take the plunge.

He made a reservation at a French-style bistro, where the tables were covered in wipe-off red checkers, and flickering candles were stuffed into the necks of empty wine bottles.

A burger bar would have suited him better, but Ruth had nagged about going to Le Château Piaf for quite some time now. If this was what it took to get her in the mood for what he had in mind, he was willing to let her have her way – in the hope that he could have his.

Before arriving at Le Château Piaf, Ruth had eyed him a little warily.

'You look jaundiced,' she'd said as he'd paraded around their bedroom in the nude.

Her noticing the colour of his complexion had not been his intention. He had purposely straightened his shoulders and held in his stomach, in fact done a pretty good impression of a wedge of cheese, in the hopes that she might notice an improvement in his erection.

Was there no difference at all? Deflated ego equalled deflated erection.

He was too proud to ask her if she'd noticed any improvement. She could have done this by throwing herself to her knees, taking his pride and joy into her mouth, and half choking on its length.

Leave it to the ambience, the food, and the wine of Le Château Piaf, he said to himself.

Be patient.

Over the meal, and after a good few glasses of chilled white wine, he told her of how things were at the warehouse, but not with regard to his quest for Samuel's secret.

She listened, but there was a faraway look in her eyes that he hadn't seen before.

Was she listening?

He put her to the test.

'Do you know what I'm going to do to you when we get home?'

She said, yes dear, but her eyes were studying the other diners.

'I'm going to rip off your clothes, tie you to the bed, and rape you with a cucumber, then a banana, then the handle of one of your golf clubs.'

'Hmm,' she said.

Had she heard him, or was she agreeing?

The wine made Simon an optimist.

When they got home, he tried to rip her clothes off, and got pushed away.

'I'm quite capable of undressing myself!'

The sharpness of her retort did not sink into his muzzy head, so when she was at last naked, and about to put on her nightdress, he came at her with the golf club. He would have tried the cucumber, or the banana, but it was too far to go to the kitchen in his condition. After all that wine, he was not sure he could make his way back up.

'Get away, you filthy pig!'

The words hit his ears at the same time as the golf club.

She beat his back, and his arms as he raised them to cover his head.

That night, still half-dressed, he slept in the spare room.

In the morning he took a good look at himself, decided he did look jaundiced, and made an appointment to see Doctor Zahlevi.

Once he'd checked Simon's medical insurance, the doctor was pretty sympathetic. 'You look ill.'

'That's why I'm here. Am I jaundiced?'

Ordered to open his mouth, he did so.

Ordered to undress, he did that too.

The doctor took a blood sample. Then he asked for a urine sample. Simon obliged, glanced at his watch, and did his best to guess at what the bill was likely to be.

Over the top of his gold-rimmed glasses, the doctor eyed him with shrewdness rather than sympathy.

'I'll get this analysed. It'll cost, but it could sure be worth it. I'll ring you later with the results. It won't be too late. I'm off on my yacht this weekend, so I don't want to hang around.'

Simon left it at that, but wondered how much of his bill was going towards running the doctor's yacht.

As promised, the doctor did ring later.

'Is it fatal?' Simon had been worrying about it all morning, more so even than the bill.

'No,' the doctor replied. 'It's tea. You've been drinking too much of it. Too much tea means too much tannin. Too much tannin means you go a funny colour – orange at its worst, or a faint shade of yellow at its best.'

'Thanks, doc,' said Simon. He sighed as he threw the first box of tea into the wastepaper bin. 'You've made me a very happy man.'

'No problem. You've made me a very happy man too. My fee is in the mail. Make me happier and pay it within seven days.'

# Chapter 9

Sloe-eyed and dark-haired, Petrushka, whose daily rate for modelling for the top names in *haute couture* was enough to keep a family for a year, let her clothes drop to the floor, and stood naked, hands above head.

'I'm ready for the next frock, Cupie darling,' she called out. She emphasized the word *frock* as though it were some cotton slipover from a downtown store, not a top of the range design by Corinne in green silk.

Cupid, her dresser, did not appear.

She frowned and let her hands fall to her slender and oh-so-boyish hips.

'Give me a shout when they're ready for me, will you?' she said to one of the dressers.

The dresser, who did not answer by virtue of the pins she was holding with her teeth, only nodded.

Petrushka ventured further between the chromium rails on which hung every type of outfit from the daring to the divine, the elegant to the ridiculous.

'Nice,' she murmured, as the hanging garments brushed against her naked skin. 'If I wasn't in some kind of hurry, I'd stay a bit longer.'

But she was in a hurry. She was expected back on

the catwalk within ten minutes.

'Cupid. Where the bloody hell are you? I'm ready for the next one.'

At the back of the noisy dressing room, in a recess that led to the fire exit, she found her dresser.

'Cupie, darling. What's the matter?'

He was leaning against the wall, his body trembling as he rubbed his buttocks up and over an old-fashioned conical fire extinguisher. His trousers were somewhere around his knees, and his male part, brown and rigid, was waving free.

Wide-eyed, he was staring at the garment he held in his hands. It was green, the colour seeming to tremble almost as much as he did.

Petrushka recognised the silk gown that she was supposed to be wearing.

'Cupid!'

His legs shook, and he groaned as he let the fine silk run through his fingers.

'This is so gorgeous,' he said and crushed the material to his face.

'This is my next frock!' Petrushka snatched the dress from him. She gasped as a tingle of what felt like electricity ran up her arms and made her nipples tingle.

Cupid, his brown, shaved head glistening like polished teak, immediately came to his senses. The glazed look left his velvet-brown eyes, and a sudden blush came to his dark skin as he pulled up his trousers.

'I'm sorry. I don't know what came over me.'

Petrushka, impressed by the size of his manhood, kissed him affectionately, patted his penis, and put it away for him. She loved him, and he loved her. Of course, because of his sexual predilections, physical confirmation of that love had never occurred between them.

She kissed him again. 'Never mind, darling. Get me into this, will you.'

Perhaps it was the feel of the silk over her naked skin that made her flesh tingle, or perhaps it was the warmth of his hands setting the material straight over her shoulders, her breasts, and her buttocks. She couldn't be sure. But what she did know was that her affection – no – her lust, for Cupid had intensified.

The silk was very sheer, and very slinky. In response to its touch, her nipples hardened, and the areolae around them became plush as velvet cushions.

The dress caressed her flesh rather than covered it. As she glided through the dressing room, the other models, the other dressers, the other designers, all fell silent.

But she was hardly aware of them. The silk licked at her hairless sex, trickled like water over the roundness of her behind, and moved with her thighs.

Her hair, which was almost black and reached her waist, complimented the green simplicity of the dress. Her shoes were strappy, gold and high. She moved with the grace of a gazelle, the strength of a leopard, along the catwalk.

A hush descended on the buyers, the guests, the rich and the privileged as she floated past. There were many there to buy, many more there to be noticed.

But she did not notice them.

On another occasion, Cupid and what she had found him doing might have been the reason for her enigmatic smile. His homosexuality had always been a desperate barrier between them – mostly erected by him.

But today, it was not Cupid who made her smile. Today, it was the fact that her dress was made of green silk, and not only did it suit her visually, it also suited her on a more personal level. How it did what it was doing, she didn't know. All she did know was that the sensations it was igniting in and around her erogenous areas were eminently pleasurable.

Those watching could not know that, with each subtle movement of her body, her legs, and her arms, each jiggle of her naked breasts, the silk was arousing her.

As if in a dream, she walked to the end of the catwalk, then turned and walked back, twirled, and twirled again, before regaining the dressing room.

Everyone clapped as she walked through where half-dressed models were getting ready to follow in her footsteps and gain the accolades and dollars that only the truly outstanding received in this profession.

The clapping, the congratulations, the sheer admiration, only penetrated her mind on a very superficial level. Vaguely, she was aware of them, yet as in a dream; as if they were not quite real, and what she was experiencing most definitely was.

Cupid was still where she had left him. He was leaning against the wall, his hand over his chest.

'My heart's thumping,' he said. 'And I'm so ashamed. I can't believe what I did. I'm sorry.'

'Don't be.' Her voice floated. She was barely aware of it. She was only aware of her need for sex; of her need for him.

'Do you feel it?' he asked her, his palms flat against the wall behind him, his eyes falling to her dress.

'Yes. I feel it.' Her voice was warm as honey, her eyes

bright with a strange, green fire.

She reached for him, and her hands cupped his face.

He opened his mouth to protest that women weren't his thing, that he was what he was, and why couldn't she accept that?

But no words came out.

The silk of her dress brushed against his body. Everything she was feeling, he began to feel too. Somehow, she had transferred her sensations to him. Each knew of this phenomenon, and both reacted to it as only a man and a woman can.

Their lips kissed, their arms entwined.

Petrushka the beautiful moaned as she felt the hardness of the muscles beneath the darkness of Cupid's skin.

'You are so African,' she said, her breath hot against his ear. 'Do you know that? Do you, my Zulu warrior?'

'I'm from Harlem,' he gasped between her kisses, 'and I'm more of a Dodger man.'

Conveniently, his zip was still undone. With a little help from her hands, his trousers again fell to his knees.

He gasped, he moaned, but he did not protest.

Her hips pressed against his, so that again the rounded nose of the fire extinguisher was between the cheeks of his behind.

Preconceived ideas about what he liked or disliked about a partner – especially when it came to gender – flew out of the window.

They were hot, they were passionate, and in time both were naked, the green silk dress sliding to Petrushka's ankles, and resting upon Cupid's boots.

An aura of green light eddied around them as Cupid

sucked in Petrushka's lips, and fondled her breasts.

His member was hot against her belly; the head of the fire extinguisher was equally hard between his buttocks.

Petrushka slid her hands down to his behind, and smiled inwardly and outwardly when her fingers touched the solid object that so ably divided his behind.

'I will ride you, my beautiful African,' she said. And Cupid helped her mount.

As she divided her lips and his penis entered her, Cupid gripped her behind, then pulled her towards him.

Once impaled on the rich hardness of his member, she thrust herself onto him, her muscles drawing him in, swallowing him whole. At the same time as she thrust against his belly, his buttocks pressed harder against the fire extinguisher until the head of the cone was embedded in his anus.

Waves of green light filled both their minds as they gyrated together, the green silk swirling like sea water around their feet. Also like water, their arousal swirled upwards from their groins, from Cupid's buttocks, and down from her breasts. Climax was accumulating along his penis, around her vagina, and throbbing in her clitoris.

'Ahh,' cried Cupid, as he shuddered from naked head to naked knees. His voice shuddered with his body. Never had he experienced such an orgasm, one that was in his penis and in his behind. He had done her, yet had been done himself. The very thought of it made him want to do it all over again.

'At last, my beautiful African,' Petrushka called out. 'At last!'

How many times had she dreamed of feeling the hardness

of this big, black man against her flesh? How many times had she imagined his length filling her pussy, discharging his seed into the deep confines of her womb? Many times. Too many times to mention, but like a lot of extremely beautiful and sensitive men, Cupid had made it clear that he was not a woman's man. Men were most definitely his habit. Today, that habit had been broken.

'I don't understand it,' he murmured as he rested the heat of his cheek on her shoulder. 'I just don't understand it. I'm gay. I've always been gay.'

Petrushka patted the smoothness of his shaved head.

'Do not concern yourself. There are no women, no men, only sexuality. Now,' she said, lifting his chin with her finger, 'shall we try this again?'

A number of people expressed an interest in the chic green silk number that the famous Petrushka had been wearing.

'I'm sorry, but it is already sold.'

Celicia Corinne was the one making the excuses. Secretly, she had not been at all surprised that Petrushka had forgone her hefty fee and taken the dress instead. Although Celicia's first instinct had been to make money from garments manufactured from the green silk, her attitude had changed. A strange protectiveness had come over her. Watching Petrushka gliding down the catwalk had captivated her imagination and ignited a new resolve to keep the green silk to herself. The secret of the green silk could, she hoped, be kept 'in house'. Why should the general public have access to such a unique article? Would they appreciate its unusual properties? No. They would not.

'But, Celicia, darling . . .'

Always the shrewd businesswoman, Celicia smiled. 'Perhaps I could make it for you in blue. Blue would suit you, my dear Joanna, especially with your hair and complexion.'

'You think so?'

The ageing movie star was obviously flattered, but then Celicia knew she would be. Flattery was something she could give in plenty. Besides, it means a lot when you've kissed sixty goodbye.

'Certainly, darling. Let me make it for you in blue, but only for you in blue. For no one else.'

'Marvellous, darling. Simply marvellous.'

Celicia smiled in the same way that Petrushka had smiled as she had walked the catwalk. There was a glazed look about her eyes, a liquid movement about her limbs.

Today, contrary to normal routine, Celicia wore a pair of skimpy green panties that were no more than a triangle of fabric. The fabric was soft against her skin, yet elicited the most uncommon responses from her sensitive flesh.

Such a small thing, and yet so delightful. A mere scrap, and fashioned from green silk.

# *Chapter 10*

Simon had taken up golf with a view to increasing his business contacts. Ruth had presented him with that particular reason. Of course, she had also presented him with others, such as fresh air and exercise, plus the fact that she enjoyed hitting that small white ball with that skinny stick. Socializing with useful business contacts had been the only reason to finally persuade him. On this particular morning, it was the Brewsters they were partnering.

Clem Brewster was head of a big law firm that, besides having an office in New York, had one in San Diego, Houston, and Washington.

He was a big shot and big shots were always useful.

As Ruth went into the rough to help Marge Brewster look for her wayward ball, Simon got talking to Clem – mostly general business gossip.

'I hear Schweitzer's selling his property down on Crane's Wharf.'

'Yep. Made a mint from that old place. Going for redevelopment. Store, in-house sports complex, offices. That sort of thing. I'm handling the legal formalities.'

Simon laughed. 'My, that old man's going to have one big pile of money to spend. I wonder what he'll do with it all.'

Now it was Clem who laughed. 'Buy a body – a young wife – just like old Sam Levy did. What a way to go, eh?'

He winked, licked his lips, and slapped Simon on the back.

Rather than admit just how much old Sam's erection had become an obsession, Simon laughed too.

He left it to Clem to speak first.

'Heard you bought old Sam Levy's warehouse.' Clem peered impatiently to where the women were kicking among the long grass.

'How did you know that?'

'I drew up the papers. Remember? I did most of old Sam's legal stuff – even his matrimonial business.'

'You did, yeah, sure you did. You would, wouldn't you?'

Simon was aware of his mouth becoming dry and his words tumbling out with surprise rather than coherence.

'Yeah!' Clem went on. 'Knew old Sam for years. Knew all his wives too. And the others.'

'Others?'

'Other women. A wife wasn't enough for old Sam – perhaps with the exception of the last one. But then, he was eighty. Had to call it a day some time, I guess.'

Simon gulped and eyed the lawyer's greasy face in the vain hope that he might see something else there. Nothing gave. He asked the question he'd been asking ever since old Sam's funeral.

'How did he do it, d'you reckon – satisfy all those women?'

Clem sniggered, but still looked in the direction of his round-assed wife and the slimmer Ruth.

'Beats me. Did have a rigid routine, mind you. Early

rising: early to bed, obviously.' He sniggered again. 'Drank an odd concoction every morning too.'

'Concoction?' Simon was all interest. 'What sort of concoction?'

Clem pursed his wrinkled lips before he answered. 'Raw eggs. Garlic. Milk.'

'All together?'

'Far as I know. Must have worked wonders. I hear the old man still had a stiff one even laid out in his coffin. Is that true?'

Simon nodded. 'Yes.'

'Jogged a lot too. Swore by it. Said the earlier in the morning he went out jogging, the better he was. Reckoned the early bird always got the bigger worm.' Clem laughed again, then winked. 'Could be the worm he was referring to was his own John Thomas. What do you reckon?'

'Could be.' Simon's laugh was nervous. His thoughts divided entirely from business and golf.

Although his eyes were fixed on Marge Brewster's generous buttocks, the stirring in his pants was inspired by what he was thinking, not by what he was seeing.

On the following Monday morning, Simon arose at five o'clock, threw open the windows, and jogged on the spot.

Ruth snored on and spread herself over the warm spot he'd left in the bed.

'Now,' he said to the bathroom mirror, 'do I drink my breakfast now, or do I go jogging first?'

He looked at his reflection and instead of seeing the Simon of today who had a wife, a number of businesses, and other such adult encumbrances, he saw again the small boy who had eaten three hamburgers (much against his mother's advice) and then gone swimming.

He wagged his finger at his reflection. 'Learn your lesson! Never exercise on a full stomach, Simon, my son.'

Well, he'd learnt his lesson and he never wanted to be as sick again as he had been on that day.

'Exercise first – then eat.'

Simon got on his jogging suit that only came out of the closet when the day was fine and warm, and even then, only at weekends.

As he jogged through the downstairs lobby, the janitor threw him a knowing look then shook his head.

'Won't last.'

Simon pretended he hadn't heard him. After all, what did he know? He was only a janitor. Did he have a pecker and a sex drive that would last him into his dotage?

Head held high, Simon bounced on his soles as he ran the hard sidewalk, then took to his heels across the street to a small park where he and Ruth had done their courting.

Used to be nice in here, he said to himself. Ignoring the shrieking of brakes and the equally loud yell of the taxi driver, he bounced his way across the road, through the park gates and along the gravel path.

Birds were singing. Nice, he thought. Never realized they got singing so early.

A squirrel ran across his path in hot pursuit of a windblown paper bag.

In the days when he and Ruth had lain and fumbled on the grass, there had not been any litter, or none that he could remember. The trees and the bushes had bloomed in wild abandon, as in equally wild abandon he had run his hand up Ruth's skirt. In response, she had always opened her thighs, her hips thrusting towards his hand.

Just thinking about her, him and the long grass, made his organ go hard. His body might be in the present, but his mind was in the past.

Like his body, the park had changed. Now the foliage had a more straggly and neglected air about it, and at this hour of the morning there were no lovers lying in the grass.

Funnily enough, there were no other joggers either.

Was it too early?

He glanced at his watch. Five ten. Perhaps he'd make it a little later tomorrow. Who knows? These early morning runs might turn into quite a social occasion.

He smiled at that, and imagined long-legged lovelies wearing those cute little shorts that left the cheeks of their bottoms in view. Perhaps if he was lucky, one of those lovelies would drop her shorts and let his hands wander over the tightness of her bottom. As his rod grew, he would follow the curve of each buttock with his fingers, delve into the cleft between, and explore where her buttocks ended and the lips of her pussy began.

Then, with luck, she would mew with delight as the heat of his mouth kissed her cool flesh, and the wetness of his tongue traced feathery strokes over her pert cheeks.

Ah, bliss, he thought to himself as his member became heavy with desire.

Then he heard footsteps. Someone was running along behind him. For the first time, it occurred to him that not only joggers went running early on a morning. Muggers might have the same habit.

He became nervous, swallowed hard, and tried to persuade

himself to look over his shoulder. No, he told himself, keep calm. But he did increase his speed. Despite him running faster, the footsteps were getting closer. His heart thumped and so did his head.

'They'll catch me,' he puffed. 'They're bound to catch me.'

He couldn't keep ahead of them. It was impossible. But at least, he thought to himself, I can turn round and see who it is about to mug me. One glance was enough. Two women were running behind him. Just two women. He smiled and automatically slowed his pace. What did he have to fear from two women?

The answer came very swiftly.

He let out a loud yell as two well-muscled bodies thumped against his, and two pairs of strong hands dragged him into the bushes.

Dry twigs scratched at his face, his feet slid on damp earth as he struggled, but firm hands dragged him in then held him down.

'This is a knife, citizen, and it's pressed against your throat.' The voice was surly. He recognized business when he heard it.

He had been about to yell, but didn't need them to tell him where the blade was pressing. He could feel it, could imagine its sharpness digging into his skin, slicing into his jugular and letting his blood run free.

Two female faces looked down at him: two sets of Spanish eyes that were dark lashed, but hard as nickel plate.

'Give us your cash and cards.' The voice was darker than her eyes.

'Or we give you this,' said the other. She pressed the flat

of the blade to a spot just below his jaw.

That's my jugular! His brain screeched. He wanted to faint.

'I . . . I haven't got any money with me.'

'Then give us your credit cards!'

He swallowed again and squeezed his eyes shut.

'I haven't got them either. I came out to jog, not to spend money.'

'Don't be so funny, mister.'

The first face came closer. The knife pressed harder.

I'm going to die, he thought to himself. I'm going to die before I'm even half the age that old Sam was when he snuffed it.

He glanced down at his crotch. There was the sign of a pyramid in the soft grey of his jogging pants, all that was left of the vision of tight buttocks and skimpy shorts.

'No money! No cards!'

The first mugger spat the words at him then tore his watch from his wrist.

The other was eyeing his crotch.

'Well,' she said thoughtfully. 'Look what we've got here. You've got no money, no cards, but you do have one hell of a hard-on!'

Her friend looked to where she was looking. She began to smile, then nodded to her friend.

Simon cringed as the girl pulled down his pants. His hard-on refused to lie down.

The girls mewed in unison as his member became exposed to the morning air.

He opened his eyes, and surprised himself. Regardless of the knife blade and his predicament at the hands of these women, his member stood proud and – dare he think it – impressive.

Obviously, the girl who had pulled his trousers down thought so too.

'Nice one,' she said in a low, purring type of voice.

Simon moaned as she ran her fingers up and down his length, then groaned some more. The little minx pinched at his balls, so he cried out.

Then she dug her fingernails into the crown of his stem.

This time, he did not cry out.

This time, his mouth was full.

The mugger who held the knife had got her breast out and had popped her nipple into his open mouth.

What could he do but suck on it?

Against the smothering breast he could not see what the other girl was doing, but he could feel her. The touch of a thick bush of pubic hair tickled the tip of his shaft. Warm liquid ran like honey from an open vagina and trickled over his balls.

He could not groan, he could not move, but then, he didn't want to.

Moist and firm, the mugger's sex moulded around his. Soon, her pubic hairs were rasping against his belly as she rode him.

Vaguely, he was aware of her moaning, but also aware of his own helplessness, and also his own pleasure.

He took a gasp of air between the left tit being removed from his mouth and replaced by the right.

Hard buttocks thudded against his thighs. Now he could hear her moaning, could also hear the soft splat of a wet sex against his groin.

Was this being raped?

If it was, he had no objection to it, no objection at all.

With obvious enthusiasm, he sucked on the stiff nipple and dared to reach and squeeze the tit to which it belonged. It was soft as sponge, but very acceptable.

I'm being raped by two women, he told himself. I'm being raped by two women! In response, his penis jerked and his hips lifted from the damp grass as he thrust up into the woman who was riding him.

He might have cried rape, might have protested more if only to perversely encourage their actions, but his mouth was full, and not only of flesh, for as he pummelled and sucked on the soft breast, something hot and sweet squirted into the back of his throat. Milk! He was drinking milk, and once he had tasted that first squirt, he couldn't stop sucking.

It was as though he had returned to being a child, to being dependent upon a woman for his bodily well-being and his daily sustenance. And yet, such comforting thoughts also served to heighten his desire: they were using his body, taking all that he had. Yet in turn, he was taking from her – this one woman who took pleasure from him – feeding on her milk.

The milk was warm, her breast was warm, and the female channel that slid so demandingly up and down his stem was warm also. He was drowning in warmth, suffocating in the close proximity of female bodies that fed him milk – milk that spurted into his mouth from one woman just as his own milk would spurt into the other.

Greedily, he sucked at the tit, his climax rising as a naked bottom slapped more urgently against his pelvis. She was coming. He knew she was coming, and also knew that soon this tit, this succulent object that filled him with milk and with desire, would be taken from his mouth.

At last, she cried out and thudded down on him, her sexual lips wet against him as his fluid spurted into her. Unable to cry out himself, he bit the nipple that was in his mouth.

'Ouch!' cried the woman to whom it belonged, and Simon suddenly remembered the knife.

The raping vagina departed from his loins. To his deep regret, the invading breast left his mouth.

The owner of it looked towards his now limp member.

She moved nearer to it and touched it. It moved, but not very energetically.

'I can't wait around for you to get hard again,' she said to Simon. 'You've given my buddy something, and I've given you my milk, you greedy little sod. Now you've got to give me.'

She took off her trousers, and facing towards his legs, she straddled his face.

Female scent filled his head. Her sex was hot and wet against his mouth and his nose.

'Lick it,' he heard her say. 'Lick it and put your tongue in me. Make me come. And do your damnedest, because as you're doing that, I'll be playing with your dick – and my knife's still in my hand.'

With an energy and dexterity he didn't know he had, Simon licked at her swollen clitoris, and dived without hesitation into her yawning vagina.

As he licked, gulped, and dived, he was aware of the coldness of the knife blade being rested against his stem, the hardness of the handle pushing between his legs, and pressing against the softness of his scrotum.

'Faster,' she called over her shoulder. As she shouted, the flat of the blade hit against his sac.

Whatever speed he had been going, it doubled. In his mind, he could see himself dead in his coffin and his own dick not stiff and upright like old Sam's, but lying beside him – cold, inert and entirely separate.

Spurred on by his own fears, his tongue seemed to grow and become more dextrous, more skilled in its probing.

With his fingers he opened her dark-haired lips and where his tongue could not reach he probed, tickled, tapped, and caressed.

'Keep going,' she cried. 'Keep going!'

He did, and so did she.

Strong thighs rubbed against his face as she bounced up and down on his mouth. Just as his tongue divided her inner lips, her outer ones separated over his nose.

At times, he felt he was drowning in her musk, her wetness. He was at her mercy, and when her final release came, she sat on him, her slippery flesh quivering against his face as her climax washed over her. He thrashed his arms, fought for breath, and for a moment, truly thought his end had come with her climax.

He blacked out, and when he eventually came to, the two women were gone, but not without leaving a sign that they had been there.

Where the stickiness of their fluids still adhered to his face and his sex, they had stuck handfuls of leaves: Not nice flat maple or plane leaves, but small ones from willow, and prickly bits of holly.

'Ouch!' he exclaimed, as he tried to pull them off. He did

what he could. After all, he could not afford to linger. He had a warehouse to oversee, and a mission to accomplish.

He brushed himself off, rearranged his clothes, and jogged wearily home.

By the time he got there, Ruth was up and about. He tried to head straight for the bathroom without having to answer any awkward questions, but he was unsuccessful.

Her hands were on her hips. Her mouth was set firm and her skin glistened with moisturizer. 'So,' she said, crossing her arms, 'what gets you up so early?'

'I've been jogging.'

She shook her head and tutted just like his mother used to do. 'I don't think it's good for you.'

'Why not?'

'It's brought you out in a rash – a red one all round your mouth.'

He didn't answer. He rushed off to the bathroom, closed and bolted the door, then reached for the medicine cabinet.

There was some ointment there guaranteed to soothe mild irritation caused by bites or stings.

Quickly, he unscrewed the top, slapped a load of it over his face, then let down his trousers.

# *Chapter 11*

Katie O'Flanagan, who had very red hair, and very green eyes, was not a woman to be denied what she wanted. At the fashion show where Celicia Corinne was showing her latest designs, she had been smitten by one creation and one alone. It had swirled over the model's body as though it were making love to her, and equally, the model had seemed responsive to its touch.

Katie was observant about such things. Others might have been fooled into thinking the model was walking that way in a bid to enhance the swirl of the silk. But Katie was a woman of wide sexual experience and knew that as the model's hips swayed, the inside of her thighs would brush against her pubic lips.

Silk, she told herself, does have an arousing effect when worn against bare skin. But Katie had a strange intuition about this particular dress. This dress, she decided, would do things for her that no other dress could do. She wanted it, but if her judgement was anything to go by, Celicia Corinne had seemed more interested in making an impression with the dress than in making money from it.

That in itself intrigued her. But of course, it was also green. Green was the colour of her eyes. It was also the colour connected with her nationality, and besides that, best complimented by hair as red and hot as her blood.

But Celicia Corinne had been adamant about the dress. No amount of money would persuade her to change her mind. Katie had been disappointed, but not downhearted. She was a resourceful woman, and pretty sure she had an ace up her sleeve.

Gregory Maynard was a cool guy, who had a hot body. This was something Katie had found out pretty quickly since coming over from Ireland for a holiday in New York. Gregory was married, but not bound by morals. His wife, he had told her, was frigid. Not exactly an original line, but in his case – from what she had found out after a few discreet enquiries – a truthful one.

Gregory was also workshop and stores manager of Celicia Corinne's fashion house. He knew who was making what, from what, and where any spares might be hiding.

'I kept some spare,' he told her.

'Any reason for that?'

He smiled. 'I'm an observant guy, and the minute green silk is mentioned anywhere near Celicia or those pet boys she keeps in tow, their eyes light up. That material has sure got something nothing else has – nothing that I've ever come across, anyway.'

Katie's face lit up, and her eyes filled with a promise that Gregory Maynard could not help but interpret salaciously.

She touched his cheek and ran her fingers along his lips. 'Will you bring it to me, Gregory, darling?'

Gregory took her fingers in his and kissed the palm of her hand. His eyes burned into hers, his voice rasped with lust. 'Whatever you want, Katie darling. Whatever you want.'

'Yes,' she had murmured. 'Whatever *I* want.'

Ever since she had reached puberty and her breasts had sprouted and her hips begun to curve, Katie had found it easy to get her own way.

In Galway, where the sea was as green as the grass, and the mountains as blue as the sky, she had blossomed from a long-legged adolescent into an equally long-legged woman. Unrestricted by the rigours of underwear she had run through the green meadows and bathed naked in the sparkling sea.

Among the young men, many a wet dream was centred on the vision of Katie O'Flanagan, and in older men, many a memory was invoked by looking at her. Even those who by virtue of their calling should be eternally celibate, were tempted by her creamy flesh. Many prayers for forgiveness were muttered in darkened bedrooms and many a priestly penis refused to lie down and go to sleep.

Celibacy had been put to its greatest test when Katie had taken up hang-gliding. Like a bird, she had soared on the thermals, revelling in the freedom of soundless flight and sharing the view of the rolling hills, rivers and valleys only with falcons or very low-flying light aircraft.

Of course, there was an increase in light aircraft once one pilot had informed another that Katie preferred to hang-glide in the nude, her breasts hanging earthwards, and her bottom kissed by the rays of the sun. Such a thing could only be expected to cause trouble.

It had been a hot July day when she had soared higher than normal, and the pilot of a light aircraft had become so captivated by her charms, he had flown too close to her and created a turbulence that sent her in a downward spiral.

Nothing she did stopped her from going ever downwards, but at no time did she panic.

On seeing the spire of St Oedocus monastery, she said a silent prayer and closed her eyes.

Her nylon wings jolted, and just when she thought the end was nigh, the ghost of a thermal lifted her again, but only enough to soften her landing. She came down just over the wall of the monastery, and before passing out, was aware of the smell of earth and vegetables.

On waking, she was still aware of the smell of dark earth. The place she was in was also dark, though there was enough light to distinguish terracotta pots ranged in strict order of size along a series of shelves.

There were also garden implements, a length of hose-pipe hanging on the wall, and two or three wheelbarrows.

Besides being aware that her harness was gone and she was still very naked, she was also aware of a figure between her and the door.

'So. You're awake.' He spoke sharply.

He came closer. She could see he was a monk; could see his habit dropping to his sandalled feet. He wasn't old, but he was no youth. If he hadn't been a priest, she would have ear-marked him as a potential lover. His eyes were dark, and so was his hair which rose high in the centre of his forehead and curled somewhat wildly to his shoulders.

It was hard not to regard him as anything but a handsome man, but besides being lustful, Katie never forgot to be respectful. Reminding herself that this was a holy man, Katie had immediately tried to cover her nakedness with her hands. It surprised her to find she could not move. Her hands were tied to either side of her head. Automatically, she tried moving her feet. They too were tied, one ankle to an iron ring in the wall, and the other to a heavy iron vice.

The monk smiled triumphantly. 'It's no use struggling. You can't get free to run wild in here, you little demon. You're not going to tempt my brethren, I can assure you. And you're not going to tempt me!'

She stared at him before answering. Did he really think she was a devil? A supernatural being snatched from legend and superstition? Or did he merely mean that as a woman, she could not help but be a temptress, and as a man, he could not help but be tempted?

'And what makes you think I'm here to tempt anyone?' she asked.

He glared. The firm jaw remained firm. The mouth did not smile and the air of resolute piety never left him.

'Providence brought you here. Providence can sometimes be the devil. Sometimes not. Anyway, I'm not chancing anyone else being provoked by your charms into doing things they might regret.'

'So let me go.'

'No.'

'Why not?'

The monk acquired the sort of look she'd only seen before in stained glass windows. His eyes looked towards heaven. Saintly, she thought to herself, he looks saintly.

His nostrils flared as he took a deep breath, then looked directly into her eyes.

'I'm going to sit with you all night and endure your nakedness. By gazing on your flesh, I will attempt to test my own resistance and, with God's help, I will resist.'

'And in the morning?'

The saintly pose vanished. 'In the morning I will release you.'

Thankfully, it was a warm night: not that such a fact stopped her nipples from hardening and a heavenly tingling from travelling over her naked body. Her responses might have been due entirely to the fact that the monk's eyes never left her flesh. On the other hand, perhaps she was merely reflecting or imagining what he was feeling. The difference between them, of course, was that she would not resist such temptation. With undisguised hunger, she would have fallen on him if she could. But of course she could not.

Sometimes as he stared at her, the monk shivered. Sometimes, almost as though it was all too much to endure, he closed his eyes and muttered a few words that might or might not strengthen his fortitude.

Katie was aware of her body being bathed by the light of the moon as it entered through a small window above her.

It kissed her breasts with its silvery gleam, accentuated the flatness of her belly, the curve of her hips and thighs. In its cold brightness, the redness of her pubic hair turned to gold.

Before tiredness overtook her, she heard him gasp and mutter a few more prayers.

Wearied by her flight and her landing, she drifted into sleep.

In her dream, she landed in a meadow where a handsome shepherd lay her down in the grass and somehow staked her out there so he could do with her whatever he liked.

The dream became more vivid, the touch of the shepherd and her responses more real until it came to her that she really was being touched by something.

Had the priest yielded to her charms?

Slowly, consciousness returned, but she did not open her eyes. She did not want him to stop what he was doing. Instead, she murmured some unintelligible sound that would make him think she still slept.

She moaned as her nipples responded to the touch of something cold and hard: a finger?

She couldn't be sure. Anyway, it didn't matter what it was. It was pleasant.

The cold hardness ran over and beneath the curve of her breasts. It dallied there, then scratching slightly, moved down over her belly.

Was his finger that long, she asked herself. Did he never cut his nails?

Her curiosity was swamped by the sensations running through her body. As if she were enjoying a pleasant dream, she murmured through half-closed lips, her body undulating beneath the unseen touch.

The exploration continued through her rich tangle of red-gold hair. It went further, dividing her plush lips and slithering over her inner folds of flesh.

So long, she thought. So long, and so hard. What can it be?

There was no time and no reason to dwell on such a question. Tremors of aroused sexual response ran through her body. Her nipples pouted for attention; her buttocks rose from off the hard bench on which she was lying. Despite her ankles being tied, she could bend her knees, and open her legs.

That very long, very hard device was now nudging at her vagina which was brimming with moisture and aching for invasion.

Like a hard-skinned snake, it entered. She moaned, feeling it slide easily into her.

Sure it's not thick, but it's certainly long, she thought to herself, and still it kept coming. Good God! How much more? Would it keep going until it came out of her mouth?

'No!' She could not help crying out.

All movement stopped. As though she had been momentarily disturbed by a nightmare, her voice faded into murmurs.

There was movement again; a pleasant in and out movement. Yet whatever the length was within her, it was enough to still be pressing against her sex, arousing her clitoris, and thus sending shivers of delight throughout her body.

She rose with it, flowed with it, let the sensations it ignited take her higher and higher towards her climax.

Her hips bucked, her back arched, and cries of delight escaped from her lips.

Then it came; washed over her like the waves of the sea, tingling up over her belly and down through her thighs.

Only once the last spasm of orgasm had melted away did she open her eyes. The monk was looking at her, his eyes wide, his mouth open.

Katie smiled. 'Was that as good for you as it was for me?'

His mouth snapped shut. He raised his eyes to heaven before he spoke. 'I resisted falling for your charms, your enticing murmurs and the snake-like wriggling of your body. I did not touch you. I did not violate you.'

Katie had laughed. 'So what did?'

'This,' he said as he wound a length of garden hose back

onto its spool. 'This did it. I resisted touching you. I resisted entering you.'

Even now, three years later, it amused Katie to think about that first meeting with Brother Ignatius. It amused her even more to remember his gasp of surprise when he had at last released her and she had reached for his member, tugged it only a few times; heard him **gasp**, and seen the wetness that appeared among the folds of his habit.

It had been their first meeting, but not their last. After that first encounter, they had met regularly, and had played out the same scene over and over again. Indeed, the garden hose had become softer and more pliable at one end on account of the lubrication to which it was so frequently subjected.

And Ignatius had never entered her. On the contrary, he pleasured her, and rather than her touch him, he now required that she tie him up, hoist up his habit, and beat him with that same hose on his bare backside. It was only what he deserved, he told her.

So far he had escaped entering her, but not for much longer. Judging by the vibes she had got from that green silk dress, his days of resisting her advances were numbered.

Gregory Maynard, who worked for Celicia Corinne, just had to say yes to what she asked of him. Unlike Brother Ignatius, he couldn't wait to divide Katie's legs, and have her sweetly-accented voice murmuring into his ear.

That night, Gregory arranged to meet her at the New York Hilton. Under his arm, he carried a box, and in that box was the spare dress he had made.

A smiling and expectant Katie let him in.

'Here it is,' he said and held the box out to her.

'Marvellous!' she exclaimed, her eyes bright with excitement. 'How can I ever repay you?'

Gregory, perhaps looking a little bashful, or perhaps a bit apprehensive, shoved his hands into his pockets, but managed to put into words what he truly wanted.

'Let me see you in it. Let me see you in it with nothing on underneath.' He tossed his head to throw back the lock of corn-coloured hair that had fallen over his eyes. His eyes shone like chips of deep blue sapphire.

Almost as though she was newly released from a convent school, Katie's mouth fell open before she smiled. Not that she was much like a nun when she *had* been at school. On the contrary, even there, her beauty and obvious zest for sexual adventure had been the undoing of two priests, one bishop, and countless nuns.

'All right. Wait here.'

She went into the bedroom and closed the door behind her.

For a moment she lay against it and clasped the box to her chest.

Was it imagination, or had a tingle run from her breasts to her groin?

She arched her back and pressed the box against her hips, closed her eyes and sniffed the air. Again, she was in the potting shed back at the monastery, and Brother Ignatius – he of the firm chin and smouldering eyes – was running a length of garden hose up, down and in her body.

She opened her eyes again.

'Get your clothes off and put the dress on.'

It was her saying the words, and yet in some way it wasn't. Prompted, was the word that sprung to mind. Yes. She had been prompted because in the time it had taken for her to leave Gregory and go into the bedroom, his request had been smothered by something. What was that something? Sensation? Emotion?

In a sudden effort to gain control, she threw the box onto the bed, and just as quickly got out of her clothes.

Naked, she eyed the box. Her breasts started to heave more quickly as she ran her tongue over her lips and felt the first oozing of sexual fluid tickle the tops of her legs.

Slowly, she walked to the bed, took the cover from the box, removed the tissue, then removed the dress.

She gasped as the faint tingle of electricity ran from her fingers to her nipples and her moist pubic lips.

Was it evil, she asked herself as she let the green silk dress drop back onto the bed.

Don't be silly. It can't be. It's far too lovely to be evil.

Again she picked it up, then murmured long and low as its silky coolness fell over her body.

Almost at once, she wrapped her arms around herself as her body tingled and swayed beneath the fine material.

Her nipples hardened, her hips moved gently from side to side as the silk clung to her belly, her thighs, and even the curls of her pubic hair.

Suddenly, the arms that were holding her were not her own, but those of Brother Ignatius who so pleasured her, yet so adamantly avoided having true carnal knowledge. As she gazed into his face, she wondered when his eyes had altered colour. Surely, they had been brown? But these were green, and somehow, it didn't seem to matter.

113

Gregory. His name came to her mind. I must go to Gregory.

The arms that had held her now dropped to her sides.

'I'm beautiful,' she murmured as she gazed at her own reflection in a mirror. 'I'm beautiful and I'm sexy. I feel,' she said, speaking to the reflection as though it were another person, 'as though all my sensuality is being pulled to the surface, changed from fantasy into reality.'

'Then go back into the other room and do what you want to do.'

Just as before when the voice had come to her, it did not seem real. Yet it was real. It was her voice – yet not her who had mobilized it.

She smiled at the red-haired, green-eyed reflection that now looked doubly beautiful in the green silk dress. 'Yes,' she said wistfully. 'Yes.'

Gregory got to his feet when she entered. In her absence, he had removed his clothes. At the sight of her, his erection – which was already hard and upright – seemed to increase that much more.

'You look incredible!'

She smiled. 'Good. Then you'll have no objection to taking me out.'

His erection wavered, retreated a little. 'Out?'

He was surprised on her insistence that he don what looked to be a monk's grey habit and sandals, but just looking at her in that slinky dress, her nipples clearly visible, he could not help but agree to her wishes.

Katie's eyes sparkled and her flesh tingled as she drove them away from the hotel and into an area that looked as though it had changed little since the turn of the century.

Street lighting diminished as they travelled down side roads and past crumbling brownstones where traffic was as scarce as people.

Eventually, she drove through a gateway in a high wall. On the other side of the wall, there was no light except for that lent by the moon.

A thin mist lay close to the ground, and ancient tombstones stuck up like jagged teeth among coarse grass and ragged weeds.

Crouched like a spider in the centre of its web were the old ruins of an abandoned church, its windows unglazed and unseeing in the shadowy darkness.

'In here?' asked Gregory.

'Certainly, Brother Ignatius.'

Gregory laughed. 'Brother Ignatius. So that's my name for this evening, is it? So what's the fantasy to be?'

Her eyes still sparkling, Katie smiled at him. 'You'll see. I'm sure you'll enjoy it.'

Once there would have been a door to open, but the door had rotted long ago. They walked straight through where it should have been and down the aisle to the stone altar.

'What now?' asked Gregory. He trembled as he said it, suddenly aware of strange sensations racing through his body as he brushed against Katie in her beautiful dress.

'Will you do all I ask of you?'

She kissed his chin after saying it. Her breath smelt sweet, and her closeness intoxicated his senses and sent his pulse racing.

'Yes. I'll do anything you want me to do.'

'Bend over the altar.'

The tingles that had laced through his body pierced his

brain like white hot needles. He did as she asked. He didn't know how she managed to tie his hands to two corners of the altar. But then he didn't care either. He was hers – all hers – to do with as she pleased.

In his belly, his muscles tightened as firmly as the knots that held his hands. Between his legs, his balls hung as heavy as lead, and the tip of his penis tapped against the stone of the altar.

Katie stepped back and surveyed her handiwork.

'Do I tempt you, Brother Ignatius?'

'Oh, yes!' Gregory's voice trembled.

'But you mustn't be tempted, my holy brother. You have taken a vow of celibacy. It is wicked of you to even think such carnal thoughts. And you don't want to stop at just thinking those thoughts, do you? You want to press your hot little penis into my pussy, don't you, Brother Ignatius? Is that not correct, my darling brother?'

'Oh, yes. Yes!'

Gregory almost screamed the last yes, and his legs trembled as she lifted the rough cloth of his habit.

Katie ran her hands over his bottom. His flesh was hard, his skin slightly hairy. Under the influence of the green silk, the darkness of the old ruins, and the fact that she could not see the face of this man, Gregory was – to all intents and purposes – Brother Ignatius.

'I am going to have to punish you for thinking such lewd thoughts, Brother Ignatius – just like I always do. And then, when I have done that, you will do something you have never done before. You will put your penis into me. For the very first time since our meeting, you will enter me and fill me with your seed. Does such a thought inspire you?'

'Yes!' Now he did scream, for at the same time as she ended her sentence, she scratched each naked flank with her nails and left red stripes where there had only been whiteness.

A burning was in her body, in her mind and in her eyes as she raised a strip of sapling above her head and landed it in a fierce blow across Gregory's naked behind.

He yelled out, confused and affected by pain and by pleasure as both the strip of green branch and the green silk of her dress touched his body.

With each blow, his hips jerked forward so that the head of his penis jabbed fiercely at the stone altar. It was as if the carved niche his penis entered was not made of stone, but flesh, and not inanimate, but a woman.

'Do you confess your sins?'

The heat in his behind intensified as the strip of sapling again connected with his flesh.

'Yes,' he shouted. 'Yes. I'm a sinner. I want to fuck you. I want to get into your pussy, into your mouth, and even into your behind.'

He groaned, and closed his eyes, aware that despite her treatment of him, his penis was getting ever harder, ever larger.

The green eyes of Katie O'Flanagan narrowed as she studied her supplicant, her fan, her disciple.

She flung the supple branch to one side, and raising her dress, climbed onto the altar, her legs either side of his face. As she manoeuvred herself forward so that her sex was against his mouth, she let the green silk drop over his head.

Instantly, his tongue, his lips, his teeth were upon her. As her hips heaved onto his mouth, she scooped her breasts out of her bodice, holding them, playing with them. At the same time, she threw back her head and enjoyed what was happening to her.

Closing her legs, she clamped his head tight to her and mewed with delicious desire as his tongue flicked at her clitoris and dipped into her moist vagina.

Jerking again and again, she came against his mouth, and leaving her breasts still exposed, she got down from the altar and again picked up the sapling branch.

'You have touched me! You always promised yourself that you would never touch me. But you have. Are you sorry for that?'

'No. No, I'm not.'

He cried out as she beat him again and again so that his buttocks were red enough to warm her hands on.

'Then I will give you a second chance. Do you want me to give you a second chance?'

'Yes,' he cried out. 'Oh, yes.'

'Very well. I have had your mouth in a similar way as to how you wanted mine. Now I will have your cock.'

She slid up between him and the altar and ripped open the front of his habit so that the bareness of her breasts was against his naked chest.

He moaned in her ear and struggled against his bonds.

'I want to touch your breasts.' He said it plaintively as a child does who wants a special treat.

Katie smiled up at him. 'No. I won't let you touch them, but I will let you suck them.'

Like a man dying from hunger, Gregory pressed his lips first to one breast, and then to the other.

Sensations of such exquisite delight, such sensual deliciousness, ran through Katie's body, and through his. As Gregory sucked her breasts, Katie raised her skirt and pressed her belly against his. Without hindrance, his penis entered her body, and as one, they moved together, thrust forward, retreated, and thrust again. The green silk clung between them, held them together, fused them into a sexual whole.

Katie dug her nails into Gregory's naked backside, and in response, Gregory nibbled at her nipples, bit at the curve of her breasts, and nipped at their slopes.

In one movement, one spasm of sensual delight, they both climaxed, their breath hot and mingling, their sexual juices mixing and running in warm rivulets down their thighs. When the last tremor had disappeared, Katie got out from under him.

Exhausted, Gregory slumped against the altar and closed his eyes. 'Is that it?' he murmured.

'Do you repent of your impure thoughts, my darling Brother Ignatius?'

Gregory chuckled faintly against the cold stone. 'Oh no,' he said. 'Most definitely no. In fact I thoroughly . . . Ahh!'

The sapling again landed on his hot backside. By the time she stopped, he was moaning quietly against the cold stone of the altar.

He winced as the coolness of her hand ran over his burning buttocks.

'My, my, darling Ignatius. But your behind is so hot and soft, and my pussy is so cold, I do think they badly deserve each other. Don't you now?'

The thought of Katie's pubic hair against his behind was

119

too much for Gregory to refuse. His desire and his erection
revived.

'I suppose so.'

The sapling with which Katie had chastized Gregory's
behind had a thick end as well as a thin. The thin end was
obviously more whip-like and suitable for beating the man's
behind. But the thick part had a use of its own.

Gregory moaned as the coolness of her hands caressed
his bottom. 'That's delicious,' he said. 'Oh my God!' he
added, as her fingers slid into his crack and divided one hot
cheek from the other. 'Oh my God!' he exclaimed again as
her fingers explored his crack and dived cheekily into the
puckered mouth of his anus. He still purred with contentment
as her finger entered him.

'I'm glad you enjoy it, my son,' said Katie in the sort of
voice she'd heard a visiting cardinal use back home in
Ireland. 'It's going to get even better, and you, my son, are
going to have more than a finger in there.'

Gregory gulped, then cried out as the thick end of Katie's
sapling was pushed into his anus. His knees bent, and a
hollow feeling came to his stomach.

After first making sure that the branch was firmly
embedded in him, Katie again scooped up the hem of her
dress, and like a fairy-tale witch mounting her broomstick,
she cocked her leg over the protruding branch.

She wrapped her arms around her steed and one hand
around his penis. With the other, she clung to his waist.
Gregory gasped, then moaned with pleasure, surprised that
the intruding branch could heighten the sensation caused
by her hand.

His bottom nestled in the curve of her belly and thighs,

and as she rode the branch and jerked her pelvis against him, he did the same so that his stem continually slid over the palm of her hand.

Katie too was moaning and gyrating as the rough nodules of the branch rubbed against her clitoris and the lips of her sex.

She rode the branch, jerked her sex against Gregory, and Gregory, in turn, jerked in her hand and against the stone altar.

Katie cried out as her third climax ran in violent shudders throughout her body.

Gregory, his sensations accentuated by the hardness in his behind and the rasp of stone upon the tip of his penis, came with her, his seed spurting against the altar from where it ran in thick trickles to the ground.

# *Chapter 12*

In Simon's opinion, Ruth's mother was a bit of an old dragon, but to Ruth she was a saint, a godly woman who she should have listened to long ago. Perhaps if she had, she would never have married Simon. But then, at the time, their relationship had been formed and directed by their sex drives and that curious little something that might be termed a tickle under the heart that can't be scratched, or might just as easily be termed 'let's make it legal and respectable to get our leg over'.

Anyway, in three days it would be Ruth's mother's birthday and Ruth had made a decision to go shopping for a birthday present.

The day, however, did not begin well. For a start, Simon got up at the crack of dawn, donned a tracksuit – a thing he'd only ever worn at weekends, and then only to lounge around in. But this time was different. This was a weekday, and a day in which he had gone jogging for the first time in his life.

If it hadn't been so early in the morning Ruth might have been suspicious of his motives, but in her experience 'the other woman' was a creature of dark nights and city lights. A mistress was definitely not the type for the hours before seven in the morning. She was also, in Ruth's opinion, not the sort to go for a guy who had early morning bags under his eyes. Neither was she likely to be turned on by his equally baggy tracksuit.

Cuddling down into the warmth he'd left behind him in the bed, she dozed and in her befuddled sleep, remembered the man he used to be, the woman she once was, and the fervent energy with which one body had pleasured the other.

When only half awake, she let her hand touch her breasts, then run down between her legs – just like his used to do. Her little passion bud so furtively pouting from between her pubic lips hardened and tingled beneath her touch.

Funny, she thought to herself, that when Simon's not here, my passion arises, and when he is here and I look at his familiar face and body, nothing happens. Sad, she thought, and continued to divide her pubic lips and delicately tap at her neat little bud. She kept tapping until her flesh tingled with climax, her breath came in quick gasps and a familiar, oozing wetness seeped over her thighs.

Her masturbation had so far proved the high spot of the day, and once she was smelling of sex, she got out of bed and showered, determined to be dressed, unappetising and therefore unavailable when Simon returned.

When he got back, he had a rash over his face. One comment from her and he was gone into the bathroom, the door firmly locked behind him.

That in itself would have been okay. He was a man trying to take care of himself and she couldn't knock him for that. Who could guess? If he improved that much, she might fancy him again like she used to.

In the kitchen he refused the breakfast she had prepared for him and instead swallowed some evil-looking concoction that he insisted would give him greater energy and staying power.

'Keep your hands to yourself,' she told him, yet somehow, inside, something was telling her to let him touch her, to let him play with her breasts, finger her sex, and run his palms over her round buttocks.

Perhaps she might have relented then and there if Simon hadn't suddenly turned green.

'What's the matter?' she asked him.

He didn't have time to answer. He was off, and the bathroom door was swiftly slammed behind him.

Ruth stood outside shaking her head as she heard the liquid he had drank gush into the pan.

'How about a plain bagel for breakfast?' she called.

'No,' came the weak reply. 'No. I don't think so.'

The shops helped her to forget that she wasn't happy, and buying a birthday present for her mother made her feel that much better again. Her mother liked antiques, so Ruth bought a very nice silver snuffbox that the assistant assured her could very well have been used by a gay English lord in the days when 'gay' meant 'happy'.

With a sigh of satisfaction, Ruth left the shop and stepped forward in the hopes of hailing a taxi.

'Excuse me.'

The voice came from somewhere on her left. She glanced at the woman, but not recognizing her, assumed that she was hailing somebody else.

'Excuse me. Can I talk to you a moment?'

This time the woman was right beside her. This time

there was no doubt that it was her, Ruth Tye, that she wanted to talk to.

'What do you want?'

Ruth looked the woman up and down. She was dark – obviously Hispanic, she thought to herself – and she was on crutches. Did she know anyone who was racially and physically disadvantaged? What's more, did she want to know them?

No, she said to herself, she did not. She attempted to raise her hand and flag down a cab. The woman's hand touched her arm.

'I am so sorry to stop you like this, but I think you bought something at an auction recently that I wanted to buy. I remember you walking past me with your friend, and when I asked the auctioneer about who he had sold my lot to, he described you and I remembered what you looked like.'

Ruth regarded her suspiciously but as she didn't feel threatened by her, she decided to hear whatever the woman had to say.

'Yes,' she said. 'I did buy something at an auction. I bought a chest, that's what they call it in Europe, a chest – not a box.' She laughed lamely. 'In fact,' she went on, 'I haven't even bothered to open it yet.'

She detected disbelief in the brown eyes that looked at her with such longing, such passion.

'You have not even opened it? Then there was no point in you buying it, in which case, if I could buy it off you for the same price you paid for it . . .'

'Oh, no. I don't think so.'

'All right, all right. I give you ten dollars more than you paid for it. Ten dollars for your trouble.'

Ruth shook her head and held up her hand. 'No. I don't think so. I think I want to keep it. It's a pretty little chest. It looks very nice in my bedroom.'

She thought of it sat in her closet, unseen since the day she'd bought it and she'd sensed its presence creeping across the carpet towards her.

'Twenty dollars?'

'No.'

'Thirty?'

'No. I don't want to sell it.'

'Okay. I double the price.'

Ruth stared at her in disbelief. Why would some dusky woman from some Caribbean island be prepared to throw her hard-earned dollars away on a chest? She made a mental note to open it the moment she got home.

'No!' This time she said it adamantly. 'I told you. I like the chest. It's pretty.'

'Okay. You keep the chest, I buy the contents.'

Ruth looked puzzled. What was more, she knew she looked puzzled because she felt puzzled. What was it about the blasted chest and this blasted woman? And what was in the chest? Now her need to open it was irresistible.

'No. I won't sell it. Not the chest or the contents.'

In a sudden determination to escape this woman and her increasing bids for the chest, Ruth raised her hand and waved it at a cab that had just dropped someone else off. The driver saw her and slid to a halt in front of her.

'But if I should give you an extra fifty dollars . . .'

The last words drifted through the open door of the cab before Ruth shut it behind her and shouted her home address at the driver.

She didn't see the woman mouthing her address as though trying desperately to remember it. Ruth was far too absorbed in her own thoughts. What was in the chest that could be so valuable as to make this woman almost throw her money at her?

The first thing she did when she got home was to get the box out of the cupboard.

The second thing she did was to take off her clothes and put on the green silk body that she found wrapped in tissue in the chest.

Never had she felt such silk. It's almost, she thought, as though it has a life of its own. If I didn't know what it was, that it was only an item of clothing, I would swear it was alive, swear it was caressing my body.

She ran her hands over her ribs and hips as she looked at herself in the mirror. Never mind that she was the wrong side of thirty; her hair was still dark, glossy and curled around her face. Her breasts were round and high, her belly flat but not lean, and her hips perfectly curved.

'I look beautiful,' she said to her reflection. 'And I look sexy.'

The third thing she did was to answer the door to the delivery boy. It didn't matter that she had almost no clothes on. For some strange reason, it seemed the most natural thing in the world to answer the door dressed in nothing but skin and green silk.

With bulging eyes and hectic thoughts, the delivery boy, who was around eighteen, deposited the box in the kitchen and took the money from her outstretched hand. As his eyes danced over her body, a flush of embarrassment reddened his cheeks, and there was fear in his eyes. He tossed his blond hair, and headed for the door. He would have made it if his fingers hadn't brushed against the green silk of the brief garment that Ruth was wearing.

'Don't go,' she cried as he started out of the door.

He stopped in his tracks and stared down at his fingers. He flexed them, then ran them up and down his thigh as if he were trying to remove something very sticky.

Then he looked at her, smiled, and without any hint of his former embarrassment, ran his eyes from her glossy hair to her painted toes.

Like a siren, she thought as she smiled back at him; I am like a siren – one of those mythical and irresistible women who lured the Argonauts onto the rocks.

'Stay,' she said as she ran her hands over the firmness of his body. 'Stay and deliver something better than groceries. Take something better than cash.'

'You bet!' He folded his strong arms above his head and hooked off his T-shirt. Ruth ran her hands over his youthful firmness and kissed his naked flesh.

As he closed his eyes and moaned above her, she undid his jeans and slid them to his ankles. She slid with them and relishing the warmth of his genitals, took each of his balls into her mouth. She sucked on their peach-haired softness, tasting a taste that was man, that was youth, and that was ultimately memorable.

Once the juices of her mouth were saturated with his taste, she left her fingers to play with his balls while she licked his shaft, then enveloped his crown with her mouth.

Above her, the boy – whose name was Dean – groaned with pleasure and threw back his head. 'No one's ever done this to me before.' His voice was hardly distinguishable from his breath. It sounded almost as though he was being strangled.

As only an experienced woman can, Ruth sucked on him until his penis pulsated and he cried out something very loud that although not quite a word, communicated exactly what he was feeling.

Ruth sucked and sucked until her mouth was filled with his essence – until she had swallowed all he had to give.

The boy reached for her breasts, and despite the fact that he had just ejaculated into her mouth, his erection again rose hot and strong.

'You are a very wicked lady,' he said as her hot kisses rained upon his lips, his chin, his cheeks and his chest.

'Should I be punished for being so wicked?' She laughed as she asked it, but in her mind it wasn't really her voice that was saying such a thing. It didn't even seem to be her body that draped itself over the back of a dining chair.

Almost as if this was the sort of hazard he faced every day in his job, the delivery boy took charge of the situation. Although Ruth's bottom was high over the back of the dining chair, the boy did not seem content with that. He placed another chair seat to seat against the first. Then he moved her hands so that they rested on the seat of the second chair. Her bottom was raised so high over the back of the first, that her toes barely touched the ground. Her breasts swung free, her stomach tightened.

Never in all her married life had Ruth done such a thing as this. If Simon had ever suggested such a deviation from the 'norm', Ruth would have told him to take a cold shower while she locked herself in her room. But today Ruth was not herself. Today she was doing this thing and, what was more, wanted to do this thing.

There was pleasure in giving pleasure, and if this handsome youth's pleasure was for her to be presented like this, then she would oblige him.

Even as the boy stood back and admired his handiwork, her flesh tingled and her nipples grew. Ruth purred like a cat as he leaned forward and slapped playfully at each of her hanging breasts so that they tapped against each other.

'I like you like that,' he said as he flung his jeans and his other clothes to one side. 'I think I am going to enjoy you like that, you wicked woman. I'm going to play with you until you beg me to take you again in any way I choose.'

'I'm sorry for being wicked,' mewed Ruth, although she wasn't truly regretful at all. Somehow they just seemed to be the right words to say. 'But I just can't seem to help it.' That at least was the truth.

There was no sign of pleading in Ruth's voice – not the sort asking for pity anyway. She was asking for him to do things to her, to make her squirm, to make her writhe with pain and with pleasure, and strangely enough, they both knew this.

Lovingly, he fondled her buttocks and with the wonder that only the young and the innocent possess, he gazed at the lips of her sex which peered from between her thighs.

Ruth closed her eyes and groaned as his finger probed between the thickly-haired lips and entered her aching portal which seeped with moisture.

'Do you like that?' he asked – as if she didn't!

'Yes,' she moaned. 'Yes. I like it very much.'

'But you're a wicked lady,' the boy said, a sudden cruelty entering his voice as he withdrew his finger. 'Wickedness is

meant to be punished. My teacher in third grade told me so.
She used to like taking my pants down and beating my bare
behind with her hand or a ruler, or even a book. That's what
I'm going to do to you.'

He gave her no time to protest. He bound her ankles to
the legs of the chair, her wrists to the back rungs of the chair
on which her hands rested.

To her further surprise – and also pleasure – he gagged
her mouth with a pair of her own pantyhose.

She heard him rummaging in her bedroom, but not for a
moment did she think he was stealing anything from her.
Instinctively, she knew something else was directing his
actions, and that something was also contributing to making
her feel more sexually aroused than she had been for years.

Tremors ran over her flesh, and she moaned with a
longing to touch herself, to spring from cover that tiny
button between her legs. Almost as though she'd become a
creature of fluid rather than flesh, she undulated, her breasts
swaying slightly as she wriggled her bottom in an effort to
rub her inner thighs against her aching bud.

'Oh, hurry,' she moaned against her gag, but of course it
did not come out as words – only as a mumble.

'Quiet!'

The flat of his hand slapped one buttock.

Ruth repeated her mumble.

The flat of his hand now slapped the other buttock.

In open invitation, she wriggled her bottom again.

'More,' she cried into the musky scent of her pantyhose.
'Give me more.'

The boy, so encouraged, did give her more, and as he
slapped each buttock in turn, the heat of his penis slapped

gently and rhythmically against her thigh.

'Give me that!' she cried. 'Give me that!'

But of course her demands were still only mumbles, and Dean was still demanding her silence.

'Wicked woman,' he said.

Lovely words, thought Ruth and tingled all over.

'You deserve a spanking just like the ones my teacher used to give me,' said Dean. 'But I couldn't find anything like she used to use, but I did find your hairbrush.'

Ruth trembled and murmured even more.

'Silence,' crowed Dean.

Her murmurs died to mere quivers in her throat. She was still trembling – with excitement rather than fear.

Do it to me, she was saying in her mind, please do it to me.

Bristles brushed like fine needles over her bare behind as the hairbrush landed on each cheek in turn.

A piquant warmth crept over her flesh and lured more fluid from her aching sex.

More mumbles fell in a torrent against her gag as her body moved in response to what he was doing.

Again and again the hairbrush landed, its bristles stinging the soft gap between her cheeks and the even more sensitive divide between her legs.

The tingles of sexual arousal that lingered in and between her labia increased on each contact with the hairbrush.

I like this, she thought to herself. I like this!

The thought both mystified and excited her. Yesterday, she marvelled, I would not have enjoyed this, I would not have admitted that there was pleasure in this.

But yesterday faded as waves of delight ran through her

body. Along with logical thought, yesterday's inhibitions were swamped by her new sensuality which made her nipples hard, her sex wet, and her flesh tremble with delight.

He stopped smacking her with the brush.

By looking back at him between her breasts, she could see that he had fallen to his knees, his face level with the lips of her sex.

As though his eyes were hers, she imagined what he was seeing: the black-haired lips pouting from beneath the pink flesh of her behind.

'I've never seen a woman's part this close up before,' she heard him say.

He placed one hand on each of her buttocks, and in doing so, transferred some of their heat to his palms.

She murmured sweetly, twisting seductively beneath both his gaze and his touch.

Her sex ached with longing. Surely he could see that, could perceive the oozing of moisture running like ripe sap from between her black-haired lips?

If Ruth could have seen the expression on Dean's face, she would have known from the redness of his cheeks, the dryness of his lips, and the sparkle of his eyes, that he could see the glistening fluid. As though it were the sweetest honey, sheer nectar, he licked along its route with the tip of his tongue, and Ruth trembled.

With the youthful curiosity of someone who has never had such close proximity to a woman's sex before, he dipped his finger between her fleshy lips.

Ruth groaned into her gag, twisted in her bonds and gripped the invading finger with all the strength of her vaginal muscles.

134

Longing rushed like a bush fire through her body. His finger was in her, but it was his manhood she wanted; that length of flesh, that rod of iron, used so far, she didn't doubt, only on giggling co-eds, never on a woman like her, and never in circumstances such as these.

'I have to! I will! I will right now!'

This was Dean talking. And yet it was as though it wasn't him.

Passion flooded her being, and climax ignited deep in her belly as his penis pushed into her with all its youthful vigour.

Instantly, as though it were eating at his flesh, or at least sucking him further in, her muscles gripped him, held him, and lubricated his vigorous length.

In and out he went, thrusting with all the vitality, all the unbridled excitement of youth.

Ruth braced her legs, and as her breasts swung back and forth like two juicy melons, a ripple of orgasm ripened in her sex, raced through her loins, and rose in her belly.

As if fearful they might be trying to escape her body, Dean gripped her swaying breasts, and as he gripped them, he thrust that much harder, that much more vigorously.

Blended, moulded, the two became as one: one mass of flesh, two people made into one purely by their most basic, most powerful instinct.

'Same again next Thursday,' said Ruth to Dean as she handed him her order for next week.

'You can be sure of that, Mrs Tye,' returned the young man who now had no look of youthful innocence in his eyes, no flush of embarrassment on his cheeks.

He kissed her before he left, and for a moment, Ruth

found it difficult to let go of his beautiful body.

Sighing regretfully, she waved him goodbye, but couldn't help but think of another young man who had been just as attractive in his youth, and just as vigorous. Who was that? she asked herself. But her memory was misty, and her body still tingled from her encounter with the delivery boy.

I'll think on it, she told herself, and closed the door.

# Chapter 13

Much as he tried, Simon could not find out exactly what it was that had made old Sam the man he was – or had been.

Again and again he had gone all around the warehouse, the offices, the loading bays – in fact, everywhere he could think of – in an effort to find old Sam's secret.

Even after his ordeal at the hands of the girl muggers he still gave it one last try, then, exasperated, walked out at lunchtime telling Josie that he was taking the afternoon off.

'Where shall I say you are if anyone asks?' said Josie.

It didn't take long for Simon to think of an answer. 'At the movies.'

It was an off the cuff response, but the idea of disappearing into the blackness of the cinema was suddenly appealing.

Following his rape in the park, getting to the cinema turned out to be more of an ordeal than he could ever have dreamed of. Even getting to his car sent prickles of sweat over his skin.

Parking the car was okay, but getting from the car park in through the doors and into his seat was another ordeal. At the slightest sound, the lightest footstep – someone whistling a tune, someone running – he broke out into a sweat and counted to ten before looking over his shoulder.

A movie was already in progress when he took his seat. He was still sweating and shivering slightly.

Bliss, he thought to himself as the darkness enfolded him. The movie was rough, tough, and fairly explicit. Watching what was happening on screen automatically took his mind onto other things, things that had happened to him, things that had happened to other people.

He thought of Ruth and how she used to be when they were courting: such an old fashioned word, courting. But to his mind, it still had an air of mystery around it. Have they or haven't they, it seemed to ask. He and Ruth most definitely had. From memory, he could smell the scent of her hair, her perfume and those areas of her flesh he had liked to smell best: beneath the curve of her breasts; beneath her arms, the crook of her elbow, the juicy, erotic smell of her sex and the tops of her thighs.

His penis rose in his lap and he tried to cover it with his hands.

He swallowed and stared at the screen, very much aware that his erection had not diminished.

As he lost interest in the movie, he began to look around him. The place was half-full. He narrowed his eyes as he tried to focus. He never had seen very well in dark places, but he hadn't brought his glasses with him and didn't need them to watch the movie anyway.

There were mostly couples to the front of him, and behind too, if the sound of kisses and subtle moaning was anything to go by.

He looked to his right. Vaguely he was aware of a man with very blond hair sitting there. The man looked at him and appeared to nod.

That's friendly, he thought, and smiled – mostly to himself.

He squinted a bit more and looked in the other direction. The rest of the row would have remained empty if a woman hadn't come in from the other end, disturbed the man, then got Simon to his feet.

'Sorry,' she whispered as she squeezed past him.

Simon almost passed out with pleasure as the cheeks of her bottom grazed the head of his hard rod.

'Sorry,' she said again. 'I should really have come in from the other way.'

'No problem.'

The feel of her buttocks passing over his penis ensured it remained standing.

He kept looking at her, smiling, and was sure she kept smiling back.

He winked at her, and thought she winked back at him.

He waved his fingers, and was almost sure she did the same.

The next time he looked, she was gone from her seat.

For a moment he was disappointed until, as he stared at the screen, he felt movement around his knees, fingers opening his fly and dragging his stiff member into the open.

As he gulped and stared, his fingers gripped the chair arms. What was she doing?

Her mouth swallowed him, her lips firm but pliant around his stiffness.

His gasps curled around his throat, his fingernails dug into the soft material of the chair arms. He stared at the film with renewed intensity. He refused to look down at her in case he found it was only his imagination playing tricks and she was not there at all.

But it did not feel as though she were a mere fantasy. Strong lips sucked on his stiffness; a prying tongue poked into the eye of his rod and licked around his crown. He could almost have fainted.

It didn't take long. Not long at all. In one almighty gush, he shot his semen into her mouth.

As the last throb faded away, he closed his eyes, relishing the dying throes of his beautiful orgasm, his chest heaving as his breathing returned to normal.

When he opened them again, she was back in her seat.

He had to move closer to her. He had to thank her and perhaps ask her if he could see her again.

In the darkness, he groped each chair arm before sitting himself next to her.

'Thank you for that,' he whispered.

This time, he was close enough to see her frown.

'For what?' she asked in an angry whisper.

'For that blow-job you gave me.'

'What! How dare you!'

He cried out as her hand slapped his face.

'Manager!' she shouted, and shot to her feet.

'But I don't understand . . .'

Simon looked back to where he had been sitting. He could just about discern the figure of the man who had been four or more seats along. Like the woman he was now sitting next to, the guy had blond shoulder length hair. The man's face was turned towards him. As realization dawned, Simon knew the man was smiling.

'Good God!' Simon shouted, and before the manager or

anyone else had time to grab him, he was out of the cinema, his feet flying to the car park as they had never flown before.

'Damn the muggers,' he exclaimed as he ran past many a rum-looking individual. 'And damn the bloody movies!'

# *Chapter 14*

The same Gregory who had enjoyed a night of perverse passion with Katie O'Flanagan had not been lying when he had told her that his wife was frigid.

Molly had soft brown hair and eyes. Her expression could have looked softer if she'd wanted it to. But Molly had her reasons for maintaining a stiff veneer. All her life she had conformed to what was expected of her by parents, teachers, and priest. She was always the one in class who did everything right, respectably and religiously, and as marriage was a respectable estate in which men and women lived together, Molly had duly conformed to that too.

Being a person who did everything right and properly, of course she had not indulged in premarital sex, so on her wedding night had been considerably shocked at the length and thickness of the appendage that was supposed to enter her. Up until then she had assumed that an adult penis looked exactly the same as a baby's, only bigger; about the size, in fact, of a large button mushroom. A hard-on was something she'd heard whispered of, but had never enquired about. Therefore Gregory's erection had come as something of a shock.

Being a woman who took her wifely duties seriously, she

143

had endured its penetration, but had never since made any effort to encourage it unduly, which was why, slim and supple as she was, she had endeavoured to look as dowdy and stick-like as possible.

There were no sides to Molly. She was as straight mentally as she was physically. Black was black, white was white. There was respectability and there was immorality, and sex, whether it was inside marriage or out was firmly entrenched in immorality.

But Gregory was ever an optimist. Once he had seen the effect of the green silk on Katie O'Flanagan, he automatically assumed the erotically-charged material would bring about a transformation in his wife.

He had laid enough material aside for such a plan as this. Once the sewing room workforce were off home, he took to one of the machines himself and in no time had run up a kimono-style wrap that would cling to the most meagre figure and make it as voluptuous as the Venus de Milo.

When he had finished it, he held it up to the light and admired its slinky lines and the strange light that emanated from the soft material. He smiled at it as though the woman he had in mind was actually in it. Shame it wasn't Katie O'Flanagan, but she had flown back to Ireland.

This item was not for any client, but was designed with his wife in mind.

Alternately whistling and humming a happy tune, he went home to his apartment which was on the second floor. Still full of optimism, he took the stairs two at a time, threw open the door, and singing a fanfare that had no words but plenty of feeling, he held out the green wrap which he had wrapped up in brown paper.

His wife eyed him cautiously. 'What's that?'

'Something for you, my darling.'

'What is it?'

'Take it out and see.'

Her lips pursed, and she crossed her arms over her chest. 'I don't want to see. It might be something filthy. Some flimsy garment you bought in one of those dirty sex shops like the one you bought me before that had eye-holes to poke my nipples through and no crotch.'

Not so happy now, Gregory shook his head emphatically.

'No. This isn't at all like that. It's a wrap. A truly beautiful garment made from beautiful material. I made it especially for you.'

'Why?'

'Because . . .' Momentarily, Gregory was at a loss for words. He tried again. 'Because I wanted to see how beautiful you looked in it.'

'Oh. And to look this beautiful I would, I presume, have to wear no clothes under it.'

Gregory sighed and his smile disappeared. 'Of course. It's a wrap. It's not designed for anything to be worn underneath.'

'Filthy beast!'

Molly attacked him with a bread basket which was the first thing that had come to hand. Judging by her fury and the look in her eyes, she would have preferred something more substantial and much heavier.

The parcel went up into the air.

'Give me that,' she shouted.

At first, Gregory was hopeful that she would indeed open it, and once she did . . . But his hope was short-lived.

Molly, the parcel in her thin hands for a bare half-second, threw it out of the window.

'There,' she exclaimed, rubbing her hands one against the other. 'There! That's what I think of your dirty mind and your dirty clothes. Out into the alley with it. Out with the garbage and the cats. That's where such things belong!'

John Rixey was thinking about the ripe breasts and the loving arms of his beloved Darlene when his attention was drawn to the raised voices so far above him.

He smiled to himself. He'd known Gregory and Molly a long time and thanked God that he had never been so desperate as to marry a woman like her.

Still, at least Gregory was married. Not like him, courting Darlene for years and waiting on her mother to either remarry or snuff it. In all honesty, he'd prefer the former. That way, Darlene wouldn't have to go through a period of mourning before they married. Time was now of great importance to him. Soon, his job in the computer industry would take him to Phoenix and he wanted Darlene to come with him. But her mother: what would they do about her mother?

He was about to walk on when a parcel came flying out of the window of the second-floor apartment and landed at his feet.

He had no doubt where it came from, and for a moment he was in two minds whether to shout up and ask whether he should bring it up to them. But Molly was still shouting at Gregory, so wasn't likely to hear him.

He shrugged, bent down, and picked it up.

Because it had landed with such force, the brown

paper had split open in one corner.

John frowned and touched the soft material that now showed through. Even in the darkness of the alley there was a faint luminescence about it. Almost as if the colour or the cloth were alive, a kind of electricity tingled over his fingers and ran up his arm. A strange kind of contentment flowed over him, a churning, softly touching contentment that made him think of bed, soft limbs, and the sweet smell of passionate sex.

Unable to resist the lure of the sparkling fabric, he ripped the paper away and, letting it fall to the ground, held up the green garment.

'That's pretty,' he said as he saw what it was. 'That's very pretty. My Darlene is sure to like that.'

His eyes shone as he thought of her and his penis jumped in his pants. Wow, he thought, just thinking of that woman makes me feel randy.

Darlene did like the wrap.

'It's beautiful,' she said as she took it from him.

John beamed at her. Love was in his eyes and on his lips, and sexual desire was thudding against his zip.

Darlene kissed him.

'Trust you to buy me a sexy little number like this when Mom's away at the Sunshine Citizens' Club Annual Vacation.' She smiled at him in a kittenish way and stroked his growing erection.

'Try it on,' he said in a hushed voice as he began to unbutton her dress. 'With nothing underneath.'

'How else?' she said, her breathing quickening as her fingers fought with his around the buttons of her shirt and the zip of her trousers.

147

John was staggered at the vision of Darlene's naked body even before she slipped her arms into the sleeves of the slinky garment.

'Do you like it?' she asked as she tied it at the waist. In an act of obvious provocation, she tossed her head and ran her fingers through her long tawny hair.

John stared at her. Was it just the material doing this, or were her breasts firmer and riper than before, her waist smaller, her hips more curvaceous?

He swallowed swiftly but made no attempt to curtail the emotions or desires he was feeling.

'I want you,' he said breathlessly. 'I want you so bad, I think I might faint.'

Still smiling, her nipples pouting and her eyes sparkling, she took his hand. 'I wouldn't want you to do that, darling. There are things I want you to do, but fainting isn't one of them.'

In the cool green and white of her bedroom, and on the satin whiteness of her bed, they lay naked, his clothes on the floor, and the green wrap underneath them. A green mist rose from it, hovered as if uncertain it was needed.

Their kisses were hot, their caresses full of both love and passion. His body was hard against hers, and her skin was like satin against his.

His penis prodded her belly, and her hips jerked invitingly towards him.

'I love you, John,' she whispered against his ear.

'I couldn't bear it if you didn't,' he whispered back.

'Do you feel it, John? Do you feel that something sensational is happening to us, something almost magical?'

'Yes,' replied John as his penis divided her succulent sex

and entered her body. 'Yes. I feel it.'

'Oh John!'

'Oh Darlene!'

'I feel so passionate, John,' said Darlene as her hips jerked in the first throes of orgasm.

John slowed his thrusts so she could get the full benefit of his pubic bone on her clitoris. Between each thrust, he murmured against her ear. 'Do you think – the magic – will work – on your mother? Do you think – it might help – us get married?'

'How – could – it – do – that? HOW? HOW? HOWWWwww . . . ?' she at last cried out.

'I – don't – know,' murmured John as the first shot of semen burst from him. 'I – DON'T – KNOWWWwww . . . !'

The magic that both had sensed stayed with them till dawn when, finally exhausted from their sexual Olympics, they rested and sleepily talked about their hopes and dreams.

'I know we've been going together for a long time, John, but I can't just leave her. After all, she is my mother.' Darlene stroked his thigh as she spoke. 'I owe her something, and you know what she's been like since Dad died.'

John sighed. 'If only she could find another guy. I've got four weeks to accept that posting in Phoenix.' He kissed the softness of her hair, and as his penis began to revive, he murmured softly against the nape of her neck. 'I don't want to go without you, babe. You know I don't.'

Darlene yawned and squeezed his arm. 'Sure. I know. And I want to go with you; believe me I do. Anyway, Mom does have another guy. Old Jake's been after her for ages.'

'So why doesn't she marry him?' John yawned too and huddled against Darlene's back so that her buttocks were pressed against his stiffening stem.

'She reckons she's not up to it. Besides, she says she doesn't fancy him.'

John sighed. He was a patient man, but even the most patient come to the end of their tether. Silently, he prayed that the magic that had sustained tonight's passion would assist in resolving his problem.

Let her get laid, he said in his mind. Please let her get laid. Then, as the blood rushed to his penis, he gently pushed its head between Darlene's buttocks and on into her vagina.

# Chapter 15

Rosie Smith came back from her Sunshine Citizens' Club vacation having yet again kept old Jake Feldman at arm's length.

It wasn't that she didn't like having a man fancy her. On the contrary, the prospect quite delighted her. But really – at their age? Wasn't sex something the firm and beautiful did when forty was a long way off and high school not that far behind?

She smiled to herself when she thought of Jake. He was a big man and in his youth must have been really something to look at. Nowadays he had white, close-cropped hair and his shoulders, although as broad as they'd ever been, stooped slightly.

But Jake was still attractive. His jaw was strong and his eyes were blue. There were plenty of other women at the Club who would loosen their pants for him, but Jake seemed to have eyes for no one but her. That fact alone made her blush even though she was seventy-five.

On coming back to the apartment she shared with her daughter, she quickly read the note that said Darlene had gone to a conference and wouldn't be back until the following evening.

It was something she already knew about, but Darlene liked to make sure she hadn't forgotten. Darlene, she decided, fussed too much. Such consideration sometimes niggled her as it did now.

'My memory's not that bad,' she said to the piece of blue paper. 'What do you think, I'm gettin' old or something?'

She didn't answer her own question and avoided looking in the hallway mirror. Instead, she looked around for something to do – something to occupy her mind – if not her body.

The apartment seemed so silent without her daughter, so she turned on the television. She stared at it, listened to the banalities, decided it was pure trivia, but did not turn it off. She needed the background noise. Needed to know she was not alone, as if the people on the screen were real and keeping her company for the afternoon. Rosie decided to do the ironing as she watched these people who laughed, sang and chattered on the screen in the corner. Just as she started sliding the hot iron over the first item, the telephone rang.

'It's me,' said Jake.

Rosie's heart skipped a beat. 'Oh. Hi. Nice to hear from you.'

'Did you enjoy the vacation?'

'Yes. You know I did.'

'We could have enjoyed it even more, you know. Just you and me.'

Rosie blushed. 'Perhaps we could, but at our age . . .'

'Age? What's age got to do with it? It never dies you know: not love, not passion. It's always there – always will be there till the day you die.'

'That may be so, but . . .'

'But nothing. How about you coming out with me tonight?

152

I know a nice little restaurant where we could bill and coo in a private corner. How about it?'

Rosie gripped the phone more tightly and tried not to click her teeth. 'I don't think so, Jake. It's kind of you to ask, really it is, but I've come back to an empty apartment and a load of ironing and cleaning. You know how it is when you've been away and come back with a trunk full of dirty washing. I don't want to leave it for Darlene. She fusses over me enough already.'

'Sure,' returned Jake sadly. 'Sure. I know what it's like to come home to an empty apartment.' She heard him sigh and felt suddenly guilty. 'But if you should change your mind, give me a ring.'

'I will,' Rosie replied. 'I promise.'

She sighed as she put down the phone. 'Poor Jake,' she said as she affectionately patted the receiver. 'I'm too old for all that stuff. Something pretty drastic would have to happen before I'd ring you. Like the years rolling back and my body being as firm as it used to be.' She chuckled and shook her head. 'That wouldn't be just a miracle, that would be sheer witchcraft!'

She chuckled some more as she realized what she had said. Witches were always depicted as old crones – old crones like her. So much for magic.

It was after ironing her daughter's green silk wrap that she changed her mind.

Once or twice during ironing it, she had stopped and rubbed her fingers together as a current of something remotely electrical ran up her arm. Is this thing trying to electrocute me, she asked herself.

But whatever had ran up her arm also held her like a

magnet to the iron and the green silk garment beneath it. An infusion of something indescribable ran through her body. There was something alien about it, yet also something familiar. It was as though a shrivelled and dry area within her had been touched by a magic wand and burst into new fruitfulness.

When finally she put the iron to one side, she gazed at the wrap with wonder and ran her hands over it. Sensations and desires she had not felt for years swept over her body.

'My, but you're a beautiful wrap,' she said, and picked it up.

Almost as though it were a lover, she hugged the garment to her chest and moaned with pleasure as it moulded itself to the contours of her body.

'Yes. I know,' she said softly. 'I have to take my clothes off to wear something like this.'

She didn't know who had asked the question, and wasn't too sure in her mind as to whether she had even replied. But she took off her clothes and put on the wrap.

Without her clothes, the silky fabric clung to a body that had taken on a certain suppleness that had not been there that morning. To her surprise, her flesh tingled as it responded to the sensuous touch that belongs only to silk and, perhaps, to satin.

Before phoning Jake, she put the ironing away, turned down the lights, and put some romantic music on the CD player.

'Jake, darling,' she said in her sexiest voice.

'Well hi there.' He sounded surprised. 'Have you changed your mind? Are you coming out with me to that cute little restaurant?'

'No, Jake. I'm not. I'm lonely in this apartment all by my little old self. Darlene's away overnight at some conference. Come on over.' She took a deep breath. 'I'm all ready for you. Do you want to know what I'm wearing?'

He hesitated. She sensed his surprise. 'Sure,' he said at last. 'Sure I would.'

'Nothing,' she replied. 'Only a green silk wrap. It's real soft and slinky against my skin. It's turning me on. My nipples are standing out against it. The material's moulding itself to my belly, my thighs, and even to my pussy. I'm feeling real sexy, Jake. Real sexy!'

'You are?' Jake's voice trembled. 'Then I'll be there.'

Even though he'd stopped on the way for flowers and chocolates, it wasn't long before Jake was ringing her doorbell.

'Jake, darling. You shouldn't have.'

The last thing Jake could remember doing was talking to her on the telephone. Getting into a taxi, buying chocolates, buying flowers, all became hazy. The sight of Rosie standing there in a glorious green robe that clung to her body in all the right places, robbed him of his memory.

She noticed his hands shook as he handed her the flowers and chocolates.

At last he regained his senses. 'My God, Rosie, but you certainly look something!'

The silk of her wrap rustled as she moved. Jake gasped, then trembled as she pressed her body against him.

'So do you, Jake,' she said as her hands played over his chest and her mouth sought his. 'So do you.'

'My, Rosie,' Jake exclaimed as his arms wrapped around her and his hands caressed her back. 'You sure have one hell of a body.'

Jake meant what he said. Rosie was seventy-five, but the body pressed up against him looked and felt forty years younger than that.

As she opened his shirt and the cool silk of her robe rubbed against his bare flesh, new vigour rushed through his veins.

His shoulders straightened, his muscles hardened, and a sudden rush of hot blood pumped into his penis. He felt young again. He threw back his head and groaned with pleasure.

Rosie took him by the hand and led him to the bedroom.

Beneath the cool cotton of the sheets, a woman who had experienced much love and much passion, made love with a man who had experienced a lot of sex and had had many lovers during his life.

They were instruments mellowed with age and moving to a tune they both knew well, a melody that had lain dormant in their memories, out of sync with their bodies; until tonight, that is.

Beneath his soft caress and hot kisses, Rosie murmured, moved and tangled her limbs with his. Beneath her touch, his penis hardened and prodded at her belly.

She ran her hands over his shoulders and felt the strength that was still in his muscles, the hardness of his bones.

As though her back was as supple as it had been at seventeen, she arched it, raised one leg, and thrust her hips towards his shaft.

His penis nudged against her pubic hair which was still dark, still silky; then easing through her plump lips, he pushed it through the slippery moistness of her sexual folds and into her vagina.

Rosie mewed with pleasure, then closed her eyes and left it to her other senses to respond to what was happening to her. When she opened them again, all she could see was a green mist that seemed to be shining around them both.

I'm drowning in it, she thought to herself as she moaned with pleasure, I'm drowning in it – in sex, and I don't care. I want to drown in it. Jake is in me and I'm enjoying it. I feel like a young girl again. My sex is juicy, my temperature is rising, and so is my climax. I want Jake to make me come. I want to do everything I used to do. Everything!

'I'm coming!' she called out against Jake's ear. 'I'm coming!'

With a sigh, a groan, and a tensing of one body against the other, they came. Shivers of orgasm rippled through Rosie's body. Vibrant pulses of energy forced copious amounts of semen from Jake's well used tool.

They rested. They bathed together, and as they did these things, they talked.

'I want to do more,' said Rosie, her eyes sparkling.

'So do I,' said Jake.

As they dried each other with thick towels, each studied the other's body.

How beautiful she is, thought Jake as his eyes wandered over her firm bosoms, her flat belly, and her gently curving thighs. Even her face. There was barely a blemish, let alone a wrinkle. Like a young girl, he thought. How come I never noticed that before?

'You're beautiful,' he said gently.

Rosie, immersed in her own thoughts, smiled and blushed. How powerful he is, she thought, her tongue licking at the dryness of her lips as she surveyed his broad shoulders which now showed no sign of stooping. His chest was as hard as a twenty-year-old's. So were his thighs and the nine-inch member that reared so ready from his groin.

'What other things do you like to do?' Rosie asked as she ran her hands down over his arms. 'Sexually, I mean.' She threw her wrap on the floor so that they both stood on it.

Jake smiled and looked down thoughtfully at his stiff penis.

'Look at it,' he said, and wiggled his hips so that his member swayed from side to side. 'It's been many places, done many things. I was in the Marines, remember, so I did get around a bit. But the best, the absolute tops was when some woman in the Middle East took it in her mouth and sucked it in. Sucked me near dry, she did.' He chuckled as he brought the memory to mind. 'From what I recall, she belonged to some minor princeling and had been specially selected for the job of sucking him off on account that she had no front teeth.'

'Is that so?' said Rosie, her eyes bright in consequence of the thoughts erupting behind them. 'Well, Jake darling, I think I can do even better than that. There are some advantages to being old.'

She turned from him. At first, it seemed her teeth were her own again, but eventually, she managed to take them out, and put them in a glass. Then she dropped to her knees before him.

'My God!'

Jake threw his head back as her toothless mouth sucked him in.

'That's incredible! Incredible!'

His eyes were closed. His hands were on her head.

Memories of a hot land and hotter flesh blazed in his mind as a mouth without front teeth – no – without any teeth, sucked on his penis.

He groaned as his member jerked and tapped against the back of her throat. There was nothing – nothing to compare to the suction of a toothless mouth drawing his essence to the surface.

Rosie herself was surprised. With her cheeks hollow and sucking with all the power of a high velocity vacuum cleaner, she held his balls and felt them heave as the first semen rushed along his stem.

Old memories came flooding back to her as the warmth of his semen hit the back of her throat. As though thirsty for the essence of man, of life, and of all the things that go with it, she drank of him, sucking for all she was worth until the last droplet trembled on her tongue.

She swallowed, and finally let him go.

Rosie and Jake beamed as they told Darlene of their intention to get married within ten days.

'That quick?' queried Darlene, then added with a smile, 'Why the rush? What have you two been up to?'

Out of sight of Jake and Darlene's mother, John caressed Darlene's behind. This was the chance they'd been waiting for. Their wish had come true. John was smiling and so was Darlene.

'Time isn't on our side,' said Rosie as she looked up at Jake. 'We've got a lot of living to do.'

'Wow. Then I'd better think of buying you a wedding present.' Darlene squeezed John's hand as she said it.

'Trousseau present, Darlene,' interrupted Rosie. 'I'd like

a trousseau present. I'd like that green silk wrap of yours. Do you mind?'

Darlene laughed and shrugged her shoulders. 'No. Of course I don't.' This time it was her turn to look into the eyes of the man she loved. 'John and I have no need for a trousseau. We'll take it all as it comes. In fact, what say we make it a double wedding? Better make the most of us being around before we go off to Phoenix with John's company.'

'That's a fine idea.' Rosie hugged Jake's arm to her, and Darlene wanted to cry.

Instead, she kissed her mother's soft cheek and hugged her.

'Be happy, mom.'

Her mother was going to be happy. Darlene was sure of it. She and Jake looked like two young lovers, not a man and a woman way past their prime. It didn't matter that Jake had a stoop and his muscles had wasted away to soft flesh. It didn't matter either that her mother was not the supple beauty she had been in her youth; that her breasts were flabby and her hips carried too much weight.

In each other's eyes they were beautiful: in each others arms they were desirable and that was all that mattered. If the green silk robe helped them achieve that effect, then all well and good.

# Chapter 16

Since the episode with the delivery boy, Ruth Tye had kept the green silk garment under lock and key.

Not that she didn't think about the experience; in fact, she even dreamt about it.

'It's haunting me,' she said to herself. 'It's haunting me, and I think I want it to go on haunting me. Am I going mad?'

It had occurred to her to talk to Hannah about it, but somehow she just couldn't find the right words to even begin.

On one occasion, it had even crossed her mind to find out where the woman on crutches lived and ask her to take the chest off her hands. But she hadn't. Almost as if it were a mongrel puppy that she couldn't bear to get rid of, the chest remained.

Simon, on the other hand, was still looking for the secret of old Sam's erection.

He had decided, on account of his recent excursions into sex, that it wasn't him at fault, but Ruth. After all, Kitty's foot had made him come; so had the two girl muggers in the park, and even, dare he admit it, the blond-haired guy at the movies.

Yes, he said to himself, it's her that should be drinking the tea. The thought truly inspired him and brought the hint of an erection in his pants.

Owing to the fact that he had thrown away old Sam's secret cache of tea, he went out and bought some – oh, at least ten varieties – and took them home.

Under Ruth's suspicious gaze, he made the first pot.

'Try it,' he said as he poured her a cup.

'No. I don't want it.'

'But you like tea, don't you?' Simon surprised himself by staring at his wife's ripe breasts as he tried to force the tea on her. As he did so, his erection grew.

She saw him look and covered them with her hands.

'Yes,' she said. 'But I don't want any at this moment.'

'Try it.' He tried to pull her hands away from her breasts. Their warmth inspired him to greater effort, and his erection grew that much more.

'No.'

'Go on, try it.' This time he pressed the cup into her hands.

'No,' she shouted, and threw the cup onto the table. The tea slopped into the saucer.

Unperturbed, Simon poured her another.

'Then try this one.'

This time he grabbed hold of her head and pressed the cup to her lips.

'No!' she screamed, and spat it out in a hot brown stream.

'Drink it!' cried Simon, now overly excited by the feel of his penis digging against his wife's curved hip.

'No! No! No!'

Ruth struggled and his fingers tightened. At the same time, his penis became too big for his trousers and busted his zip.

Ruth seized her chance and his dick. She slapped at it, twisted it, and left Simon clutching his crotch and moaning while she ran and locked herself in her bedroom.

It was from there that she called the police.

Simon was in the bathroom wrapping a cold flannel around his bruised and now shrunken member, when the police rang the doorbell.

Of course, he didn't know they were the police until he opened the door, and in his haste to open it, he left the wet flannel in situ and his zip half open.

'Okay,' snapped a burly six-foot-high and four-foot-wide Irish cop. 'What seems to be the trouble here?'

'Him,' shouted Ruth who had run out from her refuge when Simon opened the door. 'He tried to poison me.'

Paralysed with fear, and speechless due to the pressure of the Irish cop's hand around his throat, Simon did his best to shake his head.

'No,' he rasped.

'Get the evidence,' said the big cop to the black guy with him.

The black guy was thorough, the Irish cop unyielding, and Simon was only babbling on account of the thick fingers grasping his throat.

Ruth was telling them tearfully about how her husband had tried to force the tea down her throat. 'He's trying to poison me!'

'We'll get it checked out, honey,' said the black guy as, with gloved hands, he gathered up the offending crockery and put it into a small brown box.

Simon gagged as his throat was released. 'But I only wanted her to drink the tea. It would have made her . . . it would have increased her . . .'

It was no good. Not only could he not bring himself to put his motive into words, the cops had disbelief written all over their faces.

'You're making a big mistake,' he cried as they manhandled him towards the lift, out into the street and into the back of the black-and-white.

Down at the station they strip searched him for any trace of the poison he had used. They were dead serious in their task. Their expressions remained solemn until they came across the wet flannel. Then, they became mute before bursting into laughter.

'What you trying to do? Make a bigger bulge in your pants?' asked the black guy, a smirk on his face and a sneer in his words.

Only when it came to taking a statement did what they had seen with their own eyes and what he told them – that is the truth – become believable.

'You say your wife's a bit frigid and you'd heard that tea would do the trick?'

Simon nodded.

Sympathetic glances went from one cop to another. A few sighed and shook their heads.

Later, once the lab had thoroughly tested the crockery, they took both him and it back to his apartment.

Without looking at Ruth, Simon went straight out to the kitchen.

He smashed the teacups and saucers in the sink, then

after adding the tea bags, flushed the lot down the waste-disposal.

Ruth went back into the bedroom and locked the door.

Simon sighed, threw off his clothes and lay out on the couch and fell asleep.

Ruth lay awake. Every so often she glanced towards the locked bedroom door. Her eyes wandered further in the darkness and detected a green haze drifting from beneath the closet door.

Unable to resist its power, she got out of bed and opened the door. A faint aura of green light danced around the chest in which the green garments lay – the body that she had worn and the silk pyjamas. Dare she get them out, put on the body and invite her husband to don the green pyjamas?

The temptation was extremely strong and caused her bust to heave and her breath to catch in her throat.

Hesitantly, she reached out and touched the smooth wood, the bright brass of the chest.

A different Ruth came into being. Just by touching the wooden chest, shivers of desire ran through her body. Suddenly her mouth and lips were dry. She licked them, swallowed as though her throat too needed moisture in it: not just any kind of moisture, but a warm, sticky kind that came from deep within a man's body.

Quietly unlocking the bedroom door, she slipped off her clothes and tip-toed across the carpet to where Simon lay snoring. His bare body was striped with alternate fingers of light and shade that came through the parallel slats of the blind. There was no other light except for an odd green luminescence that seemed to waft around her thighs.

Was the green mist following her? Or was it purely that

she wanted to imagine its presence was still with her, making her nipples tingle and the moist lips of her sex swell with desire?

Even as she knelt on the carpet beside him, Simon did not stir.

Judging by the movement of his eyelids, she guessed him to be dreaming.

What of, she asked herself. Sex, she replied. What else?

As her own breath quickened, she gently stroked his stomach with her fingertips. Beneath her touch, his muscles tensed and he murmured in his sleep.

His cock rose from its tangled nest and nodded as though it were pleased with what she was doing.

Ruth's bottom lip dropped as she watched it grow in size. It's me doing this, she told herself. Me making his body do things while he sleeps.

The idea was intoxicating and brought a sparkle to her eyes.

Power was the word that came to mind. Her, Ruth Tye, born Ruth Lipman, had power over this man who lay so helpless, so lost in his own sweet dreams.

With a nervous shiver, she let her fingers travel into the soft down of hair from which his penis rose rigid and strong. She gasped softly as she smelt its warmth and felt it tremble and grow. How full of life it is, she said to herself. Look how it pulsates as his blood rushes into it.

Glowing in the dark like a silver pearl, moisture seeped from his glans. Tentatively, she slid her fingers up his stem. She paused, then, very gently, tapped at it.

His whole member trembled.

Ruth paused and glanced at his face. Simon mumbled

something in his sleep – something indecipherable. Softly, his pelvis and limbs undulated as though he were enjoying his dream; and enjoying what was not a dream.

Being careful not to breathe too heavily, Ruth wrapped her fingers around his stem and slowly began to pull on it.

Simon continued to murmur as she hastened her stroke, then slowed it, then hastened it again.

Slowly, Simon turned onto his side. The tip of his penis kissed one breast before burrowing between them.

Ruth bit her lip to stop herself from sighing with pleasure.

Simon brought his leg up so that his knee no longer rested on the couch but was pressing against her pubic divide.

She sucked in her lips as the pressure of his kneecap caused her clitoris to burst into flower and her body to sway so that the seepage from his penis lay sticky in her cleavage.

Quickening in tempo, one hand rode up and down his length while the other fondled the heat and the soft down of his balls.

Like a soft cocoon, the green mist swathed their bodies. Within it, they writhed gently; Simon against Ruth's breast bone, inspired by the ministrations of her hand, and Ruth from the pressure of his knee against her sex.

Ruth opened her eyes, closed them, then opened them again as she perceived the green mist trembling around her, eddying, swirling, gathering in a never-ending helix of movement whose intensity seemed to be a reflection of her pleasure.

Faster and faster it moved and whirled, swirling in ever more concentric oscillations until, as her climax peaked and crashed like a tidal wave throughout her body, it grew bright and burst into a myriad of green stars around her.

Her mouth was wide open and she thought she'd cried out.

She couldn't have, she told herself as she disentangled her hand from Simon's penis and damp curls.

Briefly she touched the area between and beneath her breasts. Semen lay like warm cream and reminded her of her thirst.

Bending her head, she took the head of his maleness into her mouth and sucked out the last of what he had to give.

After she had gone back to bed, Simon slowly opened his eyes. He'd read enough of Stephen King to know what a succubus was: some creature that came to you in your sleep and sucked the life essence out of you.

He looked along his body to where his penis lay soft and sleepy among his crisp, damp hair. He touched it and felt its wetness, then looked towards the bedroom door. It was still closed; locked and barred against him. A green light glowed from beneath it.

# *Chapter 17*

Cupid, the brown-skinned dresser with the body of an athlete, was nobody's fool.

When Petrushka had found him hooked like a split plum over the head of the fire extinguisher, he had been staring at the green dress that she had been waiting to wear. Right from the very start, he had felt its latent energy transfer from the fabric to his fingers. Pins and needles had travelled up his arms and throughout his body. His eyes had stared at the dress, and stared also at his own limbs, his own chest, belly and penis as the sizzling current had rushed through him. Yet he couldn't see anything. No green flame just beneath his skin; no verdant iridescence flowing through his veins. All the same, he had felt its presence taking him over.

In bed with his lover, Johnny Bow, he told him about the strange fabric – and Johnny Bow, who was six foot, blond and extremely likable, told him he would see if he could get some of the same stuff when he next took a delivery to Celicia Corinne's workshop. Cupid was too nervous to take some for himself. Besides, Corinne watched like a hawk the moment she thought anyone was taking too great an interest in her latest find.

True to his word, Johnny got chatting to some of the

machine girls. They eyed him as if they could eat him. Johnny gave them the come on, used every trick in the book to get them gasping for his body. Not, of course, that they had any chance of having his body. Johnny was in no doubt that his lover, Cupid, was bisexual. Johnny was not, but that didn't stop him using his obvious good looks to get what he wanted.

'My old granny's making me one of them quilted comforters,' he told them. 'She's doing it in patchwork and using all different shades and patterns of green. Got any spare pieces you don't need?'

'What do we get in exchange?' asked a bubblegum-chewing girl with bright red lips and a mop of blonde curls.

Johnny smiled. 'How about dinner?'

'How about a fuck?'

Her answer was quick – even surprising. But Johnny still managed to smile. 'Before dinner or after?'

'Before I give you the bits of material.'

Johnny struck his most provocative pose and smiled casually. 'Depends on what the material is, honey. Best silk, you're on; crap calico, you're out.'

'Follow me,' she drawled, and to the catcalls and wolf whistles of the other women, she sashayed down through the lines of sewing machines. Johnny was just a yard or two behind her and already planning how best to get out of her clutches. This, of course, meant admitting at just the right moment that he was as queer as a nine-dollar bill.

The store room the bubbly blonde took him into was lined with shelves on which lay plastic bags full of various bits of material in a myriad colours. All off-cuts. All stuffed into plastic bags, numbered, and labelled.

'Green,' she said suddenly, reached up and brought a bag down from the shelf. 'I think this is what you want.' With a knowing look in her eyes, she pulled out a piece of green silk from among the cotton, crepe, and other stuff in there.

'That's pretty,' said Johnny as he scrunched it in his meaty fist. 'Granny will like that.'

His expression altered as something resembling licks of tiny nettles ran up his arm.

'My God,' he muttered. The stinging sensation ran quickly from his fist, up his arm, across his chest, then shot like an arrow over his belly and between his legs.

Fuck her, said a voice in his head.

But I . . .

His protest was swamped with something more powerful than his own will, his own nature.

His breath caught in his throat. Immediately, without him having to think about it, his rod stood to attention.

Johnny's mouth fell open. Lust burned in his body and brightened his eyes. With obvious intent, he looked at the red-lipped blonde in a different way than he had before.

Desire already burned in the wide blue eyes of the curvy blonde. Like Johnny Bow, she had a tingling racing up her arms, settling around her nipples, and diving between her legs.

The bits of material spilled from the plastic bag as the blonde let it tumble to the floor.

Cotton, calico, synthetics, linen, satin and silk lay like a tumbled bed. The blonde's clothes, and Johnny's, were quickly added to the pile.

The girl's long, white arms reached for him, and he

shuddered as he felt the soft silkiness of her fingers on his shoulders.

Johnny reached for her breasts, grasped them tightly, and pulled her closer. Stiff and big with passion, his penis tapped against the blonde's tight belly.

Every vein in his body was pounding with something more than blood and stood out from his flesh as if about to burst. He gasped his desire into her ear. 'I want you,' he said. 'I want to fuck you.'

'Then do it,' she answered. She sounded impatient. 'Do it in any way you want to do it.'

Perhaps influenced by his own sexual preferences, Johnny turned her over onto her hands and knees. The blonde's breasts swung back and forth as she thrust her bottom back against him. She wriggled and murmured with pleasure as the head of his weapon slid between her buttocks then nudged at the puckered mouth of her anus.

Johnny, a man experienced in such things, was well aware of his need for lubrication. Normally, Vaseline would have done the trick. But this was a woman. With her, there was no need for artificial assistance. Help was already here. With a contented sigh, he dipped his member into her seeping channel and then for the first time ever, plunged deep into the body of a woman.

He cried out at the sheer ecstasy of it; the piquant way her muscles drew him in, held him there as though they were sucking out his very soul.

Waves of desire flooded over him: urges to thrust, to bury himself deep within her made him forget that women were not his thing; that they were vessels needed for procreation and not for outright pleasure. Only men could give that.

Only like could truly enjoy like. At least, that had been his creed. But now, his previously held beliefs were forgotten as green mists swam before his eyes. His penis was hot and his pelvis hotter as he thrust furiously at the moaning creature whose furrow he ploughed. She still knelt on all fours, her buttocks reddening as his pubic hair scraped against her soft-skinned flesh, her breasts swinging like half-filled bean bags.

Thoughts of merely lubricating his member so that he could slide it more easily into her anus were forgotten. Already his semen was gathering deep within him, coiling like a liquid spring before spilling over from that deep well and beginning its journey to ejaculation.

'More,' he heard her cry. 'Faster. Faster. Give me more. Mooooore . . .'

Her voice faded as she drowned in her orgasm.

The green mist that Johnny had regarded as a mere illusion, now circled her head like a soft halo before reaching out for him.

Unable to withdraw; unable to coerce his thoughts and his actions back to where they used to be, Johnny too stiffened as his semen poured from him into her; from the man into the woman.

Johnny Bow left Cupid in the dark as to what he'd had to do in order to get hold of the green silk, but in an effort to quell any unnecessary questions, he had brought home the whole plastic bag of bits and pieces.

'I couldn't take just one piece,' he explained with that lazy smile of his. 'I had to take the lot. It was a take it or leave it situation. Some little blonde insisted.'

Cupid believed him. Cupid knew him well. Not for a moment would he have imagined that Johnny and the blonde had fucked themselves dizzy in that dark little store room with all those bits of cloth beneath them.

They'd done it in all ways. It was as though, Johnny thought to himself, sex was a new toy – one he hadn't had before. It seemed logical. After all, he had never had sex with a woman before, and now he had, he couldn't get it out of his mind.

After the first copulation, she rode him. On the third attempt, he'd tied her wrists to the top shelf on which the bags and rolls of remainders were stored. She hung there, her legs tight around his waist as he thrust his weapon into her, his fingers squeezing, pulling and prodding her breasts so that she closed her eyes and moaned about how wicked he was, and how he was hurting her.

But of course she didn't really mean it. In fact, he was convinced that, like him, she had loved every sex-filled minute.

'I'll make you a little posing pouch from this piece, sweetheart,' said Cupid as he held up a triangle of the shiny green silk. 'And I'll make myself a natty little shirt from this bit.'

Cupid was true to his word. He made Johnny his cute little posing pouch that accentuated the form and size of his penis. It didn't cover much, but then it wasn't really meant to. The triangle of cloth added mystery at the front. The waistband was not much thicker than string, and neither was the piece that ran between the cheeks of his behind.

Cupid made himself the 'natty little shirt' which exposed his chest to his midriff. Two thongs came down from the

waist and dived through his legs, and likewise, between his buttocks. He was pleased with the effect the shirt created: a deep vee exposing his chest, and an inverted one exposing his penis.

Of course, if Johnny had hung around, he would have tried its effect out on him. But Cupid's mother, who was Baptist and full of fire and brimstone, was due home, so no naughty novelties that night!

Careful as always not to offend his beloved mother, Cupid hung his latest creation in the closet between a navy and beige striped blazer, and a red velvet jacket with a black braid trim.

'I sure hope you've been behaving yourself while I've been away,' said his mother. She did not smile as her son kissed her respectfully on each cheek.

'Of course I have, mother.' She was never 'mom'. Common, she'd always told him. I prefer to be called mother. 'Don't I always?' Cupid added.

His mother nodded curtly.

He went to a meeting with her that night and obediently drank his hot milk and ate his crackers before settling down beneath the bedclothes.

For once, he was glad of the rest. His job was demanding, and so was Johnny. Anyway, he liked his mother fussing over him and always did his best to please her when she was home. When she was not – well, then he was a completely different man.

As he dozed he heard her dusting and fussing around his room; opening drawers, tidying them; tutting as she put this away, folded that, and put his things exactly where *she* liked them to be.

Vaguely he was aware of the closet door opening. It seemed a far away sound, so deeply was he slipping into sublime contentment.

Clothes rustled, and coat hangers grated against metal.

How good my mother is, he mused as he drifted further into slumber.

Then he heard her scream.

His eyes snapped open. He sat up quickly, eyes wide, fingers tightly clutching his bedclothes. 'What is it . . . ?'

His heart thumped in his chest. The shirt. He knew it had to be the shirt.

'What is this disgusting abomination? Have you been wicked again, my son? Have you been toying with devilish things and playing with wicked parts of your body?'

'I . . .'

She didn't give him time to answer.

The thongs of the green silk garment flicked across his shaved head as she beat him.

'Wicked! Evil child! Did I bring you up to this? Did I? Would that your father were here! Would that no-good, sex-mad creature was here to see what his son has become. Well, my son, you might be good in the fashion business, but this item here is one you'll not be wearing!'

With that, she opened a drawer and took out a pair of scissors.

Before Cupid's horrified gaze she began to snip away at the green silk.

He was sure he saw it glow with that odd iridescence that had made him enjoy both a fire extinguisher and the female delights of the model Petrushka.

But his mother's religious zeal was too much even for the power of the green silk.

Once the garment lay in a pile of odd-shaped pieces, his mother scooped them up and threw them out of the open window.

Cupid, his mouth and eyes wide open, held his head in his hands and began to moan. His latest and sexiest creation was gone.

Like green snow, the pieces of silk fell to the darkness of the alley below.

Cupid's mother did not stay to watch them fall.

With pursed lips and a firmness in her arms that only the truly sanctimonious can achieve, she slammed the window shut and slapped the palm of one fat hand against the other.

'There,' she said as she dragged the bedclothes off her son. 'Now, my son. We have a good deal of praying to do.'

With that, she dragged him onto his knees, and keeping a firm grip on his ear, she forced his confession out of him.

# *Chapter 18*

'Goodnight,' said the doorman before slamming the back door of the Amorous Angel nightclub.

'Goodnight,' replied Dorothy Flaybot, whose stage name was Flamingo.

But the doorman was gone, and as the door slammed shut, the pink neon light above it, depicting a naked woman with wings, went out too.

Dorothy sighed. Tonight, for fifty dollars, she had taken off her clothes.

She had used every trick in the book to ignite the audience to breathless arousal. Instead, all she had got was insipid and horrendously polite applause.

'What can I do to spice up my act?' she asked herself as she turned from the main alley and into a smaller one that ran between two apartment buildings. 'I'd do anything to get them up on their feet and demanding my body.'

She shook her head mournfully. Perhaps she was getting old. No, she told herself. You're only twenty-nine. Your body's still firm, and given the chance, your sex life could be great too.

But it isn't at present, countered a small, strange voice in her head. Half-convinced that someone was behind her, she looked over her shoulder. At the point where she had decided to throw aside her exotic dance act and get herself a job waitressing or brush up on her computer skills, a soft shower of green silk floated like confetti around her.

'What the hell . . . ?' she began, then burst into smiles of joy and of wonder.

In the darkness, the pieces of silk glowed with an eerie yet soft green light.

Gently, they touched her face, her breasts, and as she held out her hands, they landed on her palms.

'They're so beautiful,' she said out loud.

In a sudden rush, she began to gather up every scrap she could.

She shoved bits into her pockets, her bag, and even into her pants.

'That's nice,' she murmured as particles seemed to slide of their own accord and skim over the naked lips of her well-shorn pussy. In her profession, pubic hair was not required.

Dorothy, or Flamingo, as she preferred to be called, had a small basement apartment that was fairly big, but also rather dark by day. Not that it mattered much, seeing as she was usually asleep during the day.

This morning, as she tipped the pieces of green silk out from her clothes and her bag, her apartment was suddenly brighter.

'It's the silk,' she said, her voice echoing around the empty room. 'The lamp is reflecting light from it.' Whether she just looked at it, or whether she touched it, the silk gave her a good feeling.

'Take your clothes off,' she said, and just as she had in the alley, she looked over her shoulder to see who had spoken.

'Silly bitch.' She laughed out loud.

All the same, she could not ignore the idea in her head and the urge in her body.

Soon, she stood naked. The bits of cloth shone on the table before her.

'I know just what I need to liven up my act,' she said to herself. ' I need a new outfit. Something sexy and utterly irresistible.'

Normally after a night of cavorting half-naked beneath the spotlights, she would have collapsed into bed and not woken up until five the next evening.

But tonight her body tingled with energy.

By midday, the new outfit was finished.

At nine o'clock that night, she arrived at the Amorous Angel.

At ten she was announced.

As the music started, she stepped into the spotlight.

A gasp erupted from the floor.

All eyes were upon her, all breathing increased as her limbs, belly, breasts and behind swayed with the music.

Small as the bits of green silk were, she had fashioned them into the most scintillating, the most erotic costume ever seen at the club.

Like clusters of shining leaves, pieces of silk clung around her nipples, but did not hide them. Showers of silk dived from her hips and between her legs. Smaller pieces peeked out from between her buttocks, and others shone from among the sparkling sequins of her flesh-coloured tights.

Whistles and shouts of approval rose from the audience. The more they shouted, the quicker her limbs moved and the more her body slipped rather than strained into various erotic contortions.

She swung her breasts and her nipples shone slightly green in the spotlights. A roar went up from the audience.

She bent over so that her bottom was towards the featureless faces that stared relentlessly at the stage. She looked over her shoulder at them, sensed the expectant atmosphere, the breathlessness of those that watched her.

She wriggled, and for the briefest of moments, those in the audience perceived they could see her tiniest hole, winking wickedly green among the false leaves of green silk that were sprinkled along her divide.

The wildest roar of approval was reserved for when she bent over backwards, legs open.

The leaves that appeared to cover her crotch opened with her legs. Pink flesh glistened like fruit from among the soft green leaves.

'More!' shouted the audience as if it were one. 'Give us more.'

And as the plumage of Flamingo buried the more mundane Dorothy, shivers of excitement ran through the audience, through the bar staff, the musicians, even the manager.

Dorothy was Flamingo, and Flamingo had taken the place by storm.

Not content with remaining on the stage, Flamingo moved among the tables and invited those present to poke between the leaves that circled her nipples and entice her tight little buds to greater prominence.

For others, she bent over and let them tickle her behind and the cleft in between with one of the clinging leaves.

One man poured his drink over the leaves so that they

dripped as though just drenched by a storm. Then, to roars of masculine approval, he bent his head and licked and sucked at each glistening leaf.

For another, she bent over so that her breasts pointed to the ceiling and her legs were wide, her pink flesh peeping from amidst the cluster of false leaves.

She groaned as cold champagne was called for and poured over the false leaves that clung so well to her denuded pubic lips.

One man after another licked and sucked at her flesh until every trace of champagne was gone. Once it was gone, more was poured, and more mouths licked and pleasured her.

As the last drop was licked away by one man, another was between her legs, his tongue wedged inside her.

Like a tree in the wind, her hips moved, and her legs, although braced, trembled with pleasure.

Shivers of climax ran over her skin, and she cried out that her act was finished.

From that night on, Dorothy, or Flamingo as she now insisted on being called no matter what the time of day, never looked back. Not only did the takings at the Amorous Angel increase, but her sex life improved with it. A famous agent came along to see her act and offered a position in a better class of club. Flamingo refused the offer. At the Amorous Angel she had a great following, a good salary. Besides that, the sheer sensuality of her act had attracted the love and attention of the owner, who although not young, was reasonable to look at and very wealthy.

Flamingo now counted herself to be successful. She was certainly happy.

In the dead of night, when the man who was now her husband slept soundly beside her, Dorothy who was really Flamingo, blessed the night she had walked home through the dark alley and been showered by a fall of green silk.

# *Chapter 19*

Simon had walked about in a daze ever since the night he had dreamed that a succubus was sucking his blood and his marrow out through the end of his penis.

The details had remained hazy until he remembered the intensity of his ejaculation, the shivers of orgasm that tightened his stomach and made his legs tremble. He also remembered hearing soft footsteps tip-toeing across the carpet, and the green glow coming from beneath the bedroom door.

He could have got up there and then, knocked on the door and demanded Ruth let him in; accuse her of having done something whilst he slept that she refused to do when he was awake.

But he didn't do that. As though his body had suddenly turned to lead, he lay there and relived his orgasm again and again. Purely by imagining it, his penis rose and secreted another flood of warm, white fluid.

But what was the green glow he had seen coming from beneath her door?

Suddenly, the quest to find the secret of old Sam Levy's sexual longevity did not seem so important. Ruth was suddenly a lot more interesting than she had been. If she could suck him like that when he was asleep, what could she do when he was awake?

The thought inspired him to new hope, new ideas. Had enough of the tea trickled into her body to ignite her passion? He really did not know and all his thinking was getting him nowhere.

He made up his mind to do everything in his power to find out what made her tick; to experiment with whatever method old Sam had used to reawaken his wife's passion.

With new vigour, he recommenced his mission, but nothing seemed to work.

'I need a miracle,' he said out loud in the confines of his office. 'Otherwise, I'll be dead before I ever get to the bottom of old Sam's secret.'

On a Tuesday morning, he received a phone call from Miami.

'Hi, Simon, sweetie. It's me.'

It was Kitty Levy. Ruth, Sam and everything else fell from his mind. His pants became full of hot penis.

'Kitty,' he exclaimed, as sweat broke out over his face. 'To what do I owe this pleasure?'

His free hand automatically touched the front of his trousers. A hot hardness pressed against his fingers.

'I was just calling to ask if you'd found my things – you know – my body suit and Sammy baby's jimjams.'

Simon's brain clicked into gear. 'Oh, those. Yes, yes. I remember.'

'Have you found them?' She sounded suddenly impatient.

'No, I'm afraid not. They're not here in the warehouse or the office, but I will give it another going over if you want me to.'

'I'd appreciate it, Simon, sweetie. I really would.'

Her voice was all sugar again.

Simon remembered her sounding like that when the sole of her foot had played against his groin beneath the white cloth of a restaurant table.

As he thought about that occasion, his fingers pulled down his zip. The heat of his erection fell out of his trousers and lay heavy in his hand.

'How are you getting on down there? Made any new friends?' he asked, unwilling to lose the sound of her voice at this stage.

She laughed. It was casual, but carried a hint of wickedness. 'I've made lots of new friends. Some are better friends than others. Some have lots of money, others have other – ' she paused ' – assets.' She laughed again. 'That's why I want my beautiful green silk things.'

Simon, whose hand was working up and down his penis with increasing excitement, tried to laugh too, but it came out a little choked. 'I bet you look gorgeous in green.'

'I do,' she said slowly. 'The body suit has very thin straps. The material clings to my breasts. Nothing of their shape is hidden from view. You can see my nipples and those cute little cushions around them. Even my navel is easily seen before the silk dives between my legs.' He heard her sigh; thought she was going to stop; didn't want her to stop. Keep going, keep going, his brain shouted. His hand moved in time with his thoughts.

He heard her gasp, then purr with pleasure.

'Even between my legs, the silk clings to me, caresses me as if it were a second skin. The folds of my flesh smile through it. It divides them and kisses my clitoris.' He heard

187

her murmur, murmured with her, then groaned as she groaned.

'Is it hot in your hand?' she said suddenly, her voice rushed, her breathing heavy. 'Are you coming?'

Simon didn't ask her how she knew. It seemed only natural that she should know. 'Yes,' he gasped, '*yes!!!*'

'So am I!' she exclaimed loudly. 'So am I!!!'

Simon closed his eyes and flung back his head as a flood of semen filled his palm.

There was only the sound of breathing – hers and his – before Kitty spoke.

'Did you enjoy that, Simon sweetie pie?'

Simon took a deep breath before he replied. 'Oh, yes. Yes, Kitty, I did. Tell me, how did old Sam ever keep up with you?'

Kitty laughed. 'Must have been those cold baths he had every morning and evening. It does a lot for the circulation, you know. Rushes to the best bits of the body, so I understand.'

'Cold baths. My goodness. What a thought.'

He thought of Ruth. Would she be persuaded to take a cold bath with him? He could try.

Kitty's voice interrupted his thoughts. 'I'll ring you again tomorrow round about four to see if you've had any joy.'

'I'll look forward to that,' he said, his voice trembling, his eyes glazed, and his fingers, now sticky, tightly squeezing his penis.

He sat thinking after he'd put down the receiver. Then, with a smile on his face and whistling something from a Broadway show, he reached for a sheet of paper, wiped the semen from his hand, and threw it into the bin.

Tonight and tomorrow, he would attempt to persuade Ruth to take a cold bath with him.

When was the last time he had seen her naked?

He couldn't remember the actual date, but he did remember what she'd looked like. Her breasts were ripe and full as melons, her belly curved to a profusion of black pubic hair which burst from the moist valley between her silky white thighs.

'Oooh, Ruth, but I'm coming for you girl,' he said, and looked down at his member before tucking it away behind his zip. As if agreeing with him, it stirred, stiffened slightly, and emitted a last globule of semen.

He sighed. If only Ruth had been on the end of it. But she wasn't so he put it away and went back to business.

# Chapter 20

At first Ruth was touched by Simon's apparent consideration for her. It had been a long time since he had run a bath for her, and a longer time since they had bathed in it together.

'It's ready,' he said, and beamed as he came out of the bathroom.

Ruth looked him up and down. He was wearing his bathrobe. She frowned. 'Are you having one too?'

Simon read the signs that told him a twosome was out of the question.

'I'll have one after,' he said, shuffled his feet, and slouched into the bedroom.

'Take it easy. Let her have the bath to herself this time. Give her the chance to get used to it.' That was how he spoke to the stiff penis that peeked out from between the folds of his bathrobe. It nodded before it diminished and slid back into the warm nest of hair behind the towelling.

'Ahhhhh!' The scream from the bathroom was blood-curdling.

Simon flattened himself against the bedroom door. Could that sound possibly represent obsessive sexual desire? He bit his lip and a lead weight clunked from his stomach to his balls.

Clunk, clunk. His penis shrivelled.

'What the hell do you think you're playing at?' screamed Ruth as she slammed open the door he had been leaning on. 'The water was stone cold. You could have damn well killed me!'

Simon used his hands to communicate. He was stammering too much to say what he wanted to say.

'Cold baths can be good for you,' he at last blurted out.

Ruth, still shivering, wrapped herself in towel after towel.

Her eyes blazed as she stared at him, and her teeth chattered as she put her opinion of him into words. 'You cretin! You mangy-assed idiot! If you ever, ever do that again, I'll cut off your dong and stuff it up your ass! And believe me – I would do it!'

Simon crossed his legs and buried his hands in his crotch.

'Ruth, I didn't mean to hurt you. I really didn't.' He made a great effort to move closer to her; to sit beside her on the bed and touch her shoulder. She shook him off.

'I'm sorry, Ruth. All I wanted to do . . . All I wanted to do . . .'

He took a deep breath and at last put into words all the things he felt about her. 'I wanted it to be like it used to be. I wanted you to be as sexy as you used to be. For me to make love to you just as I used to. I've been asking around as to what can help put a bit of sparkle back into sex – you know – married people's sex. Someone suggested a cold bath.'

Ruth glared at him querulously. 'And what idiot told you that?'

He hung his head before he answered. 'Kitty Levy.'

Ruth's jaw hung agape. When she did speak, her voice

was even more strident than usual. 'And when did you speak to her?'

'She phoned me at the office. Asked me if I could find some stuff she'd left behind there.' He didn't tell Ruth about meeting her in the restaurant. A talk and a hand-job over the phone was one thing: a face to face meeting and a foot-job in a public place was another.

Ruth was ready to blow up and tell him never to speak to that woman again, but what he said next stopped that from happening.

'Ruth, did you walk in your sleep the other night?'

She stopped shivering. 'What?'

Simon stared at his hands rather than at her. 'Did you walk in your sleep the other night – the night after I came back from the precinct?'

'I – I don't know.' She cleared her throat and patted at her wet neck with the end of the towel. 'Why do you ask?'

'Because I thought that something – someone – was sucking at me. You know, like a vampire or something. I could have sworn that . . .'

His voice trailed away. Even though he had been married to Ruth for years, he found it hard to talk to her about sexual matters – to describe sexual actions.

'Well, I wouldn't know, would I – not if I was asleep at the time.' She got quickly to her feet.

'Then you didn't see the green light.'

'Green light?'

Her voice was smaller now. Her eyes flitted around the room like nervous butterflies. Simon did not notice this. Simon was still staring at his hands.

'Yes. It was glowing from beneath your door.'

'You must have been dreaming,' she blurted. 'Both of us must have been dreaming.'

She swept from the room.

Simon heard the bathroom door closing and the water in the bath gurgling down the drain before the hot water faucet screeched into action.

He frowned and thought some more about Ruth and what had happened the other night.

For the first time in his life, intuition took over from logic. Ruth, he decided, was hiding something from him, and she wasn't the only one. For the first time, he wondered whether Kitty Levy had told him the whole truth about how old Sam had maintained his virility.

He decided to be more forceful the next time he spoke to her.

As arranged, Kitty Levy rang him from Miami at around four o'clock the next day.

'Hi, Simon darling. How's your sex life?'

Simon cleared his throat. Because it was Kitty on the other end of the telephone, his penis jerked in his pants.

'I'm fine. How's yours? How's that hot little pussy of yours faring down there among all those hot hunks with sweaty palms and big dicks? Had your fill of them yet? Want to come back to New York and sample mine? It's heaving you know. Swelling in my pants so that I've just got to – got to – open my zip and let it out.' As he spoke, he gasped as though he had in fact just done that. 'There it is,' he went on without giving her a chance to say anything. 'There it is. Hot and throbbing in my hand, swelling like mad as I talk to you. Just imagine how hot it would be in your hand or on your tongue. Just imagine that spit of fluid brimming from its all conquering eye as it skims down over your belly and pushes its hot head through the fleshy lips of your quim.'

The next time she spoke, Kitty sounded breathless. 'Oh, yes. I can imagine it. I can see it. I can feel it! Oh! Oh! Tell me more!'

He had her panting. He actually had her panting, begging him for more. And yet although his penis was stiffening as much from his own words as from the sound of her voice, it was still incarcerated behind the metal bars of his zip. He had to concentrate on what he was doing, on what effect he was having on her.

'But think, think, think,' he went on, his voice as low and sexy as he could make it. 'Think how best to maintain its stiffness, to maintain the beauty of the orgasm as it shivers through your sexual divide, down between your thighs, and up over your belly. Think of your nipples tingling, your flesh shivering as though a thousand, thousand fingers, a hundred and more cocks were covering your body, filling it with spurt after spurt of hot liquid. Think of how you would cope with it. Think, Kitty. Think hard.'

'I am thinking,' she cried out. 'I am thinking! I know how I would cope. Sam knew how. He showed me how.'

Unseen by Kitty, Simon's eyes lit up. His stomach tightened as Kitty gasped and sighed on the other end of the telephone. As he visualized her hand stroking her own breasts, her own crotch, his buttock muscles clenched against his chair.

'So how would you cope, Kitty darling? How would Sam have coped? How would he have maintained his stiffness?'

'The green silk,' she blurted as her voice shuddered with orgasm. 'The green silk.'

Stunned, Simon waited until her breathing had returned to something near normal. 'You mean the clothes you asked me to find? The nightclothes?'

'Yes,' she breathed. 'Have you found them?'

Simon slumped back in his chair. 'No, Kitty, I haven't. They're certainly not here. Could they have been left at the apartment?'

'They could have been, but everything there went to auction.'

Simon lifted his pen and slid a notebook under his hand. 'Never mind. I still might be able to help you. Who handled the auction?'

'Oh, Simon, I would be so grateful. Perry and Merryweather handled things. Their auction room and offices are in the basement of the Zeister building. It was a Miss Puckermouth who was handling the deal. A Miss Primrose Puckermouth.'

'You serious?'

She giggled – nervously, Simon thought. 'I know. Terrible name, isn't it.'

'Miss Puckermouth it is.' Simon scribbled on his pad.

'You will let me know if you find them?' Kitty asked.

'I'll see what I can do. I might have to pay a high price to get them back. You do know that, don't you?'

She laughed. It wasn't nervous this time, but it wasn't as confident as it could be. 'I'll pay any price you want to name. Any price at all.' And Simon knew exactly what she meant.

He took a few deep breaths once the phone was back on the hook.

'Yahoo!' he shouted triumphantly, and threw his pen in the air.

He phoned Perry and Merryweather and asked to speak to Miss Puckermouth. He was put through immediately.

'Miss Puckermouth speaking.' Her voice sounded as cracked as the old china she dealt with.

'I wonder if you can help me,' Simon began, struggling not to let excitement enter his voice. 'I'm making enquiries regarding the estate of Mr Samuel Levy, deceased. It's regarding tracing some artifacts that should not have been sold at the auction.'

'Everything had to be sold at the auction,' snapped Miss Puckermouth. 'It was a condition of Mr Levy's will that everything be sold except for his widow's personal items.'

'I know,' Simon went on, determined not to retreat before the curt words of this woman. 'But it appears that some items of a personal nature belonging to Mrs Levy were left inside a piece of furniture or trunk, or something. Has anyone reported finding anything?'

'Who are you?'

'Who am I?'

'Who are you?'

'I'm acting for Mrs Levy.'

'You her lawyer?'

'No, I'm not . . .'

'Then I'm afraid I can't help you.'

'Hang on a minute. I can get her to contact you direct, or even get Mr Levy's lawyer to contact you direct.'

'No need. I'll contact them to ascertain your authenticity, Mr . . . ?'

'Tye. Simon Tye. Mrs Levy's in Miami. She phoned me only a short while ago, and I was playing golf with Mr Levy's lawyer on Friday, but please ring him if you want further confirmation.'

'I will. Give me your number and I'll ring you back.'

He did give her his office number, and she did ring him back. She was almost as curt as before, but not quite. He wondered if she were more used with dealing with antiques rather than people; dead things more so than live ones.

'I'll send you a list of the purchasers,' she said in a clipped voice that reminded him of snipping scissors. 'But I have to warn you, some of these people are only contactable through me. Is that clear, Mr Tye? Our more exalted clients value their privacy.'

'Yes! Yes,' he answered, hardly able to control the excitement in his voice. 'That's clear! Very clear.'

He swallowed hard as he put the phone down. There was no guarantee that what he sought would be in one of those items sold at auction, but Kitty had told him enough to make him hopeful.

In his mind, he could see him and her dressed in those green silk clothes, her nipples digging like rivets into the material, her legs opening as she unbuttoned her gusset and opened the lips of her sex to his hungry eyes.

And him; bristling with sexual vigour, his heart pounding and his penis thrusting through an opening in the pyjama trousers, its one eye seeping with tears of desire.

He shook his head and the vision shattered.

'Pull yourself together, man. Just sit on your butt and wait for ole Miss Puckermouth to do her thing.'

# Chapter 21

The health of Carla Ferretti had improved since the day she had accosted Ruth Tye. She was off crutches now, and although she still limped slightly, she was beginning to look and feel her old self.

Although not overly tall, or blessed with being related to a wealthy family, Carla did have one particular asset. From her mother, she had inherited a considerable determination. With as much determination as her mother had wanted her to start a new life, Carla wanted those green silk nightclothes. She wanted to be sexy. Film stars were sexy. Models were sexy. Even those women caught having affairs with politicians had a certain aura of sexual energy about them.

Carla wanted it too.

That was why she fixed herself a job in Perry and Merryweather with a view to finding out the name and address of the woman she had seen buy the chest and its contents at auction. She knew her face and had accosted her in the street. But now she wanted to bargain with her, to offer her anything she wanted in order to obtain the brass-bound chest. If all else failed, well, she might adopt the more territorial and dangerous attitude of her younger brother who was eighteen, in the United States, and in jail awaiting sentence for stabbing someone to death.

Perhaps there had been no excuse for her brother doing that. But it was different for her. She did have an excuse to be mercenary about what she wanted. After all, wasn't it her who had put the green silk things into the chest beneath those old photographs? Weren't they hers by right? Another question came to her head. Could she stab someone to death for such clothes and such a sexual turn-on?

She didn't know. 'I would only kill for something I truly wanted,' she'd said to her friend Angelina on a day when they'd discussed such things. Of course, she had never expected at the time to run into something as unusual as those green silk clothes – clothes that shimmered and made the wearer look sleeker, sexier than they truly were. Immediately she had seen them, she'd wanted them. Oh, how she'd wanted them!

At Perry and Merryweather, she ran errands, filed bits of boring paper, made coffee, and trundled a big trolley from one department and one floor to another.

Sometimes the trolley contained small antiques for valuation. It also contained internal memos, packages, and photocopying done on the machine on the ground floor and required by the more important people on the top floor.

Sometimes, like today, she got to the machine at that point when the operator had got tired of watching endless reams trickle down into the delivery tray and was going for coffee. From the first, she had asked Carla to watch the sheets for her in case anything should stick.

'I won't be long,' the operator shouted over her shoulder before resuming her conversation with the guy in the post-room.

'Don't worry,' Carla called back. 'I'll read while I wait.'

Carla was keen on improving her English, so she read a lot of what went through the machine. Usually it was letters, contracts, or memos as they filtered through. Today, something different caught her eye. She noted the date, the address, the name of the law firm that had handled her old employer's business and personal matters. Then she saw the name Samuel Samson Levy.

'List of Purchasers and Purchases,' she said softly, as she scanned the heading.

Quickly, she glanced over to where Mary, the operator, was still gossiping with the young black guy who ruled the post-room.

She glanced at the machine. This batch of photocopying was nearing the end. She waited until the last sheet landed. Then she reprogrammed it and sent the list through again.

'Everything OK?' asked Mary who looked a little more anxious, but not enough to leave half her coffee or her conversation.

'Sure. Sure. Everything OK,' Carla replied. As the new copies came through, she shoved them beneath a large green folder that held accounts returns for the auction rooms which were also on the ground floor and next to the post-room.

'Thanks,' said Carla as Mary came back to her machine. 'I take these now.' Off she trundled with her trolley towards the elevator.

She delivered stuff to where she had to deliver it, but that night, in her one-roomed apartment that she had painted in yellow and red, she ran her brown finger down the list of items sold at the Levy auction. There it was. The chest. She ran her finger along the line to the name and address of the purchaser. She smiled. People who lived in a place like that had money. People like that expected to be burgled at least once in their lives.

It was suddenly to her advantage that during her time with Sam Levy, Carla had also done some work for a domestic agency called Chambers Charmers. They had issued her with an identification card that had her picture on it and stated that she worked for them. It was a pass card to most places that used agency domestics. When she got to the block where Mrs Ruth Tye lived, she waved it at the security man. He scanned it casually, waved her through, and turned his attention back to one of his monitors which, somehow or other, he had managed to tune in to a ball game.

Carla found her way to the apartment where Mrs Ruth Tye lived. Her expression hardened as she thought of this woman who had stolen those things that were hers by right. She could keep the chest. Keep the pictures too. None of that stuff was important. It was the green silk she wanted and she meant to have it!

She rang the bell.

There was no answer.

She rang again.

Carla immediately recognized the dark-haired lady with a heart-shaped face who answered the door. She was wearing a pale peach wrap and was holding it at the front with one hand. She smelt of something flowery as if she had just got out of the bath.

'Yes. Can I help you?'

She was frowning slightly and sounded impatient.

'I come to clean for you.' Carla adopted a heavy accent –

the sort she had discarded long ago.

'I don't think so.'

'Yes,' Carla insisted, and waved her card. 'I come to clean for you.'

'No,' the woman said firmly, and shook her head. 'I haven't arranged for anyone to call. Not today. Conceptua cleans for me on Tuesdays and Fridays. Today is Thursday. I think you've got the wrong address.'

She started to close the door.

'Conceptua ill. I come today. I cannot come tomorrow.'

Ruth paused. The woman's eyes opened wide. They were very brown and very appealing. Ruth relented. After all, she didn't want to clean the house herself on Friday, having it cleaned on Thursday was good enough. Anyway, on Friday she'd fixed to go to the beauty salon and then out shopping with Hannah.

'Okay,' she said. 'Come on in and get started. But there's no need for you to do the master bedroom.' The frown went and a furtive look came to her face. 'I'm doing something in there at the moment. I'm also expecting someone. I want you gone when he comes. Is that clear?' Her smile was weak.

Carla nodded affably, and as is the way with all seasoned domestics, she made her way to where she was sure she could find the vacuum cleaner, dusters, and everything else she might need. Ruth Tye hovered whilst Carla got all the cleaning paraphernalia out into the open. She lingered until Carla had organized her dusters and a large can of spray polish. Carla began to hum something religious and eminently reassuring as she worked.

Although she appeared absorbed in dusting and polishing every item in sight, Carla peered carefully from beneath her dark fringe as Ruth went into the bedroom and closed the door behind her.

Once she was sure of being alone, she peered into corners, closets and drawers. Of course, she couldn't expect to find the chest in a drawer, but what if this woman had discovered her hidden hoard? The prospect appalled her.

Her efforts were without success. Now where else could it be, she asked herself. Could she have put it in storage for some reason, or even, horror of horrors, discovered it had termites and sold it, or even burnt it?

But then, she countered, if Mrs Ruth Tye had opened the chest and had found the flimsy body suit, and the pyjamas, wouldn't they most likely be in the one room in the house where they truly belonged – the bedroom?

She turned the vacuum on and used it to hide the sound of her rushing feet as she careered across the carpet to the bedroom door.

She leaned against the closed door: heard nothing. She turned off the vacuum and listened again. Nothing. At the same time as reaching for her brother's switchblade and releasing the catch, she reached for the doorhandle.

'What are you doing?'

Carla spun round, the steel blade flashing as she did so.

'What are you doing?' The delivery boy had very blue eyes that were fixed on the knife she was holding. He also had a very fine physique, and youth was definitely on his side.

Slowly, without blinking, he set the box of groceries he was carrying down on the coffee table. He took a step towards her. Carla noticed he had broad shoulders. Football jock; jerk more like.

Carla's heart was beating fast. 'I have to . . .' Wide-eyed, she looked towards the closed bedroom door. Could she reach it and grab what she wanted? No. She could not. The delivery boy looked as though he meant business.

He stepped towards her.

She side-stepped and gripped the knife more tightly.

'Drop the knife.' He said the words firmly.

Sounds like a cop, Carla thought. Built like one too – just like one of those big Irish ones whose cocks are bigger than their brains.

Slowly, she shook her head.

'Drop it and you won't get hurt.' He took a step towards her.

'Come forward one more step, and you'll get hurt,' she growled.

She bent from the waist, her shoulders low, her eyes glowering up at him. Her brother had taught her how to use a knife.

The big, blond college jock folded his arms across his chest. The muscles of his upper arms bulged against the sleeves of his T-shirt. 'I wouldn't count on it, honey,' he said with a sneer. 'I've got a black belt in judo.'

'And I've got black knickers in my laundry. So what?' spat Carla. But she was not entirely unaffected by him. His eyes were compelling. He was compelling. If only, she thought, I had those green silk things. I could really have fun with him. What a dish. What a body! I'd run my hands over him, lick him all up those hard muscles, and once his dong was big and hard, I'd ride him till he screamed.

Thinking such things made her lose her concentration. She became vulnerable. The delivery boy saw his chance and lunged for her.

But despite her slight limp, Carla was quick. She ducked, and being a woman who knows when she is beaten, made a run for the door.

With the switchblade still in her hand, she ran down the corridor and knew he was running behind her. She hid, lost him, then dived off down the stairwell and didn't stop running until she reached the bottom.

At the bottom, she at last breathed a sigh of relief.

'I must get rid of this knife,' she muttered to herself as she crossed a patch of grass and went under the shade of a group of lime trees.

Carefully, she wrapped the knife up in a scarf which she took from her bag, and rather than dumping it in a trash can, she let it fall to the ground. Then she rushed off.

Her breathing was more even now. She'd lost him. She was sure of it.

'Hey you!'

'Oh, no!' she muttered breathlessly.

It had to be the big, blond delivery boy.

Her legs raced along with her heart beat as she fled across the grass and regained the sidewalk on the other side.

'Hey you! Stop!'

Would she hell!

Without giving a thought to the traffic, she raced out into the road. There was a screech of brakes as cars tried to avoid her. A taxi did not. Knocked off her feet, Carla flew over the bonnet of the taxi and landed on the road.

A crowd gathered as she lay moaning and rubbing at the injury she had received when the piano had landed on her legs. It throbbed, and without any doctor telling her so, she knew it was broken – again.

She looked up at a sea of faces – all different faces – all different colours.

'Hey, lady. I wasn't going to mug you, you know,' said a man with a dark brown face. 'I just wanted to return this to you. I saw you drop it.'

He held up the scarf she had wrapped the knife in.

'It was blowing through the grass,' he explained.

Carla whimpered and began to cry. 'I thought you were . . . someone . . . else,' she said haltingly. 'I thought you were a blond guy and were going to do something terrible to me.'

The dark brown head shook sadly from side to side. He smiled. ''Fraid not, lady. As you can see, I'm far from blond.' Suddenly, he grinned wickedly. 'And I wouldn't have done anything terrible, lady. Might have asked you for a date and got fresh with you on the way home, but that's not so terrible now, is it?'

Carla stared at him. What a hunk of a man! What a chance she'd missed. 'Oh, no,' she began to wail. 'Oh, no!'

Dean, the delivery boy, saw the woman with the knife get knocked down by the taxi.

'Serve you right,' he said, and whistling happily, made his way back up into the apartment and the bed of Ruth Tye, his new lover.

# Chapter 22

Gavin, who worked in the store room at Celicia Corinne's fashion establishment, was colour-blind. At the time an order came through from the sewing room for a bolt of blue silk, he still had his gloves on because he had ridden his motorcycle to work. A cop had stopped him and booked him for speeding, so he was in a bad humour which was made worse at being hustled into getting an order ready straightaway.

Accordingly, green silk arrived in the sewing room and not the blue as ordered. The machinists too were annoyed at receiving a rush order at such a late hour on a Friday afternoon, so did not bother to question why the colour had been altered.

'It is almost blue,' said Betty, who wore wire-framed spectacles and hadn't had much of a love life since she wore flowers in her hair and helped draftees burn their call-up papers. 'Blue is the next colour to green. In fact, it's part of the same spectrum. Blue and yellow make green.'

'Near enough for me,' said one of her colleagues.

The others went along with it. Normally, their grumbles would have gone on longer, but for some inexplicable reason, their enthusiasm for the job increased along with their conversation.

As on other afternoons, their talk turned to sex. Normally, they would stick to generalities about their love lives, but on this particular afternoon, things went further than that. There was a tingle in the air that was tangible, yet unseen. It touched each of them, alighted on busy fingers and, unbidden, travelled over their bodies and into their minds.

Memories normally hidden from public view came to the surface. Descriptions of their sexual encounters became far more vivid and personal than usual. Each one began to relate her most memorable sexual experience, her greatest turn-on. No one held anything back. It was Betty's story that truly held the rest spellbound.

'We were demonstrating outside the White House,' she said, 'and the National Guard had been called out. There was all the usual shouting and cracking of skulls. Those that weren't arrested left the city and set up camp in a place just off the main highway. We lit joss sticks and filled the air with perfume. The smoke from them and our cooking fires made the night hazy.' Sensing the room had fallen to perfect silence, Betty glanced around. The past and the present fused in her mind. Was her mind playing tricks? Was she seeing the same smoky haze she had seen then?

Let it be, she thought to herself, and felt strangely happy. She went on with her tale.

'By the time everyone had finished talking, eating and drinking, there were only five of us left – me and four guys.'

'What were these guys like?' asked Sondra, who was leggy enough to be a model, except that her boobs were far too big.

'Average to good.'

'In looks, or in tool size?' asked the same bubbly blonde who had seduced Johnny Bow down in the store room. Surprisingly, she said it without the hint of a giggle.

Betty smiled. 'In looks, mostly. Men are never average in the other department. They all vary. Some are medium, some big, and some super-dooper! Anyway, that's beside the point. Some have a good technique, and some don't. And that's what really matters.'

The sewing room gasped in wonder. No one was shocked. Betty herself seemed strange, other-worldly.

'Anyway,' Betty went on, 'there we were. Me and these guys. One guy began to kiss me. Cavalier, they called him on account of the boots and the broad-brimmed hat he wore. It was black and had two ostrich feathers stuck in the band. We took off our clothes and got down to it as the others watched. Cavalier had very dark eyes and bushy eyebrows. His hair was long and hung in ringlets. So did his beard. I remember it feeling like silk against my breasts – yes.' Her voice was soft, her eyes glazed as she recalled the memory. 'Like silk. His skin was smooth too. Surprising that, considering he had all that hair on his head and chin.

'I remember looking up at the stars as he played with my breasts. My nipples tingled. I can feel them now,' she said, closing her eyes as she laid her hands across her breasts and kneaded them as he had done. 'He wound the hair from his beard around them, and I remember humming to myself as he went down over my stomach. I thought he was going to lick me between my legs – you know, usual stuff. But he didn't. Instead, he put a teaspoonful of sweet-smelling oil into a pot of warm water. He dipped his beard into the water and began to wash me between my legs. The effect was crazy – beautifully crazy. He washed me with the hair from his beard, and dried me with the hair on his head.'

'What were the others doing?' asked Naomi, who had short red hair and a black crucifix hanging from one ear.

Betty smiled and ran her hands down over her belly. She opened her legs slightly and rocked gently to and fro as she rubbed her crotch with both hands. 'They were playing with my breasts. One was playing a guitar and making up some song for the occasion. Someone's dick was tapping against my cheek. They stretched me out – kind of like a sacrifice. It was a way-out feeling, I can tell you, to have all those hands and all those dicks around me.

'Eventually, Cavalier lay out on the ground, his rod pointing at the stars. "Come ride me, baby," he said, so I got up and slid myself down on him. It felt good. It felt real good. And then, it got even better. One of the guys – Cinch, I think his name was – got on top of me and pushed his dick into my behind. That was two holes taken care of. Then the dick that had been tapping against my cheek went into my mouth. It tasted good – like honey, cheese, and warm chocolate, all laced into one.

'I took another in my hand: that was the biggest one. It had to belong to the Glassman.'

'Why was he . . . ?' asked a curious voice.

'Shhh!' hissed someone else.

Betty continued.

'He was called the Glassman because he was covered in scars. He got high one night at some rave-up in Harlem and fell through a skylight. Had a good body, though.' She smiled reflectively. 'Good size dick too. That guy was not only black, he had the sort of dick that legends are made of. Wow! I took him in my hand. Like velvet it was – soft, black velvet.

'It was an incredible feeling, like nothing I'd had before, and like nothing since. It was almost as though I were some ten-legged animal, or an octopus – though they have tentacles, don't they? Instead there were eight testicles surrounding me, and four dicks: one in each hole, and one in my hand. I moved as they moved, slid up and down on the one that was in my sex, as another thrust into my behind. And I sucked – God, how I sucked! And as I sucked one, I tugged on another – tugged on the beautiful black tool of the Glassman.'

Betty sighed and she hummed a gentle, unrecognizable tune before she continued her tale. Her voice was soft, reflective.

'How warm the night was, all those years ago. We felt like giants: felt like life and the world were ours. Power was in our bodies, a need for living in our minds. We were lost in ourselves, our bodies; each other's bodies. We tingled together, and almost came together. The liquid that spurted into my throat and the rest of my body, was as warm as the night.'

'Did the big guy come into your hand?' someone asked.

Betty trembled, moaned, then shook her head and brought her hands back up to the work in front of her. Her eyes still sparkled behind the wire-rimmed frames. 'No. The Glassman never did that. Once he was about to come, he let it spurt into his guitar. Said it kept it fertile with tunes. After he'd done that, he held his instrument – the one attached to his body, that is – near my face so I could lick it clean for him.

Then he cradled his guitar to his chest and kissed it, told it how wonderful it was and how much he loved it: Esmerelda, he called it; his guitar, that is. He was mad, of course, crazy, but I'll never forget him; never forget any of them. Never forget that time either.'

She sighed and bent her head back to her work.

There was silence before the others too spoke of their own sexual experiences, but nothing matched the originality and the feeling of nostalgia Betty had engendered in her story.

For the rest of the afternoon, an atmosphere of dormant sexuality hung over the room. It was as though something had stirred them all into remembering and into imagining what had been and what was still possible.

Betty went strangely quiet. Something about that summer night and the feel of the silk beneath her fingers was peculiarly alike. She stared at the material, fingered it before she fed it through the teeth of the machine.

Memories of the sixties and her sexual adventures stayed with her. God, but the young didn't know what they had missed, she thought to herself. They did not know what it felt like to be full of sex, full of power. Even her daughter didn't understand her, refused to listen to her lurid tales. Elizabeth, she decided, was missing a lot, and that was a shame.

She stayed later than the others, and although the green silk was already cut out and half-sewn into garments, she had it in her head to find a spare piece, enough to make a present for her daughter. Tomorrow, Elizabeth was getting married.

'Have a good time tomorrow,' each of her colleagues called as they left. 'Give Elizabeth our love.'

'Thanks, you guys,' she called back. 'See you at the party tomorrow night.'

All of her friends had been invited. All the presents were there, all the arrangements made. But she had to do one last thing. She had to make something from this material that made her fingers tingle and her body ache for old lovers, old passions. Betty believed in Karma, believed in forces that couldn't be seen, couldn't be measured. She was damned sure she felt those forces in this material, and Elizabeth would have the benefit of it.

Everyone agreed that Elizabeth MacGee was a beautiful bride. Elizabeth herself felt beautiful. Her dark hair was piled on the top of her head and laced with tiny seed pearls. Her veil was as fragile as a cobweb, its edges scalloped and embroidered with thin tendrils, leaves, and tiny buds made from clusters of pearls. Her gown was of pure, white silk. It had a scooped neckline, long sleeves that finished in points that half covered the backs of her hands. It accentuated the fullness of her breasts, the neatness of her waist, and the slender curve of her hips. A belt, heavy with embroidery and pearls, girdled her hips, its ends meeting just below her navel and hanging in front of her.

'You look glorious, my dear.' Betty, who had just one more present to give her daughter, kissed Elizabeth's cheek.

'Thanks for everything, mom.'

'I can't believe this is really happening,' Betty said tearfully against Elizabeth's ear. 'My daughter getting married without ever having been a rebel.'

'That's the way I am, mom,' replied Elizabeth, her face flushed and her dark eyes shining. 'I'm a different generation,

Mom. The hippy bit's all gone. There isn't such a call for rebels any more; people calling for peace instead of war. All the flower people have gone respectable. You should try it yourself.'

Betty visibly baulked and laid her hand on her chest. 'Don't ever say that, Elizabeth, darling. Please don't ever say that.' She raised her eyes to heaven. 'Respectability. Me. The former Betty Buttercup Breasts. Who'd ever have thought it. And my girl – getting married.' She shook her head and smiled wanly. 'You haven't lived, my girl. I still don't think you've had enough men or enough sex to be getting married.'

'Mom!' Elizabeth blushed a little more. Her husband came and gave her a kiss on the cheek. Betty eyed him casually. He was a nice guy – not overly handsome – but nice. He was an accountant with some firm called Perry and Merryweather who had an auction room where old things were sold off.

Just like I should be, Betty thought to herself as she sighed again and bit her tongue in an effort to prevent herself lecturing her daughter on the dangers of getting hitched without having lived a little.

'I'll be all right, mom.'

Still smiling, Betty nodded.

The best man kissed Elizabeth on the cheek. He looked a little sad.

Elizabeth blushed. Her mother knew it had been hard to choose which one to marry. She had chosen Paul. Garfield was the loser. Still, he was best man.

Both men left Elizabeth and her mother to talk alone.

'I've bought you a little present,' said Betty. She handed

216

her daughter the item she had made which she'd wrapped up in suitable paper. 'I made it at work. The silk was so unusual. I felt drawn to it. It wanted me to make something for you.'

'Mom, what are you talking about? How can a piece of material want you to make something from it? Is this one of your hippy second sight things?'

Betty smiled weakly, She ignored her daughter's hurtful jibe. 'I think you'll like it.'

'I'll open it later.'

They kissed and hugged a lot more before Elizabeth and her new husband left for their overnight stay at a hotel near Kennedy Airport. Garfield was going with them to help with their baggage and take their car home.

Their flight was for ten-thirty in the morning and would take them to London. After seeing all there was to see in the capital, they would breeze off to Bath, Stratford and Warwick.

'Don't forget to see Carnaby Street,' shouted Betty. 'And try and get up to the Cavern in Liverpool, if you can.'

Elizabeth shook her head reproachfully. 'Mother. We're not going to Liverpool.'

'Never mind.' Betty waved them goodbye, a secretive smile playing havoc around her generous lips. Her daughter – well educated and employed in Wall Street – might make fun of her flights of fancy, her second sight. But she knew they were real, knew they kept her aware of what was going on around her. Never, ever, would she relinquish that old power and pretend it and the age of free love was all a load of hogwash. It wasn't, and the green silk might prove it.

Once they were in their room at the Hyatt Hilton Hotel,

Elizabeth fell into the arms of her new husband, Paul.

Garfield, with only a hint of jealousy in his eyes, trailed in behind them. 'Hold on, you guys. At least give the best man time to get away before you start doing that stuff!' Garfield put down the bags.

'Do you want a tip?' Paul asked him.

'No,' he answered. 'But I would like a drink. Those bags were heavy, and I'm all tuckered out.'

'Try this.' Elizabeth retrieved a large bottle of champagne from a shiny bag. 'Whilst you guys drink a glass or two, I'll go and freshen up.'

'Where are the glasses in this place?' said Elizabeth's new husband, as he manoeuvred the cork from the bottle.

'Who needs glasses? I'll take it straight from the bottle,' said Garfield.

Elizabeth hadn't meant to take the parcel her mother had given her into the bathroom. It just seemed as though she couldn't let go of it.

Once she had used what she needed to use, she took off her clothes and prepared to wash her face and brush her teeth before getting into the shower. The faucet was one of those automatic types that spurted into action when you least expect it.

'Damn!' Water splashed onto the clothes she had just taken off, not just a drop of water, but quite a lot. She needed to change her dress.

Automatically, her fingers went to the parcel. Before long, it was open and her fingers were trailing wonderingly over the green silk item within.

'It's beautiful,' she whispered in a hushed voice. 'Really beautiful.'

The silk whispered back to her as she put it on.

'Yes, yes. You really are beautiful.' It was as though the silk had truly spoken and she was answering its question.

Through half-closed eyes, she eyed her mirror image. Her hair and the sprinkling of seed pearls now combined in wild disarray over her shoulders. Her lips were glossy and hung open. She murmured like the sea does against soft sand. Her body undulated as though her flesh was melting.

As though it was for the very first time, she ran her hands down over her breasts, her waist and her hips. Tingles of pleasure erupted all over her body.

Her mother had done her job well. She had fashioned the silk into a full length halter-necked lounging dress. The neckline dived between Elizabeth's firm breasts. A long slit ran from the hem to an inch or two beneath her crotch.

Elizabeth was covered in a sheath of green silk, and yet she felt completely naked. Urgent desires ran through her body like molten lava. Wherever the silk touched, jolts of something resembling electricity raced over her skin.

She moaned at her own reflection, reached out, touched it. Then slowly, she pressed herself flat against the mirror and kissed her own lips.

The glass was cool against her body. The silk cleaved to her, tightened across her belly, tickled her mat of pubic hair. In response to the coolness of the mirror, her nipples grew and mutated the shape of the silk that covered them.

Paul and Garfield were on their second glass of champagne when Elizabeth went back into the room.

Her husband saw her first. 'My God!'

Garfield was halfway through telling a joke, when he

spotted her. 'Elizabeth! What's happened?' His voice seemed to be having trouble escaping from his throat.

Elizabeth tossed her head. The pearls and her hair tumbled down her back. Her lips were moist, her eyes sparkling. She raised her arms and held them out to them both.

'Come, my darlings. Let us make this a night to remember.'

Paul stared. He had not married Elizabeth because of her bedroom technique. He had married her because she was beautiful. Passion, he'd decided, would come with practice.

Garfield began to stammer. 'Look . . . here . . . I . . . don't . . .'

It was impossible for him to say more.

As one hypnotized, he watched. Green sparks flew from Paul's chest as Elizabeth touched him. A haze – also green – seemed to swathe them, clothe them in an uncanny light.

As though in a dream, the bridegroom removed his clothes. His penis was fully erect and pointing at Elizabeth's belly. His wife clasped his nakedness to her body.

'My God!'

Garfield only wheezed out his exclamation. He wanted to go – knew he should go – but for some reason, he couldn't seem to move. He asked himself if he were drunk. No, he decided, not drunk. Merely merry. He'd had a lot to drink at the wedding, but only two glasses of champagne with Paul.

'Don't go, Garfield, darling.' With one arm still around her husband, Elizabeth reached for him.

Suddenly, there seemed no need to protest, no need to run away. A green haze invaded Garfield's mind. Tingles like pin-pricks of low voltage electricity ran through his body. He was aware that his penis was filling with blood and with passion. A voice in his head told him to take off his clothes. He did. His erection was just as big as Paul's, though perhaps his penis was longer. Paul's was thicker.

There was a screen window in the room that took in a wide vista of the surrounding blocks, the passing clouds and passing aircraft. In front of the window was a very large, glass-topped coffee table with chrome legs.

Elizabeth rolled up the soft silk dress until it rested just below her chin and over her shoulders. The rest of her body was open to the view of her husband, his best man, and anyone else who happened to be able to look in through the window.

Garfield and Paul watched, mesmerized by the curves of her breasts, her belly and her thighs.

She lay down on the cool glass of the coffee table. Both men stared, their eyes sparkling, their hands caressing their erections. Neither seemed to think it strange that Elizabeth was doing this. In fact, it seemed the most natural thing in the world.

Due to the silk and their earlier contact with the bathroom mirror, Elizabeth's nipples stood pink and erect. Her legs were spread so that the backs of her knees rested against the bottom corners of the coffee table. Crisp pubic curls crowned her open lips, the folds within pink and shiny as satin. She kept her arms up and away from her body. Her flesh seemed to shiver, become hazy as she arched her back, raised and lowered her hips from the glass table.

'Yes. I agree. You go first,' the bridegroom said to the best man.

Garfield nodded. He hadn't actually said anything – not verbally – it just seemed that way. In that split moment, a little voice had been in his head. It could have been his own voice, but it might not have. It didn't matter.

Paul slid under the table so that his head was beneath his wife's buttocks, and his hips beneath her head, the tip of his penis barely reaching the table.

As he lay there, so serene, his penis so hard with desire, he stared up through the glass to the spherical perfection of his wife's backside. He licked his lips. Garfield was getting in position.

Paul's cock jerked as he imagined the best man's hands upon his wife's breasts. Immediately before his eyes, he could see Garfield's erect penis entering his wife's vagina, his balls following on, flattened as they slid backwards and forwards over the glass table-top.

Vague memories of childhood visits to aquariums came to his mind; molluscs, octopus, squid pressing themselves against glass: as if they could see through it, as if they were trying to escape.

Each time Garfield thrust into Elizabeth, Paul raised his hips from the carpet so that the head of his penis tapped against the glass of the table.

As he jerked, he feasted his eyes on the sight of Elizabeth's buttocks. They looked broader than usual; a trick of the glass, he thought. He raised his hands and laid them flat against the glass and her flesh beyond. The purple richness of her open sex was slick with juice, shiny like satin, as Garfield's member slid in and out of her vagina.

'Hurry,' he said quietly as he lay beneath the table. 'Hurry up and finish it.'

His own semen spurted against the table top and ran like melting wax down a freshly lit candle.

He cried out in ecstasy.

Above him, Garfield tensed as he gushed into Elizabeth. Elizabeth cried out. Her body writhed and heaved on the table above. Paul rolled out from under the table. His head spun a little. Faintly, as though woven by a thousand small spiders, a fragile, green mist swam before his eyes. Too much wine, he thought to himself, too much excitement.

Garfield stood up, then bent down and kissed Elizabeth. Immediately, his penis, which had been spent, which had been soft, became hard again.

'Your turn, I think,' he said to his friend whose wife he had just made love to.

'I can't wait,' Paul replied.

He was vaguely aware of Garfield having got down to the floor and taken up position where he had been. His eyes were purely for his wife; for Elizabeth, who had suddenly taken on a far more adventurous nature than he had ever thought possible.

She smiled at him. 'Make love to me.'

'I intend to.'

He knelt at the head of the coffee table, kissed her lips, and kneaded her breasts. Using only one finger and thumb, he pulled on her nipples and held her breasts suspended. Their tongues met, circled each other. Their lips sucked on each other's mouths.

He came round to her side, squeezed her breasts, ran his hands down over her belly.

Through the glass top of the coffee table, he could see his friend, his best man, Garfield, looking up between Elizabeth's widely-spread legs. He smiled at him.

'Let me show you something,' he said.

He ran his hands along Elizabeth's inner thighs. She moaned with pleasure as he pressed his thumbs either side of her clitoris before he opened her sexual lips to the gaze of his friend. Entranced by what he was seeing, Garfield stared from beneath the glass-topped table.

With a strange feeling of satisfaction, Paul noted the slippery white substance oozing from Elizabeth's open vagina. Garfield had left that there. Garfield had made love to his wife. Paul smiled at the thought, smiled at Garfield, then at his wife.

'I'm going to make love to you,' Paul said.

His wife gazed at him with half-closed eyes. She raised her hips invitingly as she spoke. 'Yes. That's it. Make love to me. Make love to me until you can't make love any more. Make love to me until we can do nothing but sleep. Please. Now. Now!'

Paul lay on her, her breasts soft as satin against his chest, her hips coming up to meet him.

There was a sweet piquancy in knowing that, as he entered her, his best man, Garfield, was watching.

His former conservative disposition re-emerged for a moment. 'Do you mind that Garfield is watching us?'

'I want him to watch us,' said Elizabeth. 'I want him to do everything with us.'

'Have you always wanted to do something like this?' Paul sounded surprised. He also sounded very happy.

'Always. It's in the genes, it was just that I never owned up to it.' She smiled and ran her tongue over her lips.

Paul shook his head. 'I can't believe this.'

Elizabeth caressed his cheek. 'You don't need to. All you need do is to like it. Do you like it?'

'Oh, yes,' he cried as the first spasms of orgasm ran from his testicles and halfway up his stem. 'Oh. YE . . . SSSS!'

She held him to her and manipulated her hips beneath him until her orgasm occurred. As the last moan of pleasure escaped her lips, she turned her head to one side.

Beneath the dark tresses and the glass of the table, Paul could see a white stream of fluid escape from Garfield and cling to the underneath of the glass.

Elizabeth let her dress fall around her as she got up from the table.

The two men sat on the floor and looked up at her as if awaiting instructions.

Elizabeth tossed her black mane. Pearls fell from her hair and rolled over the carpet. She smiled down at them.

'Pick them up,' she said.

Ever considerate, her husband reached for one.

Elizabeth's bare foot landed on his hand.

'With your teeth.'

The two men looked at each other.

Elizabeth went behind them and landed a hard kick on both bare behinds.

'Get on with it!'

They did as she asked. The green glow that emanated from her and her dress made them want to please her, want to be subservient to her wishes.

Neither made any comment as Elizabeth did a handstand against the wall. Her green dress fell to the floor leaving her body naked but her face hidden.

She spread her legs against the wall.

Through the green haze of the silk dress, she saw them, still on all fours, in front of her.

Like two donkeys, she thought, their mouths more full than their heads.

'Put them in me,' she said.

The two men looked at each other.

'Put them in me.'

Each man did as she ordered. First Paul's lips covered her and his tongue pushed the pearls into her body. Then Garfield did the same.

'We've got a while to wait for our flight. You can kill time by taking them out again,' she said. 'With your tongues.'

Garfield went with them to Europe. It seemed the best thing to do, and even though they didn't get to see as many of the sights as they had aimed to, it didn't really seem to matter. The time passed pleasantly, and even though hotel staff probably thought it strange that three people were sharing the honeymoon suite, no one made any comment.

In the manner of any career-minded, strong-willed woman, Elizabeth took charge of their itinerary.

She also phoned her mother in New York.

'I hope you liked your present,' her mother said hesitantly.

Elizabeth made a kind of moaning noise down the phone. 'Wonderful,' she said. 'In fact, I think it was the most wonderful thing anyone has ever given me. Ooooh, that's so good.'

'I'm glad,' said her mother and smiled to herself. Her second sight had grown older with her, but was still as strong as ever.

At the end of their conversation, Elizabeth put the phone down and looked at the bulge beneath her skirt.

Then she groaned loudly, cried out, and rode the mouth

that pleasured her. Outside the phone box, the world rushed by and appeared not to notice the man who knelt between her legs.

# Chapter 23

Ruth had been discreet regarding her relationship with Dean. All the same, she just had to tell Simon about the woman who had pretended she was a replacement for Conceptua.

'We had an intruder today. She told me she had come along because Conceptua was ill. But she was lying.'

'That's nice dear,' muttered Simon Tye, his concentration fixed on the list of purchasers he had received from Perry and Merryweather.

'Simon!' She tore the list from his hands.

'What's the matter?'

'Didn't you hear me? I said we had an intruder.'

Simon gaped as what she had said sunk in. 'When? What happened? What did he take?'

'She. It was a woman. She had a knife and she didn't take anything. She didn't have a chance to. The delivery boy stopped her. He chased her out of this building and across the square. She ran pretty fast for someone with a limp.'

'No harm done then.'

'Simon! I could have been killed. She had a knife, for God's sake! If it hadn't been for Dean—'

'Dean?'

Ruth blushed. 'The delivery boy.'

'How come you're blushing?'

'I'm not. Not really. It was just that – I was in my wrap – and he was there. He helped me. He saved me from that woman.'

'Did you call the police?'

Ruth shook her head. Simon frowned. For a moment, he was almost convinced he saw a look of guilt pass over his wife's face.

'Why?'

She shrugged and closed her mouth tightly. 'The delivery boy chased her. She got knocked down by a taxi on the other side of the square.'

Simon sighed. 'Just desserts then.' He picked up his list from the chair where Ruth had thrown it.

Ruth too sighed as Simon returned to studying the sheaf of papers.

Just once, she thought as she eyed the receding hair, the bespectacled visage, just once I'd like you to make love to me like you used to, to feel everything I used to feel when we were young and in love. After all, your body's still as good as it ever was. Your face is still handsome, and everything's still in working order.

She held her head to one side and let her fancies take her. Had they really been in love? Or had nature stirred their chemicals into a bubbling stew? Was it really that something they had once regarded as magical was as logical as the attraction of iron to a magnet? Had their magnetism lessened that much over the years?

Her eyes wandered over to the bedroom door. She glanced at her husband one more time, then slipped quietly away. In the bedroom, with the help of the green silk, she would relive the sensuality, if not the reality, of how things had been then.

Simon did not see her go. Kitty Levy was in his mind. He was on a promise. If he could find her green silk underwear or whatever, her body was his. The thought made his penis pulsate against his pants.

Where, he thought to himself as he scanned the list, where could those things be?

He tapped his glasses with his thumb. He was becoming agitated. There were three hundred different lots in the auction list and at least two hundred different buyers. It would be impossible to go through them all.

After sliding his glasses off his nose, he laid his head back and closed his eyes.

Kitty, he thought to himself, think of Kitty. Now. What was it she had said?

Her body for the garments. Yes, yes. There was that. But there was also something else. Something that might help him achieve the mission she had set him.

Perry and Merryweather had arranged the auction, had listed and labelled everything beforehand. But someone else had tidied, polished and packed what needed packing. Kitty's maid!

He had to phone Kitty. He had to locate her maid and ask her a few questions.

Dare he do it at home? He glanced over to the closed bedroom door.

No. He would not.

'I'm just going out to get some cigarettes from the drugstore,' he shouted.

He thought he heard Ruth reply, but didn't bother checking. She'd only ask awkward questions, like since when had he taken up that disgusting habit again? He hadn't, but explanations were something he could do without. He had to phone Kitty.

There was a phone booth in the drugstore. He remembered seeing it there when he had gone in to buy some multi-vitamin tablets and potions that represented another unsuccessful attempt to make Ruth a bit more sexy than she was. Of course, it was another failed attempt. He'd tried to explain, but Ruth had regarded the pills and potions with a jaundiced eye.

'Are you trying to poison me?' she'd snarled.

Experiences of the police and jail were fresh in his head, so he'd shelved that idea immediately.

'Did I see a phone in this place?' he asked the guy in the drugstore who was facing two baseball-capped customers across the counter.

Silently, the man pointed to a glass booth over in the far corner. His hand seemed to shake a little.

'Thanks.' Simon didn't loiter to talk to the guy. He did notice that the man had an unhealthy pallor about his skin. Anyway, he seemed to be giving all his attention to the guys he was serving.

Simon glanced a second time at the two guys in baseball caps. He frowned as he jingled some change in his pocket. Had he seen those guys before? Perhaps. He gave it no account. He went into the booth and rang Kitty.

Her answerphone bleeped into action.

'If you're after action with pretty Kitty,

'Then lick my ass and suck my titty.

'If you want to fuck me when I get home
Then leave your message after the tone.'

Stunned by the sheer lewdness of Kitty's answerphone message, Simon stammered, then, unable to get his words together, he slammed down the receiver.

He laid his head against the coldness of the glass. What a message! How the hell did you follow something like that?

He blinked as he tried to get his head together. God, all he wanted to ask her was the name and address of her maid.

'Be cool,' he muttered to himself. 'Be like Harrison Ford, or better still, Gregory Peck.'

He took a deep breath before he redialled. Again, the message clicked into action.

This time he was ready for it. He waited for the tone, then left his own message.

'With a view to you and me getting laid,
'Give me a ring about your maid.
'Just for the record, this is Simon Tye.
'Ring me at my office. But for now, goodbye.'

Breathing a huge sigh of relief, he put down the phone. His smugness turned to apprehension as he became aware that two grinning faces were peering at him through the glass.

'Hi there again,' said one of them.

Simon gulped. Those dark eyes – that deep voice. It was them, the girls who had raped him in the park.

Briefly, he wondered where the druggist had got to. He stretched his neck and peered over to the counter where he'd last seen him. No sign of him.

The girls opened the door to the booth.

'Well. If it isn't our favourite early morning jogger. How are you, big boy?'

Big boy! Has it grown ears, he asked himself, as he felt his member stiffening.

'I'm . . . uh . . . fine.'

The one who wore a red baseball cap ran her fingers down over his growing erection.

'My. I see you remember us. Now isn't that nice.'

'Let me see,' said the other. Her hand joined that of her friend. 'Yeah,' she said, smiling as she chewed a blob of pink bubblegum. 'It sure is nice to know that someone's glad to see us.'

'Where's . . . where is the . . . uh . . . guy?' Simon nodded towards the counter where the druggist had been standing earlier.

'Stretched out.'

Simon gulped and tried not to choke on his fear. 'Stretched out? You mean he's . . .'

'Not dead, stupid. We stripped his clothes off him and tied him up with those. Played with him a bit, though. Pulled on his dong and tickled his balls a bit.'

'Not much fun, though,' said her friend. 'He was too old and too frightened of us to get stiff.' She smiled provocatively and flashed her eyes. 'Not like you, though, darling. You like a bit of rough treatment, don't you, honey? Is that right?'

Simon swallowed and blinked rapidly as he heard his zip being undone. He moaned as their fingers pulled his warm penis out from its lair.

'Wow,' said the first girl. 'Will you just look at that!'

'I am looking, honey,' said the second in an awestruck voice. 'I surely am looking. Wow! What a weapon.'

'Me first.'

The first girl, who was bigger than her comrade, pushed him tight against the corner of the booth. He whimpered slightly as he felt her fumbling around between his sex and hers. Then he felt her rich thatch of sex hair brush against the tip of his penis. Moist pubic lips kissed his rod, then opened and sucked him in.

He cried out before her mouth covered his and her tongue forced its way between his teeth. He struggled for breath as the long, wet beast tickled the back of his throat.

His body felt weak, ineffectual, soft – except for his penis, that is. Rape seemed to appeal to its perverse personality.

What shame! What bliss. The big girl's body was heavy against him, and made even heavier by the weight of her friend's behind her. He was trapped, pinned against the glass which squealed as his naked behind slid against it. This girl was riding him, raping him; her hips thrusting and slamming against his.

She was quick about it. His semen was only halfway up his stem when she came. Her wet vagina was quickly replaced by that of her friend.

'I'm going to have you,' the second one murmured against his ear.

He moaned, shut his eyes, and willed his orgasm to hold back until this second girl was somewhere near to achieving her own. The consequences of him ejaculating prematurely were just too horrible to contemplate. What if they really had bumped off the old guy that ran the store? And, even worse, what if they did the same to him?

Take it easy, he said to himself, though the advice was

directed at one specific area of his body. Take it easy.

The second girl ran her hands beneath his sweater and pinched his nipples, scratched his stomach and dug her fingernails into his navel.

'Ouch!' He jerked more forcibly against her each time she did that. She seemed to like it.

What the hell, he thought to himself as his semen began to pump up his stem and into her.

Just when he thought he would be too early and might reap the consequences and get his throat cut, she cried low and long against his ear.

As his semen pumped into her, Simon congratulated himself. His timing was perfect.

'This is sure becoming a habit,' she said in a seductive voice.

'We'll have to stop meeting like this,' he said lamely.

The girls' expressions, which had been soft and shiny, now became serious.

'That's true. You're getting to know us too well. How do we know you won't turn us in?'

There was a sudden flash from a steel blade.

Simon shivered. 'Why should I?'

The knife slid under his throat.

'It would be a great shame to slit your throat,' said the first girl.

'Or cut off your Bobbitt,' said the other as she trailed the knife over his wilting erection.

'I won't!' Simon cried in a high voice as his Adam's Apple raced madly up and down his throat. 'I promise I won't. After all, I enjoy your company too much. You must have noticed that.'

There was a small moment of nothing happening before the girls' expressions softened.

'Yeah,' nodded the first.

'That's true,' added the second.

'And seeing as you've robbed this store, don't you think you'd better tie me up too?'

The girls looked at each other.

'Yeah,' said one and nodded.

'That would look real good,' said the other.

He was stripped naked and made to lie down next to the drugstore owner, then like him, he was tied up, gagged and blindfolded with his own clothes.

By virtue of the long silence that followed a certain scuffling of retreating feet, he presumed they were gone. Later other footsteps were heard. There was a quick intake of breath. Someone was standing over them. Who? Had the girls come back?

Firm fingers clamped like plant tendrils around his sleeping member. A thumb tapped lightly at its sticky head. Immediately, a new erection sprang into being.

He arched his back, thrust his hips as his penis hardened and new semen travelled along its channel.

He mumbled and moaned against his gag.

As he ejaculated into the strong hand that jerked him off, his blindfold slipped slightly. Metal. Something metal. A knife? No, he decided. Not a knife. A button; a badge. A badge. A policeman's badge.

Once he and the drugstore owner were dressed, both gave descriptions to a young policewoman with pale red hair and a freckled face.

'They tried to jerk me off,' said the drug store owner. 'But

I resisted them. I'd have none of their dirty ways.'

Poor you, thought Simon, but said nothing.

'How terrible for you,' said the young policewoman, and wiped her sticky hand down her trouser leg.

'They did the same to me,' said Simon. The policewoman's eyes lit up and she blushed slightly.

'Did they now,' she said, and leaned closer to him. Again, she rubbed her palm on the leg of her trousers. 'I bet you didn't resist.'

Simon smiled and winked. 'No. But then, would you?'

# Chapter 24

Ophelia de Pomero stared in the window of Maxim's Modes. Normally, she would just have looked, sighed, and passed by to somewhere cheaper where her money would stretch to shoes, handbag and jacket, besides a mere dress. But the one that caught her eye held it and begged to be bought.

'I can't afford it,' she said quickly, and shook her dark head.

'Beautiful, isn't it?'

A shadow fell over her. She started. She hadn't heard any footsteps. Nor had she been aware of anyone passing.

Shivers ran down her spine as she stared up at the tall man whose eyes were as green as the slinky dress that dominated the shop window.

'It's too expensive for me. Much too expensive.'

He had a thin-lipped smile. 'Nonsense. Don't some occasions demand the very best? The most expensive you can buy?'

With some misgivings, Ophelia considered his thin lips as he spoke. No teeth were visible. Instead, his mouth seemed a black void, cavernous, bottomless.

She shivered again, though not with the same feeling of

surprise as before. This time, there was a warmth to her shivers; a bit like when she showered and warm water ran over her naked body and trickled like crystal tears from her nipples.

She shifted position and thought of what she wanted the dress for. She found herself smiling up at the stranger. 'You could be right.' Her eyes went back to the dress. 'It really is beautiful, and I do want it for something special.'

'Then buy it, my dear Ophelia, buy it. After all, it is churching night.'

Creases of delight spread over her face and her cheeks shone as she came to her decision.

'You're right. You're absolutely right. I'm going to buy it.' A thought suddenly came to her. 'How do you know— ?' she began. But the man was gone.

Eyes wide with surprise, she looked up and down the street. There were few people around; two older women, laden with grocery bags, their bodies round as basketballs, talked loudly about their families as they waddled along the street.

There was a policeman leaning on a patrol car. His eyes looked her up and down as though she had nothing on. He pushed his cap to the back of his head as he clenched his fist and bent his arm at the elbow.

'How about it? Five dollars a job?'

'Get lost, jerk,' she muttered as she looked away.

Kids, old people chatting, young people shopping: there was no sign of the man with the green eyes who had urged her to buy the dress.

The dress. She looked back at it. It drew her eyes to it. Her body to want to wear it.

'What the hell!' She pushed open the door and went into the shop.

Maxim's Modes was a shop with deep carpet and well-dressed assistants. Ophelia, pretty and as sleek a pussy as ever walked the pavements, felt suddenly dull, inferior and terribly cheap.

'I want the green silk dress,' she said with a sudden surge of boldness. 'The one in the window.'

The assistant looked her up and down.

'A very good choice. Of course, it is secondhand, you know. But it did come from a very good home. The woman it belonged to was given it by her mother on her wedding day. She's started a family and has no further use for it. Do you want to know how much it is?'

Ophelia shook her head, then lifted it high. 'No. I don't. I want it, and I'm paying cash.'

The assistant sneered. 'You have cash? No credit cards?'

'No.'

Her sneer widened as, knowingly, her eyes again raked over Ophelia's slender form.

'My. There's not many people nowadays who deal strictly in cash – not unless they're crooks or whores.'

'Are you going to put that damned dress in a bag?'

Ophelia slammed the money down on the counter. Her nervousness had been replaced by anger. She didn't wait for the assistant to count it.

With her purchase in a black shiny bag with gold lettering, she left Maxim's.

'You came well near getting a hex put on you, you bitch!' The attitude of the assistant stung her badly. Why, Ophelia was as good as she was, prettier than she was, and man, did she have a future in front of her.

She swung the bag as she talked to herself. Slights were something she didn't take kindly to, and that assistant had slighted her. No matter who she was and who she wasn't, if she had the cash, she deserved some respect, and boy, did she have the cash.

Now she wanted something else. Ophelia de Pomero, whose great-grandmother had been the most popular Creole courtesan in the whole of New Orleans, wanted respect, and not just any respect. Respect from shop assistants came low down on the scale. Ophelia wanted respect from her own kind, her own sisterhood and brethren. Tonight, she might get that. Tonight could be the best night of her life. Green, she told herself, was a good colour, an earth colour. It would look good against her skin, and the gods would like that. Luke would like it too.

Luke Candeo was a pimp and a right bastard. He was also the son of Ma Candeo. His ma was the doyenne of the voodoo cult which met regularly in the stone-walled cellars beneath a tumbling tenement.

Tonight was churching night: not the churching of newcomers to the Christian religion, but that of those to the African, the voodoo religion.

Ophelia had thrown over everything she had ever known for Luke and his mother's religion. Now she'd confirmed her belief even more by throwing her hard-earned money away on a single garment.

But it would be worth it, she told herself, it was bound to be worth it.

No more tramping the streets looking for tricks. With that dress and Luke Candeo in tow, she'd go big time. She'd tell him that she'd go after the Wall Street tricks whose bank accounts were far larger than their pricks.

She smiled to herself as she pushed open the scratched brown door to her dismal, one-roomed apartment. Oh, yeah. Tonight would be the night!

In the arched cellars beneath a derelict building, candle flames wavered and smoked. Shadows tangled and wove alternating patterns on the crumbling walls. Around a glowing fire, dark figures danced to the thudding beat of African drums.

A white cockerel was tethered next to a tin bowl beneath a table. The table was plain, had grease-covered legs, and a red and white gingham top. The cockerel crowed and obligingly stretched his neck.

Someone covered the wipe-clean top of the table with a square of black velvet. No longer was it a kitchen table. By that one act, it had become an altar.

Smoke curled and wavered as voices rent the air in a curious lilting chant that tangled in the brain, and trailed icy fingers down the spine. The language the singers used could be called French, but the words and lyrics were tainted with an older language, darker sentiments inherited from a time before black ivory had been taken from the Dark Continent and brought to the New World.

The thumping beat, the mix of smells, and the flickering light made the air seem heavier than it was, the bodies unreal, the chanting eerie.

Naked beneath the sheer silk of her dress, Ophelia de Pomero entered the church of Ma Candeo.

The old witch herself, fat, naked, and glistening with

sweat, was sitting in a chair that had a long, twisting gazelle horn at each corner. They looked as though they were coming out of her head. Her huge breasts lay glistening on her round belly, which in turn fell in folds over flabby and massive thighs. Her stubby fingers curved over the bleached skulls of long-dead monkeys. At least Ophelia assumed they were monkeys, though the more gullible suggested they might be something more human.

The drums continued to beat. Ophelia searched the room for Luke. There was no sign of him. Swine! Who was he with? What other little tramp was he fucking this evening?

Stay cool, baby, she told herself. Stay cool. Tonight, the gods are with you. She was sure of it, and if the gods were with her, with their help Luke would be with her too.

The drums became more infectious. Were they louder than they had been? It seemed that way. The beat filled her head. She ran her hands over herself as she began to sway. What was that stinging sensation that rolled in prickly waves over her body? It was as though a thousand hands were covering her flesh, a thousand palms caressing her soft skin, and a thousand, thousand fingers exploring her curves, her creases, her every cranny.

Slowly, as though she were a dark and beautiful snake, she threw back her head and licked her lips. Strange sounds erupted from her throat as she ran her hands down over her long neck, her nails scratching her throat before she wrapped her arms around herself.

Her hips undulated to the incessant beat of the drums. Her hands covered her breasts and her fingers pinched her nipples. Thin wails poured from her mouth. At first they were only sounds with no words at all. Then, as if she had merely been searching for a key, she began to sing to the same tune as those chanting. But the words were different; older, even, than Africa, and darker. Much darker.

As the music and her possession overtook her, other dancers less favoured than herself moved aside.

Some dropped to their knees and hummed along with the tune she sang. The notes rose like thin needles of steel to pierce the darkness and infiltrate the minds of those who came to worship the old gods of Africa.

Soon, she was the sole dancer left upon the floor. Her body moved as though it no longer belonged to her. It was still hers, yet she had the impression she was outside of it, watching it gyrate, undulate, sway around the floor, lost in its own shocking rhythm.

The cockerel squatted as she danced around him, her hands now diving over her belly and between her legs. With bent knees, she jerked her hips backwards and forwards.

No one watching doubted the intensity of her possession. Stunned silence reigned as a green mist coated Ophelia with unholy light.

Slowly, as her hands moved, the skirt of her dress writhed upwards. The firmness of her brown thighs, and the darkness of her pubic hair were exposed to those who watched and adored.

Crying out in a voice that was not hers, she dipped her fingers into the plump lips of her sex. Sexual fluid lay sprinkled like seed pearls between her legs as her fingers slid between her labia and dipped in and out of her vagina.

Wide-eyed, her worshippers watched her abandonment. Never had they seen such a possession as this. Even Ma

Candeo, ever the most sceptical of other's possessions, and the most blessed receiver of spirit habitation, was highly impressed. Many times she had been blessed with the touch of the spirits, but never had she been aware of her possession being shrouded in a green and awful light; a light neither of earth nor of heaven.

Ophelia, oblivious to everything except what the green silk was doing to her body, gathered up her hem still higher and knotted it at the front. The silk was tight around her backside. One end of the knot hung immediately in front of her sex.

Still singing her ancient song, she raised her hands high above her head, her fingers spread and rigid. She brought them down to the straps of her dress which she pushed down her arms. She slipped her arms out of them. The dress settled around her hips. Now her breasts bounced as she danced. Her navel changed shape as her hips swayed from side to side and jerked to and fro. Her buttocks glistened in the smoky glow of the candles.

Stirred by the primeval sexuality of her dance, two men undressed and dropped to their knees.

As she gyrated and sang, they crawled to her; one in front, one behind, their brown bodies shone with sweat, the sweat of excitement, but also of humility.

The first man's head tipped to her feet. He licked her toes, then inch by inch, he trailed his wet tongue up the front of her legs, his hands following, his fingers lightly caressing.

The man behind did the same. He started at her ankles and began to move up over her calves. He lingered on the backs of her knees. The other man lingered at the front.

That they did this to her seemed to make no difference to Ophelia. Her body continued to undulate and waver like the rising smoke itself. Her feet continued to dance, her voice to chant the ancient words that even Ma Candeo did not understand.

The old woman's fingers gripped more tightly at her monkey heads as Ophelia continued her dance. Her eyes never left this supplicant who she had once thought promising, but not outstanding. So far, her own status was safe. Something more stupendous would have to happen before Ophelia would be feared by her.

She watched as the man before Ophelia licked up over her thighs before burying his head in her sex.

The man at the back licked up over the backs of her legs, then with his hands, pushed the folds of her dress up to fully expose her round, brown buttocks.

In a strangely dream-like way, Ophelia was aware of what was happening to her. If this is possession, she thought to herself as waves of desire flooded her body, then I want more of it.

For now, she accepted that the tingles running through her body were what was causing her to dance the way she was dancing. Where the song came from, she didn't know. All she did know was that she could not stop singing, could not stop her hips from jerking as though some man, some mighty phallus was inside her.

Fingers pulled her pubic lips apart as the man in front of her licked her folds of flesh. She thrust her hips over his mouth. The man behind licked her buttocks, held them apart, and probed her tiniest hole with his flicking tongue.

Ma Candeo narrowed her eyes as she watched the gyrating

girl and the grovelling men. Through the eddying smoke, the swirling green mist, she saw another figure – saw and recognized it.

'The queen is dead,' she said softly. 'Long live the queen.'

Quaking with humility, Ma Candeo listened to the voice in her head. Slowly, she got up from her chair.

With slow, measured steps, she circled the tableau before her, then tapped each man on the buttocks with her ivory wand.

The men disengaged themselves from Ophelia's body.

Alone in the middle of the room, Ophelia began to gyrate with wild abandon. Sweat poured down between her naked, jiggling breasts, and her legs began to tremble as though she had suddenly been struck with a fever. All the time, her hips jerked backwards and forwards as though towards an unknown lover.

Her chanting gave way to loud, anguished cries.

'Lie down,' commanded the old priestess in a calm, but firm voice.

Her body still jerking, Ophelia did as she was told. Even lying down, her body continued to move as though unseen hands were playing with her flesh.

Ma Candeo chanted.

Ophelia did not hear her chant, did not see her hold the cockerel up by its legs until all its blood had dripped from its slit throat and into the tin bowl.

She was only partly aware of the blood being smeared onto her forehead, then onto her breasts, her belly, and in a vertical line down the inside of each thigh.

Ma Candeo chanted more loudly, more terribly. Her

words were as old as the chant sung earlier. In that terrible tongue that only the chosen understand, she called on the Lord of the Underworld to come and take his handmaiden.

Through half-closed eyes, Ophelia became aware of the swirling mist that those watching had seen. She also saw something – someone – few could see. His eyes were like chips of broken emeralds. His face was gaunt and his chin pointed. He appeared naked, and although she did not feel revolted by his body, she knew it was not like that of other men.

A gasp of astonishment rose into the air as she spread her arms and her legs. She whimpered as she felt his hands upon her breasts. His palms were rough – like the bark of a gnarled tree. The nails of his fingers were thick: claws, she thought.

Myths and fear mingled in her mind. Nothing came of them. His weight was upon her. She welcomed that weight, heaved her belly, her hips and her sex, up to meet him.

As his phallus entered her, she screamed out loud. 'It's too big!' she cried out. 'You'll hurt me!'

She swallowed hard and tried to move her arms. They remained above her head as though they were pinned there. She tried to close her legs, but they remained steadfastly open. The shadow of Ma Candeo fell across her, and something of its coolness transferred to her fevered brain.

He moved on her; she stared into his bright green eyes as he pushed himself in and out of her, his cruel nails raking her breasts, digging into her buttocks as he raised her hips from the floor.

Never, with all the experience of her trade, had she felt so

impaled, so full of male hardness. The thought of the man
might or might not repel her; the feel of him still inspired her
sexuality and made her juices flow so she could take him
better.

Pubic hair as rough and abrasive as wire wool rasped
against her body. She moaned, cried out, and whimpered as
the might of him thudded against her, his nails digging like
eagles' talons into her numb behind.

Driven by her own insatiable sex drive, drowning in a sea
of sexual arousal, she submitted to primeval feelings. The
threads of climax rose around her nipples and in her sex.
She was soaring; in the clasp of his claws – no – his hands,
she was flying, like a princess in some fairy tale, lifted from
the earth by a scaly dragon. That's how they felt, these
sensations that racked her from head to toe.

Her climax was earth-shattering, explosive, monumental.
As though she were without bones, without muscle,
breathless, she collapsed against the earth. I've turned into a
jellyfish, she thought to herself behind closed eyelids. I'm
nothing but a jellyfish floating in a pea-green sea.

Slowly, she opened her eyes. Above her was only darkness.
She let her gaze wander to the silent crowd around her. She
was aware of gaping mouths, staring eyes. Had her possession
by spirits been that outstanding?

There was an odd smell in the air, a mixture of sulphur
and blood. She also became aware that certain parts of her
body were feeling rather tender and very hot. Suddenly, she
realized how inelegantly she was lying. She was half-naked.
Her arms were above her head, and her legs were wide
open.

'Let me help you, child.' Ma Candeo was smiling.

'Was it a good possession?' Ophelia asked as Ma Candeo helped her up.

The old woman beamed. 'The best ever,' she answered. 'You have been singled out for greatness, my child. It was the Lord of the Underworld himself who took you; not just mentally, but physically too.'

Ophelia was amazed to see everyone gathered fall to their knees. Even Ma Candeo bowed low before her.

'Now I know who is to take my place when I die,' said Ma Candeo. 'You, my child, have been chosen by the dark one, and chosen in a way that I never was.'

Somehow, Ophelia did not need this old woman to tell her this. The seed of power and invincibility was already in her mind. She could feel it growing, ripening, its leaves coming into bud, and waiting to bloom.

She smiled. Her teeth flashed white, strong and strangely deadly. She looked directly at Ma Candeo, thought of Luke, thought of revenge.

'Good, old woman. And the sooner it happens, the better.'

Ma Candeo trembled, knelt with the others, and touched her forehead to the floor.

# Chapter 25

Kitty was pretty quick telephoning him with the number and address of her ex-employee, Carla Ferretti.

With the dexterity that only the truly determined can rise to, Simon clasped the receiver with his chin, wrote the number and address with his right hand, and jerked himself off with his left.

If he was like this talking to her over the telephone, he thought to himself, what's it going to be like in bed with her?

Luckily, when he reached his climax, his wastebin was positioned not too far forward from his penis. White fluid thudded numbly into the metal bin and he moaned ecstatically until what had been hard returned to being soft.

'Be firm with her,' he heard Kitty say to him as he tried not to moan down the phone. 'Don't let her palm you off with her lies and get you going with her big dark eyes.'

Simon's voice was as weak as water. 'I won't.'

He put the phone down. 'Big dark eyes, eh?' He said the words thoughtfully and imagined the dark-haired maid and her nut-brown body. Her nipples would be a kind of sepia colour and soft. When they hardened, he could imagine them being like chips of milkless chocolate.

His penis became less soft and raised an enquiring head.

He looked down at it and frowned. 'Don't be greedy,' he said, and resolutely tucked it into his trousers.

There was no reply from Carla's telephone, so in view of the urgency of his mission, he decided to visit unannounced.

Her room was on the fourth floor of a place that might have been quite a building a hundred and fifty years before. Now it looked its age.

As he entered, the smell of urine, spicy food, and something sweet and highly illegal assaulted his nostrils.

The passageway was narrow and made narrower by a bicycle left leaning against the wall. Beyond that was a baby carriage.

A teenage girl sat on the lowest stairs. She looked up as he entered and smiled engagingly. Simon smiled back. Her skirt was very short and she was opening and closing her legs.

His eyes were drawn to the dark crevice that nestled at the top of her thighs. As she opened her legs wider, the pinkness of her sex shone like a gash of raw silk between her black crinkly hair and her brown flesh.

'Excuse me,' Simon said as he squeezed past her.

'Want it?'

Unsure of having heard correctly, he stopped and looked down at her. 'I'm sorry?'

'Do you want my pussy? It's available and hasn't been used too much. Well? Do you?'

Simon's mouth dropped open. My God! This girl couldn't be much more than sixteen.

She was young, he thought again. Her body would be firm. Her eyes were nice, and she was pretty in an unkempt and wild kind of way. But he was resolute in his mission.

'I'm not here for that. I'm looking for a Miss Ferretti. Do you know her?'

'Or what about a blow-job? Would you like me to do that to you?' She reached up and tapped his hidden member with her fingers which were long, brown and had dirty nails.

Although Simon's rod jerked expectantly, he shook his head as though he were shivering.

'No,' he said, and swallowed hard. 'I told you, I'm looking for someone. Do you—?'

'Ten dollars.'

'No, I don't want—'

'Eight?'

'No, I don't—'

'Seven-fifty. That's my lowest price. Blow-job only. If you want pussy, that's twenty minimum. Savvy?'

'No!'

Simon dashed up the stairs with unusual vigour. By the third flight, he was flagging and breathing heavily. He took the last flight extra slowly. His voice would be needed, and in order to speak, he would need some breath in his lungs.

There was a notable decline in graffiti on the fourth floor. Too many stairs, thought Simon, and for once had sympathy with the spray-can Picassos.

The door to Miss Ferretti's room was very dark because it was painted with that sticky brown varnish that had been popular around the turn of the century.

A scrawled note of her name was taped above a black plastic bell push. Simon pressed it. He didn't hear it ring, so he pressed it again. Nothing.

He shuffled his feet and looked over his shoulder at a nearby door that had opened about ten inches.

A moon-shaped face with round brown eyes stared at him. It appeared to be a child.

He felt an explanation was in order.

'I've come to see Miss Ferretti. Do you know whether she's in there?'

The child blinked, but did not answer. The door closed.

Simon looked around at the dark cream walls, the dull brown floor. Like being inside a cake, he thought, one that had gone stale and become inedible.

Again he looked to the door, but this time, rapped smartly on the wood.

'I'm coming,' he heard someone say.

A security chain crossed the woman's face at nose level. Above it, dark brown eyes looked into his.

His penis stirred as he remembered what Kitty had said. Carla Ferretti did have beautiful eyes. Her voice did not match them.

'What you want?' She spoke with an accent.

'I wanted to see you, Miss Ferretti. I believe you used to work for the Levy family?'

'Why you want to know that?'

He got out his wallet. 'It may be to your advantage.'

Her eyes fixed on the brown leather folder.

The door closed and the chain rattled as she removed it. 'Come on in. Make yourself at home.'

Where's the accent gone, thought Simon, but didn't comment. He was here on a mission, and he had every intention of carrying it out. Look what he had coming if he was successful!

The decor in Carla Ferretti's room made him wish he was wearing shades. They were in his pocket, but he couldn't be rude, could he? Never had he seen so many colours all brought together in one place.

'Coffee, Mr—'

'Tye. Simon Tye.' He held out his hand, and after tucking an aluminium crutch under her arm, the woman shook it. 'I won't have any coffee,' he answered after taking the view that rich colours hide a lot of dirt. He was convinced that her coffee cups would be as gaudy as the walls of her room, and therefore easy homes to any germs that might be hiding in a place like this.

Not that her room or her person was dirty. On the contrary, both were pretty neat. It was just that slumming on the poorer side of town brought out inbuilt prejudices that Simon would never admit to.

Carla was dressed in a pink satin house robe. Judging by the way her breasts jiggled against the glassy shine of the rustling material, she was wearing nothing underneath.

Simon made a conscious effort to stop looking at her nipples.

Carla stood watching him warily, her head cocked to one side like a curious sparrow.

'So what is it you want to know?'

'I understand that you did the final packing prior to the auction of your former employer's effects.'

'I did everything. I always did everything. Mrs Levy was fit for nothing like that. She was not a wife, you see,' she said, shaking her head mournfully.

'Oh?' Simon raised his eyebrows. Kitty was getting to be his favourite subject. 'Why was that?'

In pure Latin style, Carla pursed her lips and spat as though she were ejecting an apple pip. 'She did not look after him properly, not his house, not his food and things. Not things like that. She only looked after him in bed. Demanding little bitch, she was. On heat all the time, she was. Not that Sam didn't like his sex. He did. I knew that, mister. I knew that very well.' Her eyes smiled at him along with her lips. He was in no doubt what she was hinting at.

Simon was aware that his chin was travelling to his navel. He managed to pull himself and his lips together.

'I see. I see.' He coughed before saying what he had come to say. Carla put her hands on her hips and swayed a little.

Simon asked his question. 'I wonder, did you happen to notice some personal items of your employer's when you were sorting out the things for auction?'

'No.'

Her look said otherwise.

'Are you sure?'

'You call me a liar?'

Her accent had returned.

'No, no,' said Simon hurriedly, unwilling to upset her at this stage. 'I only wondered whether you had seen these particular items. They weren't valuable as such. They were items of clothing, just items of clothing.'

Carla screwed up her eyes as though she had just remembered something.

'You got wife with dark hair?'

Taken by surprise, Simon nodded.

'You live Plaistow Tower?'

Simon nodded slowly. 'How did you know that?' He frowned. What was she getting at?

'Get out!' she suddenly screamed. 'Get out! Get out! Get out!'

As she shouted, she beat his chest so that he stumbled backwards to the door.

Her blows still fell on him as he reached behind himself for the doorhandle.

Finally, he was out in the passage. Other doors that had not been curious about him knocking now opened and hot-looking people spewed out to see what the commotion was all about.

'He police!' shouted Carla.

'No!' Simon corrected, accurately detecting an instant animosity in the watching Spanish eyes that viewed him now with outright malice.

'You get out. Get out!'

Those who had spilled out of the doors pushed forwards behind the flailing arms of Carla Ferretti. Simon backed off down the stairs, then turned and ran.

He was fast, but still he heard them thundering down behind him.

Whether the others were less fit and fatter than him, he couldn't be sure. He only knew that, so far, he was ahead of them.

He spun round the last turn in the stairs and crashed down into the entrance hall and lay sprawled on the floor.

'For twelve dollars you can come in here.'

Simon looked up at the girl with no pants on and an urge to do business, who was standing astride him. She was pointing to an open door from which music and the crying of a baby drifted out.

'Yes. All right. Twelve dollars.'

She helped him to his feet.

In the dim light of her small apartment, he leaned

259

against the back of the closed door and heaved a sigh of relief.

'Twenty for sex,' the girl said. 'Thirty for the works.'

The girl paused to put a comforter into the baby's mouth and turn it on its side. It faced away from the room and from him. As if, he thought, she didn't want the child to see how she earned her living.

Suddenly, he felt strangely grateful and especially kind.

'The works,' he said softly, and wondered what he was letting himself in for.

He stood quite still and watched as she took off her clothes. Her waist, even her hips were slim and her legs long. Probably because she was still suckling the baby, her breasts were larger than he would have expected. Her nipples and their surrounding halos were very dark and very swollen.

'You like?' she said, tilting her head and bringing her long, dark hair forward to fall over one shoulder and caress one heavy breast.

'Oh yes,' he said, his voice hushed and his member rising. 'I like very much.'

Almost as though she were an adoring child, she took his hand and led him to her bed that had a white plastic headboard, a black surround, and piles of cushions in a variety of colours.

'I make you very happy,' she murmured before standing on tiptoe and kissing his chin. 'I make you very happy indeed.'

She helped him remove his clothes, her long fingers light as feathers upon his naked flesh.

His member jerked as she ran her hands down over his

body, cupped his balls. She took his erection in both hands and began to pull.

Murmurs of pleasure rumbled in his throat before escaping his lips. Initially, he had felt a tinge of guilt at taking advantage of her poverty, her need to keep herself and her baby. Now, he knew he was dealing with a professional, a woman who might be young in body, but was old in the ways of men and of nature.

To his surprise, she led him away from the bed and to a dark red couch. She ordered him to sit on it. He did so, his naked legs spread to allow for the weight of his balls and the stiffness of his erection.

The material scratched his back. He stared at the girl, his penis upright and jerking slightly with each movement she made.

'I will give you works,' she said with a smile, and dropped to her knees.

His thigh muscles tensed as she nipped pleasurably at his scrotal sac. She licked at it, sucked it into her mouth like kids do mounds of pink bubblegum before blowing it back out again. She did not blow it back out. Gently, she held it between her teeth and ran her tongue over it.

Chest heaving, Simon opened his mouth. He wanted to wail out just how beautiful it was, but was afraid to wake the baby. If he did that, then this whole, beautiful scenario would be over.

Instead, he moaned and mumbled how good it felt, how incredibly good.

She kissed his belly, his chest, and then his lips with her hot little mouth. Her tongue pushed in to meet his, her hands spanning his shoulders and caressing his neck.

Simon moaned with delight. His stomach muscles tightened as desire took him.

'Ride me,' he breathed against her ear. 'Please. Ride me.'

With slow deliberation, she eased her buttocks downwards until her sex sucked lightly at the tip of his penis.

'Naughty little baby,' she said. 'What are you doing to your mamma?'

'Oh, baby.' Simon ran his hands down over the smooth, brown skin of her back. He spread his fingers over each cheek of her behind, gripped her flesh firmly, then pushed her down onto his rod.

She closed her eyes and mewed like a kitten as she lowered onto him. He arched his back and raised his pelvis slightly until she was completely impaled, until he wore her as he might wear a glove.

'Naughty, naughty,' the girl murmured.

She curved her body over him, slid her hands behind his head, and brought his lips to her breasts.

He took the weight of them in his palms, and took one nipple into his mouth.

'Feed!' the girl ordered. 'Feed, my beautiful baby.'

At first, he did not understand what she meant. Then, as he began to suck her heavy breast, realization dawned. Warm milk spurted from her nipple and into his mouth. He gulped it in, swallowed it down, and remembered the time before, the mugger who had raped him in the park. It had tasted good then. It tasted good now.

As he sucked at her plump nipple, his hips jerked up to meet her sex. In turn, she slid herself up and down his slippery rod.

It was as though he had never had sex before; never had sucked a breast before.

'Enough of that one.' She jerked one breast from his mouth, then pushed him onto the other. 'Here,' she said. 'There is plenty in this one for you.'

Even before he began sucking, the swollen nipple leaked warm milk into his mouth. It trickled from his lips, down over his chin and his neck. Greedily, as though he'd skipped lunch – which he had not – he sucked on her and lapped the warm fluid to the back of his throat.

The more he sucked, the more she rode him, her buttocks slapping methodically against the muscles of his thighs.

His nose was crushed against the softness of her breast. Her smell, that milky smell of lactation, mixed with the freshness of her youth, filled his head.

If he could have eaten her, he would have. Or was he anyway? He was feeding on her, taking something from her with his mouth. At the same time, he was invading her with his penis.

The feel of it, the thought of it, excited him. All the sexual sensations he had ever experienced liquified in his body; flowed over it, in it, like some volcanic stream.

Semen rose in his stem like mercury does in a thermometer. It climbed, fell back, climbed that bit further. He pressed his fingers against her bosom so that more milk poured into his mouth. He pushed on it as though he were a feeding baby.

Finally, as her milk spurted into his throat, his semen spurted into her. What she had given him, he had given back.

Once he was dressed, he gave her fifty instead of thirty

dollars. He asked her about Carla Ferretti again.

'She not been the same since she got knocked down by a taxi.'

'Where did that happen?' asked Simon.

'Plaistow Square. Reckons some guy was chasing her.'

Simon nodded. He was vaguely aware of having heard this before, but couldn't for the life of him remember who had mentioned it.

There was a soulful look in the girl's eyes. Even before she spoke, he knew what she was going to say.

'Will you be back?'

It was hard to resist her big brown eyes and say no. But he did just that.

'No. I won't be back. But I do appreciate you helping me.'

He kissed her forehead.

'Thank you.' he said.

She shrugged her shoulders. 'No problem. I enjoyed it. Someone has to drink my milk. That little sod spits it out. Prefers the bottle.'

Simon looked over at the small bundle in the cot, wondered about individual tastes, then left.

He did not look back.

# Chapter 26

Ma Candeo's son, Luke, infamous local nark and pimp, could see that Ophelia de Pomera was not the woman she used to be.

He had expected her to be angry when he had phoned her on the evening following his mother's churching night. She was not. She was cool. Strangely cool.

'I'm sorry about not getting to the churching with you, honey, but I had a little business come up. You understand?'

'I understand.'

'Well, babe. You know how it is. Now I'm flat broke. I need some bread. I'll be over later once you've had chance to score a few tricks. Savvy?'

'Oh, yes. I savvy, but I sure won't be pulling any tricks for you any more.'

Luke gripped the phone as though he were gripping Ophelia's throat. 'Don't even think it, you bitch!'

There was pure malice in his voice now. Ophelia would know that. She'd felt his malice before. She'd felt his fist too, and the end of his leather belt across her bare backside.

'I will think what I want. I will do what I want.'

Her voice was still uncommonly cool, her words precise.

Unseen by her, Luke shook his head and sneered. Even

without the glint of gold-capped teeth, Luke's sneer was menacing – a bit like a hungry shark when it first scents blood.

Luke clenched his fist, cracked his knuckles. His voice was pure venom.

'You, honey, will do as I say! I'm coming over. I'm coming over right now!'

'At your peril, Luke Candeo. At your peril.'

The coolness in her voice froze to something akin to ice.

He shivered, then attempted to threaten with the same sort of words he'd used before towards her and a dozen other girls. The phone went dead.

With angry eyes, he stared at the phone before crashing it into its cradle.

'Bitch!' Luke was unsettled. How could one night with the voodoo crowd have altered her so much? Where was the biddable, beautiful little whore who obeyed his every command and handed over her money without protest?

He decided to follow up his phone conversation. He went to see her, but something happened that prevented him from getting her to comply with his wishes.

It took him a few days before he remembered exactly what had been said. Shaking with shame, he recalled that his anger had done nothing to persuade her to return to the streets. Vaguely, he remembered slipping his belt out from his trousers, ordering her to take down her pants so he could give her a good beating, the sort of beating he always enjoyed. Afterwards, he would normally have got her to kneel between his legs and suck him off. This time, nothing usual happened. Ophelia had been in control. It was only now he remembered going home, and getting out of his car to hoots of derisive laughter.

'Where's your strides, Luke?'

That was it. He had arrived back at his apartment with no trousers on, no underwear either. His member, which was not the stuff of which legends are made, nestled like a withered walnut close to his body. No one, of course, mentioned it further. In the days that followed, they only sniggered behind raised hands when he passed by. As the memory of his shame became stronger, his need for revenge got stronger too.

He remembered how it all started, when he heard that she was moving to a new apartment, something more conducive to her more elevated station in life and in his mother's cult.

Well he'd fix that! He had to fix that. There was no way he could let her have her own way. If he did, he'd be the laughing stock of the neighbourhood. He had to go over to see her again at her new apartment. He looked at his watch. There was plenty of time. He had been out to see another of his protégées who, although only sixteen, had a baby and enjoyed the work he had set her up in.

Now he would go to see Ophelia. He would talk some sense into her. He seethed inside, mindful of the sly glances from those he knew, the snide remarks that were becoming more blatant, more embarrassing. Well, he would fix them, because by fixing Ophelia, he would be making it clear that he would not be made to look a fool. He couldn't have it being taken for granted that he, Luke Candeo, had lost control. A filly had fled his stable. It would do his reputation no good at all.

As he drove, he had plenty of time to think of her and ask himself what had gone wrong.

Was it only six weeks ago that he had laid on a party for some of the guys, guys he wanted to keep in with? Ophelia had been her submissive, obliging self. These particular guys had been into smacking her bare backside before spreading her on the bed and taking it in turns to make use of her in any way they wanted. Sometimes only one at a time had taken advantage of her body. Sometimes more.

Ophelia had griped a bit, but after the odd slap, her groans had been less strident. After all, why shouldn't she be compliant? That was her job, a job he'd moulded her for. As her manager, he got paid for her services, and she got a cut of it. Wasn't that fair enough? To his mind, that was the way things should be. He had every intention that they would continue that way until Ophelia got too old for the job. But now, since his mother's churching night, Ophelia was a different kettle of fish.

He rubbed his shoes on the backs of his trousers before he entered the apartment block where Ophelia lived. He frowned. When had he started worrying about being grubby in her presence? He shook his head. His mother had a lot to answer for. Wait till he got hold of her.

He hadn't been there on that churching night, but he had heard something special had happened. He didn't know how special until he had gone to see Ophelia.

As he looked up at the building in which she now lived, more details of that night came to his mind. He had meant to grab hold of her and demand why she wasn't out on the street earning money. Somehow, his arms had refused to obey his brain.

'Get out of here,' she had said in a low voice that made his toes curl up. 'Things have changed, Luke. I don't want to see you again.'

Incredulous, his mouth had fallen open. 'What? What are you talking about, girl? This is my place. You're mine, and that's gospel, girl. Not my ma's gospel, but my gospel. Hear me?'

Even when he had slid his belt from around his waist, Ophelia had not moved. She had stood before him wearing a green dress that had hugged her body like a second skin. His gaze had been drawn to her eyes. They were wide, unblinking, and seemed to reflect the colour of her dress.

'You should listen to me, Luke. If you don't, it could be the worse for you. I will make it worse for you. I will make it very bad for you, Luke.'

'Bitch! Who do you think you're talking to, girl! Some two-bit punk? Some nobody?'

Her lips had curled back in an evil caricature of a smile.

He had tried to step forward. His legs wouldn't move. Neither would his arms. Sweat had broken out all over his body. It seemed for a moment that she had a mouthful of fangs. He'd blinked and looked again. Had her eyes turned to green?

'You will leave this place, Luke Candeo,' she'd said, her voice deep as a base baritone. 'You will leave this place now and never come back.'

Despite a sudden weakness invading his body, he had managed to protest. 'But it's my room. You live in it. I pay the rent.'

She'd shaken her head. 'I earned the money to pay that rent. Once I am gone, you can have the place. I will be moving to a new one, one more fitting to my new—' she paused. 'Profession.'

'New apartment? New profession? What are you talking about, girl?'

His voice had sounded far away. He had chanced to wonder if he was ill, but that had seemed a stupid thought.

'Yes, Luke. A new apartment, a new profession, a new life. You will leave here and only return when I have left. You will do exactly as I say.'

'Yes,' Luke had said. A green mist had swam before his eyes. He had felt dizzy. 'Yes. I will do whatever you say.'

What she had been saying suddenly made sense. He would leave. She would be gone to her new place when he came back. The place was his. It couldn't have been simpler.

He had done exactly that, though he still couldn't remember taking his trousers off. It was three days before he realized that foxy pussy had got the best of him. No prick-pulling pussy would ever take notice of him again. He became angry. Such a situation could not be allowed to continue. He had to put it to rights.

It was in Clancy's bar that he shouted his mouth off about what he intended doing. Normally, other men would have patted him on the back and told him to take no lip from no woman. But not this time.

Silence dropped like a curtain all over the bar room. There was fear in those eyes brave enough to look at him. Others looked away and mumbled the sort of words used by believers to ward off evil spirits.

Luke chose to ignore what the silence and the frightened expressions were telling him. He refused to accept that Ophelia was no longer the person he had used and abused.

He refused to notice that she was talked of in hushed tones and with unequalled reverence. Even his mother held her in awe.

'She's obedient to a stronger power than you, son.' She stared hard at her boy as she said it. The power of her thoughts was not strong enough to make him change his mind.

Not that he wasn't a believer in her mumbled chants and her racial memories of an Africa of blood and magic. Voodoo was a religion that even he respected. But it couldn't, it just couldn't, he told himself, have changed Ophelia that much. Today, he would prove it. Today, he would sort things out with her.

'Who you want?' asked the janitor who sat in the hallway reading a paper.

'Miss Ophelia de Pomera, my man. Remind me of her apartment number.'

The man smirked and a strange look crossed his face. 'Forgotten it, have you? Or didn't she give you it to begin with?'

Luke's confident expression slid from his face before his mouth hardened and deep hollows appeared beneath his cheek-bones. He grabbed the janitor by the throat and pulled him to his feet.

'You were saying?'

'Room 402.'

The man struggled for breath. Luke liked that. It made him smile.

Luke threw him to the floor and slapped his hands together as though he had been touching something extremely dirty.

He didn't see the man smiling as he struggled to his feet. Neither did he see the knowing look in his eyes. Luke was too busy deciding whether to take the elevator or the stairs. He chose the former. Luke never exerted himself unnecessarily. He liked to act smooth, liked to arrive unruffled.

As the elevator went up, Luke brushed nervously at his cuffs. Again, he shone his shoes on the back of his trousers. He frowned like he had before.

Third floor. One more, and then— The elevator went no further. It had stuck between the third and the fourth.

Luke shook his head and muttered things too terrible to repeat. He pressed the alarm button. Nothing happened. He pressed it again. Still nothing.

'Shit!' he exclaimed, and kicked at the door with one foot, then the other. He shouted as loud as he could. 'Can someone get me out of this fucking thing!'

No one came.

He hammered at the door with his fists. Still no one came.

'Fucking place. Fucking cow! Why did she have to move to an asshole place like this?'

As time ticked by, Luke noticed how silent everything was. Sweat broke out on his glistening head and square temples. His eyes flitted between the buttons on the control panel as if glaring at them alone would make the elevator begin to move. The elevator was fashioned from sheet steel that had small ridges running through it, but was still shiny enough to reflect his surroundings; or at least, it was at first.

After kicking and hammering on the door a few more

times, shouting at the top of his voice, and pushing the floor buttons with haphazard abandon, he sank to his haunches. He was drenched in sweat and breathing heavily. It was then that he noticed the figure reflected by the sheet steel was not him, and was not alone.

There were people there, or more accurately, bodies – naked bodies of all colours, all descriptions. He saw women copulating with all manner of outlandish things – inanimate and otherwise. He saw women mounting men, and men in turn mounting those men, enormous penises disappearing between the cheeks of their behinds, whilst others entered their mouths.

Women were trussed like turkeys as men thrust other things into their bodies: vegetables, fruits, cudgels, and candles, the flames still burning.

At first the sheer lewdness, the undoubted similarities between his own tastes and those happening in the reflection, fascinated him. He even fancied he felt the beginnings of an erection. He stroked it proudly for a moment before realization dawned on him.

Slowly, he felt his skin stretching tightly over his face as his mouth dropped open. These goings-on could not possibly be reflections; there they were within the steel itself. Still staring at what was happening, he rose to his feet. His legs trembled, so he reached behind him for support. The metal, that should have been cool, scorched his fingers.

'This can't be happening,' he shouted. 'Stop it! Stop it!'

But the figures did not stop what they were doing.

Luke swept his fingers over his shiny head, his eyes wide and staring. What was happening to him? Was he going mad?

'No, no, no, no!' He shook his head. Beads of sweat flew from his skin and sizzled as they hit the walls.

He closed his eyes. Perhaps he was dreaming. Perhaps it would all be gone when he woke up. He opened them again. The figures were still there. He could see them. He could see— Wait. There was something different about them now.

His chest felt tight, but he forced himself to study the figures that so openly copulated on, or rather in, the walls of the elevator.

Taking pride of place was a man stretched out on a wooden frame. A dark man, like him. Same height, same weight, same shape. A man exactly like him.

All the other men had disappeared. Only the women remained. He could see that their eyes were dark with hatred, their lips dripping with malice as they formed a circle and, hand in hand, walked slowly around the man.

Luke was sure he could hear them chanting. What was it they were saying? What was it?

Gradually, as if someone had turned up the volume, he heard the words they uttered.

'Here we are awaiting, awaiting, awaiting.
Here we are awaiting, awaiting, Luke, for you.
Hell is such a hot place, a hot place, a hot place.
Hell is such a hot place. It's waiting, Luke, for you.'

Luke shook his head vigorously, as if that would stop the words eating into his brain.

'No,' he shouted. 'No!'

The sweat now ran down his neck, his spine and his

chest. He stared at the scene that developed before his eyes.

The women were sticking things into the anus of the spread-eagled man, and as though they were men they rode him, thrust their bellies onto his buttocks, the front of their thighs against the backs of his.

Luke covered his genitals with both hands as the women clamped the bound man's penis into a cruel looking vice. The man's penis was no bigger than Luke's own, yet the women were stretching it, pulling it out as long as it would go, just like he'd pulled earthworms out of the ground.

The man's screams were loud, shrill and like nothing he had ever heard before.

The man screamed more loudly as the women clamped his nipples between cruel, metal clasps. Soon, there were no moments of whimpering or silence between his screams. The women were whipping him, beating him mercilessly with whips, paddles, baseball bats, and something that looked like the famed cat o'nine tails.

His scream was so terrible, so ear shattering, that Luke clamped his own hands to his ears.

It was no use. The scream penetrated his hands, his eyes, his mouth – even his very skull. He could not escape it.

Without him having noticed it rising, a green mist floated between him and the terrible scene.

Green eyes peered out of the mist, terrible eyes, eyes that haunted sleep, haunted old places, and made even the most loyal of their familiars tremble with fear.

The eyes suddenly developed a nose, a mouth. A complete face appeared.

The mouth smiled. Rows of teeth as jagged as pieces of chipped crockery showed through the thin lips.

Luke smelt decay and something more bitter, more foreboding.

'Everything is prepared for you, Luke. Everything will be to your satisfaction.'

Luke, his hands still clamped over his ears, shook his head.

'No! No!' he cried. 'I'm not coming with you.'

The face raised dark eyebrows. 'But Luke, you enrolled to come with me so long ago. A place has been prepared. There is no question of you not joining us. See?'

As he spoke, the face of the man being so cruelly tortured came into view.

The high forehead glistened with sweat. Creases of pain marked the once-handsome face. A black void appeared where there should have been a mouth. Then there was the scream.

Again, Luke clamped his hands over his ears. The scream covered him, skewered him against the hot, heaving wall.

'*Noooooo* . . .' he screamed. '*Noooooooooo* . . .'

By the time they got him out of the elevator, he was no longer screaming. He was silent. His dark brown pupils were no more than pin-pricks.

There was a stiffness about his body that had not been there earlier. His mouth was tightly shut, and what was left of his eyes stared straight ahead.

Those in the know about voodoo stepped quickly and silently to one side.

'Are you all right, mister?' someone asked.

'Shh,' said someone close by, 'or you might take the same curse he's under.'

Luke Candeo, as though responding to a silent command,

276

resumed his journey, but this time up the stairs.

The crowd who had gathered around the elevator door fell silent as they watched him go.

The janitor rubbed his neck and smiled. The new girl on the block had herself a brand new zombie – and didn't they both deserve it!

# Chapter 27

It was as Simon was studying the list from Perry and Merryweather, the auctioneers who had disposed of Sam Levy's worldly goods, that his wife's name caught his eye.

It wouldn't have jumped out at him if he hadn't also been musing about the night when Ruth had crept out of her room and sucked him off. She had denied it, but he hadn't believed her. He could have argued and been strong about it, but he hated confrontation. After all, didn't he get enough of that from his business acquaintances?

And what was it she'd said about the woman who the delivery boy had found with a knife in her hand?

Suddenly, other bits and pieces began to click together; like her blushing when she had mentioned the delivery boy. And the delivery boy chasing the woman with the knife, and her getting knocked down by a taxi.

Slowly, the list sank to his lap as he took in what he thought he was seeing. He also thought about Kitty Levy. The list, lifted by his rising penis, fluttered in his lap.

What could have been so precious that Carla Ferretti had come armed with a knife? There could only be one answer. If it was so, it also meant that what Kitty had told him about those garments was true. The possibilities excited him.

Another thought occurred to him. If his wife did have the green silk things that Kitty told him could really turn a body on, who was she using them on? He remembered the blush when he had mentioned the delivery boy – the blond Adonis who never took the lift, but took two stairs at a time, despite being burdened with boxes of groceries.

Visions of his wife having sex with the athlete from the deli immediately filled his mind. It made him hot just thinking about it. As a wronged husband, he would have to challenge her about it. He half rose from his chair.

That would be useless, he told himself. Ruth would deny it and he would cave in. He sank back in his chair again.

On the other hand, perhaps talking about it might get them both onto the right wavelength. She might soften. They might both end up getting something good out of it – like sex.

The thought made him stiffen.

He let his finger run across from his wife's name to the single item she had purchased. '*Oak chest with brass banding and clasp, plus sundry items, photographs, etc., $20.00*' in figures, and repeated in words. '*Twenty dollars.*' What was in the chest that she had bought for twenty dollars?

For once, the spending of his hard-earned cash was a secondary issue. He looked towards the bedroom door. He had a plan, a plan not only to find out where this mysterious chest was, but also to find out what his wife had done with its contents. He had a great urge in him to know what she did when he wasn't around. He had his suspicions, and yet, he wasn't jealous; in fact he was aroused by the thought of Ruth making love with someone else. Perhaps by watching, he could assess where his technique was going wrong.

Normally in the morning he would shout goodbye to his wife, then close the apartment door quietly behind him. Ruth hated her sleep being disturbed. On this particular morning, he did not stick entirely to his usual routine. He did shout out his usual goodbye, but instead of making for the elevator and the lobby once the door was closed, he sneaked back in, climbed the steps to the storage area that lay between their apartment and the one above, and lay patiently in wait.

As there was little to do lying out on dusty floorboards amid cobwebs and discarded crockery, rugs, and broken picture frames, he dozed for a while. He woke up sharply when he heard voices.

Being careful not to scrape the toes of his shoes across the dusty floor, Simon eased himself into such a position that he could look down through the small gap where the plaster of the ceiling below did not quite reach the light fitting. What he saw made him want to have Ruth then and there.

She was wearing some kind of green underwear that lisped lightly over her breasts and belly as she moved. Was this the item that Kitty was so keen for him to retrieve? He licked his lips and was aware of his heart beating fast against his ribs. Ruth, he thought to himself, looked stunningly sexy. He watched as she glided into the bedroom as she never had before, her body undulating like grass stirred by a soft breeze.

Her dark hair flew around her face as she shook her head, closed her eyes and licked her moist red lips. She was holding the hands of the delivery boy, drawing him towards the bed. Her breasts looked very full, her nipples prominent against the thin silk of her garment. Her waist looked very small, her hips curved, and her legs endless.

Simon groaned and quietly slid his hand down between the floor and his body. He felt the hardness of his penis and gripped it tightly.

'I want you to undress me,' he heard the young man say.

It was hard for Simon not to gasp. Was this *his* wife who so obediently did as ordered? Never would he have believed that a blond Adonis with a delivery van and a batch of groceries could have such a stunning effect on someone as resolutely respectable as his wife.

Though, he thought again, she hadn't always been that way. He remembered when they were first married, her naked on a couch, her sex open to him, her feet resting on his shoulders as he played and sucked at her youthful breasts.

She had protested at first. Never had they tried such a position before, but he had insisted; in fact he had been downright forceful about it.

His fingers had left red imprints around her ankles as he had forced them up around his neck. He had tied them there, fastening the scarf behind his neck, so she could not possibly retrieve them. Then, as his blood had pounded in his head, his fingernails had dug into her buttocks as he had drawn her onto him.

She had cried out, told him to stop. He had told her to be quiet, tied her hands behind her back and covered her mouth with his hand.

He sighed at the thought. That was a while ago when their passion was new. This, sadly, was now. Today, ten years later, he was watching his wife as her hands played over the chest of a young man who, although blond, resembled him at that time. Even through the thin cotton of his T-shirt the perfect shape of the young man's torso was clearly visible. His shoulders were wide, his chest broad before his torso tapered to his waist. Once his T-shirt was off, the beach-bronze of his skin and his sprinkling of gold chest hair was clearly visible.

It had to be admitted the name Simon had given him, Adonis, suited the young man. He had a very flat stomach, and very pronounced muscles; blond and beautiful; every inch the model for some lecherous old sculptor to mould into marble. Momentarily, Simon was jealous. He saw Ruth's hands – his wife's hands – caressing those muscles, her fingers following the line of hair that ran from the young man's chest and dived into the waistband of his jeans. He heard the rasp of a zip and her cry of delight as a youthful penis came into view. It stood proud from the young man's body; full of the vigour of youth, the brimming energy of his sexuality. It was a penis to be envied. A thought occurred. Was it bigger than his? Was that why Ruth looked so enamoured of it, her eyes shining, her tongue curling over her lips?

No, he told himself. That couldn't be the reason. He fingered his own penis, felt its size and its hardness. No. It compared favourably. What Kitty had told him must be true. It was the green silk garment Ruth was wearing that held the secret. All this time he'd been looking for the secret of old Sam's erection, it had already been under his own roof with his own wife.

'Get down on your knees and suck it,' he heard Adonis say.

His wife was suddenly defiant. 'l don't want to!'

Simon was disappointed. He wanted her to do it almost as much as the young man did. His heart thumped and sent the blood rushing to his head; almost, he thought, as if it were about to come out of my ears. His eyes did not leave what was happening in the bedroom below. It was his wife doing this to another man. But he wasn't jealous. In fact, the whole scenario excited him considerably.

'Do as I say!' said the young man.

Simon gulped and felt his penis grow larger as a pair of strong hands grabbed hold of his wife's hair and forced her to her knees.

'No,' she said weakly, but her hands were already around the firm length that rose before her eyes.

'Suck it.' Adonis gripped her hair tightly and shook her head like a dog does a rabbit.

Whimpering slightly, Ruth's eyes stared at what rose so proud and so firm before her. Then she parted her lips which looked more red, more moist, than they normally did. Tentatively, yet so, so provocatively, her tongue licked over her pearl white teeth before she took the end of the young man's penis into her mouth.

Simon saw her close her eyes, heard her murmur soft and low as inch by inch, she sucked in the swollen part. He licked his lips as he imagined what she was tasting, and what the young man was feeling.

'Enough!' he heard the young man shout.

'But please,' said Ruth weakly.

The young man shook her by the hair again.

'Silence. Do as I say.'

Ruth's face was immobile, but her eyes were shining.

What happened next made Simon's eyes pop in his head.

'Get under the sheet.'

Adonis threw Ruth face down, onto the bed, then covered the top half of her body with one of the sheets which had lace around the edges and had been a wedding present from Ruth's mother. If only she knew, Simon thought to himself and gleefully smiled.

Mesmerized by what was happening, Simon held his breath.

Adonis pushed all the pillows under Ruth's hips so that her bottom stuck brazenly in the air. Then he undid the buttons that fastened the green silk garment between her legs, and rolled it up to her waist.

Her bottom was now exposed, the hair and pink lips of her sex peering furtively from between her open thighs. The top half of her body was completely covered.

The sight of his wife presented in such a way filled Simon with a hot flush of desire. How lovely she looks, he thought, and grunted. His own erection was now causing him some pain, trapped as it was between his body and the floor.

With a little shuffling around and a raising of his hips, he managed to unzip his trousers and let his stiffness spring free from confinement.

As he pulled on his hot appendage he watched, transfixed, as Adonis pressed the glistening tip of his penis against Ruth's naked behind.

'Open your legs wider,' he heard Adonis say.

To his surprise and rising excitement, Ruth did as ordered. The pinkness of her sex opened like a flowering rose, one whose petals are made of satin.

Adonis gripped her hips and prodded between the cheeks of her behind. Then he tilted her up slightly so that without any assistance from his hands and with only one thrust his penis entered her black-haired sex.

A muffled moan came from beneath the sheet that covered her head and the upper half of her body.

Simon moaned too. It was Adonis who invaded Ruth's body, who jerked backwards and forwards, quicker, then slower, pulling his penis out to the very tip, then stabbing it back into her. Yet it might just as well have been Simon himself. The ecstasy, the thrilling sensations of what they might be feeling, he was feeling too.

As Adonis thrust forward more quickly, Simon pulled on his penis; as Adonis adopted a slower pace, Simon's hand slowed down too.

'Turn over,' ordered Adonis.

Simon gulped and loosened his grip on his weapon. With disbelieving eyes, he watched as his wife, her hips still held high on the pillows, turned over so that her legs were spread, her sex fully exposed.

His breath caught in his throat. It had been a long time since he had seen his wife in such a position.

An old memory surfaced. They had been on honeymoon to some hick place south of Cape Cod. The place had been a real one-horse town with little else to do except what honeymooners are supposed to do. The weather had been glorious, the sky blue, the sand bright yellow. He remembered lying with Ruth among the sand dunes. Coarse beach grass had nodded over her body from her waist upwards. Among the brightness of the sand, only the lower half of her body had been exposed, her buttocks resting on a hillock of sand. The memory sent the blood rushing round his body.

Just like she was doing with Adonis, she had spread her

legs and exposed the silkiness of her sex from between the black laciness of her pubic hair.

Simon, full of the energy and the impassioned sense of duty and lust present in any young husband, had fell to the job immediately.

Ruth had moaned as his stiff member had entered her. Like the other time with the tied scarf, he had pulled her feet up onto his shoulders and had held them there as he pushed into her.

On account of the long grass that covered the top half of her body, he had not been able to judge her enjoyment by the expression on her face. Just like now, he had only heard her moans of ecstasy. On that occasion, her body had heaved up from the sand to meet his. On this occasion, it rose from the bed to heave against the blond Adonis who delivered groceries but was now delivering something else.

As though her thighs were handles, Adonis held them in his hands, her knees between his ribs and his elbows.

Simon's fingers restarted their pleasurable caress of his stem, their movement mirroring the pace of those below.

He stifled a particularly ecstatic moan as Adonis gripped Ruth's ankles, forced her legs towards her body, and like Simon himself had done so long ago, raised them high and wound them behind his neck.

'No! Please don't make me do that. Please!' Ruth cried out from beneath the sheet. But her squeals became murmurs.

Instinctively, Simon knew she was not crying out from discomfort but from pleasure. Protesting was all part of the act. The thought surprised him.

'Are you enjoying this?' Adonis asked her.

'No!' cried Ruth from beneath the sheet.

'Good. I'm mighty glad of that. Mighty glad indeed. I'm enjoying it,' said Adonis in a sneering tone as he thrust more fiercely into her. 'I'm enjoying having you like this and that's all that matters!'

Even though the sheet muffled his wife's protests, Simon got the gist of what she was saying.

Old habits die hard. At first, Simon's fingers stilled and his member softened as he detected the condemning stridency he had become used to over the years. The effect did not last for long. As his semen drove up through his channel, and a green mist rose from the room below, he suddenly knew that Ruth was lying, that she had always been lying. His realization didn't stop there. Wasn't he too at fault? Could it be that he hadn't been truly listening to the tone of her voice, the subtle undertones that said 'do it, go ahead and do it'?

Suddenly, he felt impatient to be alone with his wife, to reassert himself as the man he used to be. How sweet it would be to have Ruth like Adonis was having her; the top half of her body hidden from view, the bottom half exposed as if it were a separate entity, a sexual haven for any man that wanted it.

Wriggles and cries made the sheet that covered her seem as if the hidden half of her body were somehow separate from the naked half: like all humans, thought Simon, their clothes hiding the nakedness beneath, their bodies holding terrible secrets, and powerful forces within.

The green mist eddied outwards and upwards from the copulating bodies. Simon's penis became hotter and harder in his hand. His fingers found new energy as his wife thrust towards the body that penetrated hers.

Heat rose up his stem along with his seminal fluid. He gasped and moaned softly. Tingling with pleasure, he jerked his hips up and down against his hand and the hard, dusty floorboards. He was coming, and so were those in the room below him.

'Take it!' shouted Adonis as he dug his fingers into Ruth's buttocks and drew her tight against him. 'Take all I've got to give you, honey.' His loins pulsated as he pulled her to him.

Ruth's limbs shivered and her feet stiffened against the neck of the delivery boy. Murmurs rolled like mild thunder beneath the sheet as she throbbed with climax.

With admirable willpower, Simon held his climax in check. Only when at last Adonis retrieved his glistening rod from Ruth's wet sex, did Simon ejaculate, his semen sticky and hot over his hand and the dusty floor beneath him.

If Simon had thought this was the end of his wife's session with the delivery boy, he was delightfully mistaken.

Adonis twisted the sheet that had covered Ruth and bound it around her wrists. As he did this, he poured hot, lascivious kisses upon her lips, her cheeks, her forehead, and her breasts.

He pulled Ruth to her feet and drew her arms above her head.

Simon ducked back as Adonis twined the end of the sheet around the main stem of the central light which was immediately below where Simon was lying.

For a moment, it worried him that he might have been seen by the delivery boy. But then, he reasoned, what if he had been? After all, this was his home and it was his wife that the young man was so pleasurably abusing.

It also occurred to him that the light fitting might not be safe enough to take such abuse.

No matter, he said to himself. If it does go crashing to the floor and puts out every light in the block, it will be Adonis who gets the bill.

Reassured, he put his eye back to the hole.

Adonis had put a pillowcase over Ruth's head and had tied it at the back so that although her eyes were hidden and she could see nothing, her nose and mouth were still showing.

'What are you going to do to me now?' asked Ruth.

Immediately she spoke, Simon's penis expanded to such a hardness that it bored its way into an adjacent knothole. He groaned gratefully, and slowly began to copulate with the dusty floor beneath him.

'I'm going to do exactly what I want to do,' Adonis replied.

The young man's words made Simon groan as if he were in pain. Of course he was not in pain, but drowning in the pleasure of knowing that what Adonis would do was exactly what Ruth wanted him to do. Why, he asked himself, had he never realized such a thing before? Why hadn't he taken his wife over his knee when she'd protested about not wanting sex?

Imagine, he thought to himself, how he would have pulled her silky pants from her white flesh, and smacked her until her creamy skin had turned a dull pink. Such thoughts gave greater intensity to his arousal as he slid gently up and down the floor, his penis firmly embedded in the tightly fitting knothole.

Although there seemed to be a green mist in the room

below, he could easily see what was going on.

Adonis was pinching Ruth's nipples, twisting them between one finger and thumb, then pulling them to full length so that her back arched and her breasts thrust forward.

'Oh, please. No more!' cried Ruth.

Adonis only laughed, and strangely enough, Simon laughed with him.

This, he realized with increasing clarity, was just what his wife had always wanted. Her words were uttered purely for effect, to add a certain excitement to the proceedings. Why hadn't he known that before?

He pondered this as the green mist rose up and through the hole in the ceiling. Simon sniffed it in and was instantly aware of an intense tingling in his nose. Tremors of a sexual nature ran from his chest to his groin. He felt his erection grow harder and groaned as the roughness of the knothole bit into his hard flesh.

Before his eyes, the young man with the big pectorals and enviable penis was now sucking on his wife's nipples. Ruth was moaning and telling him not to bite her, which, of course, meant that she wished him to bite her even more. Adonis duly obliged.

Simon was at such an angle that he could easily see what was happening below.

The delivery boy's head was on one breast, while his hand diligently kneaded the other.

He saw his wife throw back her head; was about to duck, until he remembered that she could not see him, that a pillowcase covered her eyes.

Her mouth was open, and as the young man continued to

fondle, suck and bite at her breasts, she moaned long and low.

Adonis pushed his jeans down to his knees.

What happened next caused Simon to again wonder about the strength of the light fitting and who would get the bill if it gave way.

Adonis brought Ruth's heels to his shoulders as he had before. Instead of leaving them there, he used another twined sheet to fasten them to the same light her arms were fastened to.

Simon immediately forgot his worries that the light, and even the ceiling, might fall down.

His eyes opened wide as he surveyed the sight below him. His breathing increased as he imagined what Adonis was seeing.

Adonis, whose rod shone red and rigid before him, gripped Ruth's hips and swung her gently towards his pelvis.

As if he were pulling a shoe or a slipper onto his foot, he pulled her onto his member.

Simon could see it there; so stiff, so rich with blood.

As he watched, he continued to jerk up and down against the floor, his penis pleasantly motivated by the feel of the hole he was screwing.

There was a certain smoothness about the movement of the delivery boy that did not go unnoticed by Simon. At first, it looked as if it were the regularity of the strokes that gave such smoothness. He then decided it wasn't that at all. Adonis was not the one moving. It was Ruth who was moving. Adonis was using the fact that she was suspended to swing her backwards and forwards onto his stiff appendage.

Each time he pulled her onto him, she moaned very loudly and very long. Each time he pushed her away, she whimpered like a child denied her favourite treat. Adonis was taking her, but not taking her; in fact, she was taking him, and enjoying every minute of it.

Simon himself was hypnotized. His gaze never left the scene, but as he watched, his fingernails dug into the floor and his pelvis thudded against the hole in which his member was embedded.

It didn't matter that his office suit was getting covered with dust and cobwebs. All that mattered was that those beneath were enjoying what they were doing, and he too was partaking of their pleasure.

Through a green haze, he saw them tense, heard them cry out, and cried out himself as his fluid spurted between the floorboards he lay on and the ceiling below.

His cries were hidden by their cries, and pleasure travelled like a warm breeze over his body, thrilling his flesh, and tingling his nerve ends.

The room below him became silent as the delivery boy went off to his rounds.

Ruth too disappeared. He remembered her saying she had a date at the beauty parlour and was also going to pop into the bookshop on her way back. Vaguely, he remembered her saying something about ordering a book on strange phenomena. Apart from that, he remembered none of the details. Kitty and her request to retrieve the green garments had been on his mind at the time.

The only thing that did stay with him was the green mist. Like a cloud of summer gnats, it lay around his head and eddied back and forth over his body.

'Scat!' he said, and waved at it with his hands.

He tried to move. Ruth would be expecting him home for dinner. He had every intention of appearing as if nothing had happened, as if he had indeed spent his time at one of his businesses.

He tried to move again.

'Ouch!'

Sweat broke out all over his body. He was stuck. He would have been able to move, if his John Thomas had not been jammed so firmly down the knot in the floorboards. Even so, if it had shrunk back to its normal size following ejaculation, he would have been able to move. But his penis hadn't gone back to size. It was still swollen, still hard.

'I don't believe this!'

He tried again. No luck.

'Think,' he said to himself, and that was exactly what he did. He concentrated on thinking of non-sexual things, of things and people who could not possibly turn him on, and had always, in fact, turned him off.

He thought of the fat bag lady who rummaged through the bins at one of the chain of delicatessens he owned. He thought of the big, butch security guards at the shipping warehouse where, in partnership with others, he imported European antiques. He thought of his mother-in-law. God, would Ruth end up looking and acting like her? The thought made him wince. Nothing changed. His member was still stiff and stuck firmly in the knothole.

'I don't believe this!' he cried. 'I just do not believe this!'

Each time he tried to move, the roughness of the wood chaffed at his most sensitive organ.

He moaned and cursed, but nothing he did was of any use. His penis was extremely erect and wedged firmly in the knothole.

'Time,' he muttered to himself. 'Give it time. It's bound to disappear eventually. It always has before.'

But would it, he asked himself as he thought of Kitty Levy and what she had told him about the green garments.

Suddenly, he took more notice than he had done of the green mist that wafted before his eyes. His eyeballs followed its lazy drift as it circled his head and hovered six inches above the floorboards.

This was it, he said to himself as he trembled with excitement. This was what he had been looking for. Kitty had been telling the truth about how old Sam had managed to maintain such a strong erection. The green garments had power. She'd told him about the mist and the green glow that came from them. That glow had now settled around him. Like Sam, it had chosen him specially for its erotic companionship. Due to his present circumstances, Simon was no longer sure he wanted it.

'Go away,' he shouted. 'Scat. Get out of here. Leave me alone.' He waved his arms as best he could at the glowing green mist. It wavered a little, but did not go away.

'But isn't this just what you wanted?'

'Who said that?' cried Simon, and did his best to look about him.

Boxes, old trunks, and other bits and pieces littered the low-roofed storage space. In the darkness, they were just shadows, outlines that jumbled one into the other – except for one, that is. One of them moved. A pair of eyes blinked in the darkness. They were green.

'My God!' murmured Simon as he strained to look over his shoulder.

'Not me,' said the same voice that had spoken before.

'What?'

'I'm not God.'

'Who the hell are you! And what's more, what the hell are you doing in my god-damned attic!'

Simon made a good job of appearing annoyed – bearing in mind the fact that his penis was still embedded in the floorboards.

The green eyes glittered. White fangs flashed in a smile.

'Waiting for you. You've got what you wanted, and now I want my dues.'

'What the hell are you talking about?'

'Your erection. You wanted a mighty erection just like Sam Levy had. You've got it. My green silk gave it to you.'

'*Your* green silk? And who the hell are you?'

The mouth continued to smile. Like some sabre-toothed Cheshire cat, thought Simon, and shivered as he wondered about its eating habits.

'Call me a silk merchant. Call me a man who has long travelled the Great Silk Road from Samarkand to Tashkent. Call me a purveyor of licentious commodities that no sensual man or woman can resist. As you have at last realized, my silk has unusual qualities that smother inhibitions and unlick – sorry – unlock, the most secret, the most sordid lust in people. My silk is irresistible and entirely unique. Like all silk, nothing feels like it. It will caress, arouse, as it falls over the skin. It is supple, strong, and although very cool to the touch, it possesses the ability to ignite the most ardent fire in a dormant libido. In short, it is like no other fabric you have ever come across, and you, Simon Tye, have been chosen by it.'

'Chosen by it? What for? What does it want me for?'

'To be its keeper. Think how you can use it. Imagine how many nubile women will immediately desire your body once they have fallen under its spell. Think of how your most licentious fantasy will become reality.'

Simon did think, but not quite in the way he was expected to. His prick might be embedded in a plank of red maple, but his mind was full of Ruth, his wife, the love of his life. If only he'd known about her predilection for role playing, how different things might have been.

'I don't know that I want it,' he blurted out.

'Don't know!' thundered the voice. 'Don't know!'

Simon's vision of Ruth was still vivid in his mind. Somehow, it gave him courage. 'No,' he said adamantly. 'I don't know that I need it with a wife like I've got. In fact, I'm pretty certain that I don't need it at all.'

The voice rose in an exasperated wail. 'You can't say that!'

'Why not?' Simon sensed he had hit home.

'Because no one can resist the green silk, the mist, the green glow!'

'Well I am!'

There was momentary silence.

Simon saw the green eyes blink just once before a wider smile appeared from out of the darkness.

'You'll change your mind.'

'No I won't.'

'Then I'll leave you to think about it, and I'll leave my green mist here to keep you company.'

'I don't care what you do,' shouted Simon with outright bravado. 'I won't be dictated to by a piece of material and a half-hearted pea-souper. Where did you get it from? Somewhere around Jack-the-Ripper's old haunts?'

He laughed then. He laughed mockingly, outrageously, as though the green eyes and the white fangs were of no consequence at all.

He didn't see the look of downright malice before the fanged mouth smiled.

'Then so be it. I'll leave you and the mist alone together, and you will taste its continuing power. As long as the silk is in the vicinity, the mist will stay too. Pea-souper indeed!'

'I don't care what you do. I don't care what you say. I'll sort out my own sex life,' said Simon with the sort of confidence he hadn't had in a long time. 'What do you think of that, then?'

There was no reply.

Simon twisted himself that bit further so that he could look over his shoulder without the wood of the knothole serrating the sensitive flesh of his member.

There was no one there.

'Hello,' he said nervously. 'Are you still there?'

No one answered.

He was alone; alone, that is, except for the green mist.

'Go away,' he shouted. 'Go away!'

Suddenly, he wished like mad that he had not been quite so blatant in his condemnation of the man and his stupid mist. In the darkness and the silence, he thought of all the clever things he could have said, but hadn't.

'Damn! Damn! Damn! What the hell have I done?'

Hours later, he heard a door slam. Ruth had returned to the apartment. He watched, impressed by how innocent she looked as she dressed herself after showering. She was putting on a pretty little all-in-one foundation thing of pure white lace.

He smiled appreciatively as he considered how warm her skin looked against its stark whiteness. Her hair gleamed too. He guessed she had just had it done at the beauty shop. She applied fresh make-up, made faces at herself in the mirror as she tried first this and then that.

'There!' she exclaimed. 'Let's see if we can get you going tonight, Simon Tye. Just once, let's see if you've got some fire in your soul.'

Simon groaned. 'Why now?' he moaned to himself. 'Why now?'

There was his wife all ready and waiting for him. And there was him, newly aware of what his wife wanted, willing to give her it, but with his member firmly embedded in a piece of dead tree.

Ruth picked up the green silk garment and put it back into the chest.

As she refastened the clasp, she frowned. 'I should be satisfied,' she said softly to herself. 'I've got a toy boy. Isn't that supposed to be what all women of my age aspire to?'

Her brown eyes softened as she thought of her husband and the days of passion and love before they were replaced by business and domesticity.

'They're all the same beneath the sheets,' her mother had said. 'They all think they're Valentino.'

But Simon had been better than Valentino. Simon had suited her well; dominant or gentle at the right moments.

When had he lost that sensitivity? When had she given up on him?

She remembered her mother being ill and staying with them for a while.

Perhaps, she thought, perhaps.

Ruth took another look at herself in the mirror, then glanced at her watch. Simon was late. She frowned. How annoying. Suddenly, Simon was again the fickle man who never quite came up to scratch – just the way her mother measured him. Just at the time when she felt ready to wear the green silk and see what effect it had on her husband, he wasn't home.

She switched on the stereo and went to the dresser in which she kept her best cutlery and china. Tonight, she'd make a special meal for them. Tonight, she would grace the table with the best stuff they had: the best utensils, the best food, and the best wine. She wanted it to be special.

Everything was ready, and still he wasn't home.

Ruth checked the accuracy of her watch with the longcase mahogany clock that her husband had imported from England. Both read the same time. Ruth tapped her fingers on the table and eyed the bottle of Château Rothschild that had breathed long enough.

'Damn you, Simon bloody Tye!' she said, and poured herself a glass. It tasted good, but did nothing to improve the way she was feeling. 'Damn you,' she said again.

One glass followed another. 'I did all this,' she slurred, waving her free hand around whilst the other took the wine to her mouth. 'I did all this for you – for us. Where are you, Simon? Where the bloody hell are you?'

Perhaps because there was a gap between the Tyes'

apartment and the one above, sound travelled well. Simon could just about hear what his wife was saying.

'Damn it, Ruth. Why now?' he muttered to himself. 'Why the bloody hell did you choose now to go hot and randy?'

The green mist still swirled around him. His John Thomas was so swollen that the knothole bit into his flesh. Every so often, shivers of climax ran through his body. Again and again he ejaculated into the gap between the floorboards and the ceiling of the apartment below.

Exhausted, he groaned and wished he could stop doing that, but nothing he did helped. The green mist held him enthralled. He was trapped by his own lust and his own erection.

He heard the clink of glass. How many glasses of wine had Ruth drunk?

If Simon hadn't been counting, Ruth certainly hadn't.

She was staring at the last glass of wine and talking to it as though it were a close woman confidante.

'I love him, you know. Even after ten years of marriage, I still love him. Can you believe that? Well, can you?'

She tipped the glass to her mouth and swallowed a large mouthful. 'Nothing can change that, you know. My mother told me it wouldn't last, but I didn't believe her. I stuck to him like glue, though,' she said, shaking her head, 'it did become a little less tacky than it used to be. You know – the glue got a little tired. But no matter. My mother was wrong.'

The shrill note of the telephone cut into her brain. Shakily, Ruth got to her feet and went to answer it.

All the generous thoughts and passionate emotions of the

last half hour or so, suddenly disappeared at the sound of Kitty Levy's dulcet voice.

'I'm sorry, darling. I was trying to get hold of your husband.'

'Get hold of my husband's what?' retorted Ruth, her annoyance at Simon not being home now bubbling over.

'Oh, darling. You sound upset. Anything I can do?'

'Anything you've already done, you cheap trick?'

Kitty retaliated. 'Now look here, I only phoned to see if your husband had managed to locate my property. I tried phoning him at the office, but he wasn't there. They said they haven't seen him all day.'

'Of course he's there,' Ruth retorted hotly. 'Where else would he be?'

Kitty laughed. 'Well. He wasn't with me, honey. If he had been, you might not have got him back. I'd have rode and rode him, then left him for dead! Obviously, honey, you're not performing your wifely duties. Point is, honey, if you don't someone else will.'

Now Ruth was red from the wine and from anger. 'My Simon would not do that. My Simon—'

'Your Simon,' Kitty interrupted sharply, 'wanted his just desserts once he got my stuff back. That's what your Simon is like, honey. God, didn't I hear his heavy breathing on the phone when I talked to him? I know what he was doing. I know he was jerking himself off when he was talking to me. I know all the signs.'

'You bitch! You hot-assed bitch!'

Ruth slammed the phone down.

She had to find Simon. Where could he be?

She rang his business partners. No one had seen him.

302

'I expect he's down at the Levy warehouse,' said one of them. 'He spends a lot of time down there.'

'Then I'll go there!' She called a taxi and left.

Ruth was the one with a mission now, and that mission was to finally confront her husband with what Kitty had told her about him, and what she had found out about herself.

Simon, still screwed firmly into the floorboards, wanted to shout out and get her to fetch a chisel and a saw to get him out of the fix he was in. What with the dust, and what with his exhaustion, he just didn't have the strength.

'I'll die up here,' he said to himself. 'I'll die up here among this dust and these cobwebs. My erection will still be there when I'm dead – just like Sam's – but no one will see it. No one will say, "Wow. What a big one!" and that will be sad.'

It was just as he was slipping into the deepest slough of despondency that he heard the main door to the apartment being slowly opened.

There was no sound of footsteps. No cry of annoyance he might have expected from Ruth on finding that he wasn't at the warehouse.

No, he thought to himself. This person was treading very softly, and very quietly. Whoever it was did not want to be heard. This person had no business being in the apartment.

He put his eye to the gap in the ceiling and recognized Carla Ferretti. He sucked in his breath.

For someone whose legs had been broken on a regular basis, Carla was surprisingly agile. Quickly, she opened drawers and closets as she searched for the chest and the treasure it held within.

He heard her gasp, saw her slowly reach into an open

closet and retrieve a small oak chest bound with strips of brass. Carla sighed with satisfaction. She at last had what she coveted most.

She didn't linger. She was gone as quickly as she had come, and so was the chest.

It took a while for Simon to realize that the green mist had gone too. Slowly, his tiredness faded, and so did his erection.

'Thank God,' he said, and sighed loudly.

'Ruth. I've got to find Ruth.'

# Chapter 28

Carla Ferretti set the oak chest down in the middle of her multi-coloured room which at present was hidden by darkness. Her brown eyes became touched with a hint of green as she opened it and fingered the luxurious fabric for which she had broken her legs and adopted the tactics of the streetwise.

'Hmm,' she growled as she picked up the garment and held it to her. Immediately, her body began to undulate against the soft silk. Tingles of erotic energy ran with her blood to every nerve end in her body. 'All mine at last,' she said throatily as she peeled off her clothes and threw them to the ground.

A green mist swathed her body as she slipped the green garment up over her thighs. As though its fibres were fingers, it tantalized her flesh. Her nipples hardened, and a warm wetness ran from her sex like melted honey.

The green mist ran like spilt paint through the darkness. Her body moved just like the mist. It writhed, it swayed, and had form.

Carla was aware of the mist itself taking form. Her awareness was abstract; her body was aroused, steeped in its own desire. The mist was purely a sideshow.

Green eyes and a wide mouth appeared before her.

'The green silk was meant for you,' said a dark brown voice.

'I'm glad of that. I don't ever intend to let it go – not ever!'

Carla licked her lips and threw back her head. With one hand, she fingered her nipple. With the other, she stroked her crotch and let her fingers slide beneath the smooth silk of the gusset.

'The silk is very expensive. Are you prepared to pay the price?'

'Any price,' murmured Carla, the silk caressing her most sensitive spot in a way it had never been caressed before.

The wide mouth smiled beneath the sharp green eyes.

'Very well, Carla Ferretti. My silk for your soul.'

'Yes!' Carla cried out as a shattering climax erupted from between her legs. 'Yes! Yes! Yes!'

Simon saw Ruth's car before he saw her.

The office door was open, and the flitting light of a torch lit the darkness.

'Ruth.'

There was no answer.

His footsteps were quick. He knew the place well, but not well enough to remember where all the light switches were. And anyway, where was the security guard?

The thought came to mind that intruders might have got in at the same time as Ruth.

He sucked in his breath, and quietly followed the dancing light of the torch as it left the office and went down to the store rooms on the ground floor of the warehouse.

The torch disappeared with Ruth as she entered a store room.

Simon heard a rumbling sound as though heavy things were falling to the floor.

'Damn silk,' he heard Ruth say.

'Ruth!'

Quickly, the torch spun round to catch him full in the face.

'Simon! Where have you been? What have you been doing?'

'Working,' Simon replied, unwilling to have to explain the trauma he had recently been subjected to.

'How do I know that? How do I know you haven't been with some tramp – some tramp like that Kitty Levy?'

Simon sensed her old stridency returning.

Take the cue, he told himself, take the cue.

'Because I bloody say so!'

His foot slipped as he trod on an unwound bolt of material.

'What the bloody hell have you been doing?'

'I was annoyed. You didn't come home.'

He noticed her voice was less slurred than it had been.

Simon took a deep breath, then reached for her and held her by the shoulders.

'Well you found me, and now you've found me, do you know what I'm going to do?'

'No, Simon, I do not. Tell me.'

There was a sharp tearing sound as he tore her shirt from her body and pulled it down to her wrists.

'Simon! What are you doing?'

'You know what I'm doing, Ruth. You know what you want, and so do I. I saw you with the delivery boy. You deserve a good spanking for that, and you will get it. Believe me, you will get it.'

He covered her protests with his kisses as he bound the shirt sleeves around her wrists.

He pulled her underwear down from her breasts and greedily sucked on each nipple as he did so.

'Simon!' she cried. 'You mustn't!'

He laughed. 'Oh, Ruth, my darling. I must. You know I must!'

He pulled the rest of her clothes from her until she lay naked among the bolts of cloth that she had pulled onto the floor.

For a brief moment, he sat on a bolt of cloth and shone the torch over her body, bit by delicious bit. Moonlight shining through the barred and bolted window did the rest.

'You've not been all you could have been, Ruth, my darling.'

He said it thoughtfully, but firmly.

Ruth said nothing. She stared at him, the light of excitement in her eyes.

'And I,' he went on, 'have not been firm enough.'

He pulled her up from the floor and over his lap. She groaned, protested, and even wriggled, though only cautiously. Ruth had no intention of falling from his lap and escaping the flat of his hand.

At first, Simon enjoyed the sight of her naked buttocks in the light of the moon. Then he took the torch and shone it on them so he could see them more clearly.

'Open your legs,' he ordered as he pushed her thighs apart.

Her hands, still bound with her torn shirt, rested in the small of her back.

He heard her moan as his fingers parted her buttocks. He shone the light there, saw her muscles tense and her smallest orifice contract.

His penis lengthened as he opened the lips of her sex and shone the light on her glistening folds.

Ruth whimpered, but her body trembled with excitement. He used the head of the torch as if it were a plunger, or one of those old-fashioned rubber stamps. He brought it down first on one buttock, then the other.

'No!' wailed Ruth.

'Yes,' said Simon with a new firmness to his voice.

He did it a few more times until Ruth was whimpering, and her flesh was trembling.

With his fingers, he sampled the slippery wetness of her vagina, then gently, he pushed the handle of the torch into her.

She cried out. 'No! Please!'

'Yes,' he said, and pushed it in another four or more inches.

Her groans aroused him. Before the coming of the green silk, he would have retreated – even apologized. But now he knew her better. He had seen what she wanted, seen what she was capable of.

He pushed the handle in to the hilt, saw her legs stiffen, felt her belly tense against his swollen member.

'Enough,' she cried out as he worked it in and out of her wet vagina. 'Enough!'

'Then I will give you something else.'

He let her slide to the floor where she lay with her knees

bent. She looked up at him as he undressed, groaned as he forced her onto her knees and got her to take his penis into her mouth just as she had the Adonis who delivered the groceries.

Despite his earlier ejaculations, Simon felt invigorated. Ruth, he was surprised to find, excited him more than he could ever have imagined. This, he decided, was what he had been seeking, what he had been waiting for.

Before he actually came in her mouth – which was something he would save for another occasion – he lay her down among the tumbled silks that covered the floor.

He stretched her bound wrists above her head, buried his face in her breasts, then did the same with his penis as he held her breasts tightly against it.

Gradually, he made his way down her body, kissing and sucking at her flesh as he went.

At last, he took her feet in his hands, raised them and placed them on his shoulders, then, as she lifted her hips from the floor, he pushed himself into her.

There was no green silk to aid their arousal, no magic formula that caused them to make love again and again. If there was, it wasn't caused by the silk, but by themselves, by the magic that still existed between them.

Afterwards, they lay a while and ran their hands up and down each others' bodies.

'I've been a fool,' said Simon as he breathed in the scent of her hair.

'So have I,' said Ruth.

'I should have listened.'

'I should have said.'

She kissed him.

Simon thought about Sam and his erection. One of his wives had said he had sold his soul for it. Simon was suddenly happy with what he already had.

Ruth thought of the blond-haired delivery boy. She smiled to herself. She was happy enough with Simon, but perhaps, there might come a time . . . If temptation in the form of a lithesome youth did come her way, her passion would be her own and not ignited by a garment made of green silk.

What had lain dormant had been aroused. Whether Simon knew it or not, Ruth had become a woman of passion, and he had a lot of loving to do.

# A Message from the Publisher

Headline Liaison is a new concept in erotic fiction: a list of books designed for the reading pleasure of both men and women, to be read alone – or together with your lover. As such, we would be most interested to hear from our readers.

Did you read the book with your partner? Did it fire your imagination? Did it turn you on – or off? Did you like the story, the characters, the setting? What did you think of the cover presentation? In short, what's your opinion? If you care to offer it, please write to:

> The Editor
> Headline Liaison
> 338 Euston Road
> London NW1 3BH

Or maybe you think you could do better if you wrote an erotic novel yourself. We are always on the look-out for new authors. If you'd like to try your hand at writing a book for possible inclusion in the Liaison list, here are our basic guidelines: We are looking for novels of approximately 80,000 words in which the erotic content should aim to please both men and women and should not describe illegal sexual activity (pedophilia, for example). The novel should contain sympathetic and interesting characters, pace, atmosphere and an intriguing plotline.

If you'd like to have a go, please submit to the Editor a sample of at least 10,000 words, clearly typed on one side of the paper only, together with a short resumé of the storyline. Should you wish your material returned to you please include a stamped addressed envelope. If we like it sufficiently, we will offer you a contract for publication.

# SEVEN DAYS

## Adult Fiction for Lovers

### J J Duke

*Erica's arms were spread apart and she pulled against the silk bonds — not because she wanted to escape but to savour the experience. As the silk bit into her wrists, a surge of pure pleasure shot through her, so intense that the darkness behind the blindfold turned crimson . . .*

Erica is not exactly an innocent abroad. On the other hand, she's never been in New York before. This trip could make or break her career in the fashion business. It could also free her from the inhibitions that prevent her exploring her sensual needs.

She has a week for her work commitments — and a week to take her pleasure in the world's wildest city. Now's her chance to make her most daring dreams come true. She's on a voyage of erotic discovery and she doesn't care if things get a little crazy. After all, it can only last seven days . . .

0 7472 5094 4